The Unnamed Girl

Mike H. Mizrahi

This novel is a work of fiction. Any resemblance
to actual persons living or dead is entirely coincidental.

Redtail Publishing

Visit mikehmizrahi.com

ISBN: 0692123652
ISBN-13: 978-0692123652

"Molly, I have often thought if I have to die on the battlefield, if some kind friend would just lay my Bible under my head and your likeness on my breast with the golden curls of hair in it, that it would be enough."

- *From a Civil War soldier's letter*

ACKNOWLEDGMENTS

To my amazing editor, Robin Patchen. Thanks for your brutal honesty.

To my mentors along the way: James Rubart, Sarah Sundin, and Athena Dean Holtz. Thanks for helping me to hone my craft.

To Jennifer Zemanek: Thanks for the amazing book cover.

Most of all, thanks to my wife, Karen, without whose advice, patience, and love I could not pursue my passion.

One

Scavenger

Port Republic, Virginia
June 9, 1862

The sun's defiant rays poked through the clouded sky and the lingering smoke that still hugged the ground. A gold flash of light dared to answer.

Woody's watery hazel eyes burned and itched, so he swiped an arm across his stubbly face, leaving traces of red on his tattered sleeve. Blood gushed from his head. The ground beneath him blurred and the drumbeat in his head pounded with increasing intensity, as if he had just awoken from an alcoholic binge.

He stumbled toward the mysterious gleam, now wondering if his mind had played a trick. After all, he could barely think straight, and remembered only bits and pieces of the last few hours. He had dodged countless ground-shaking explosions all around him, and charged headlong toward the mouths of ear-splitting cannons that rained death and grave injuries on his comrades. That much he remembered.

The big guns had since been quieted, but the high-pitched

ringing they left in his ears threatened to drive him to his knees.

A gentle voice sounded as he approached the patch of ground that had yielded the light. The words rang clear: *Find my family, and I will grant peace to your battle-weary soul.* A child's plea had somehow drowned out the ringing and pathetic moans of grown men calling out for their mamas. But this was impossible. He scanned the area. With the exception of a brave young drummer boy, staring heavenward with vacant eyes, there were no other children here. Thankfully. Nobody here could have uttered those innocent words. Did he imagine them?

The dead boy couldn't have been older than thirteen. His shattered drum lay by his side. Way too young for a lad to die. Woody thought about the comforting touch and the warm responses of his mother during the worst of his illnesses and injuries growing up. This boy's mother would soon be devastated that she could not be there at her son's greatest hour of need. Woody mourned for her loss. As he took a knee to close the boy's eyes, an earthquake was loosened in his brain. His legs wobbled under the strain.

He had to concentrate. Where was he? A wheat field...where? The pounding in his head made it hard to think. What had happened in this place? Woody touched his hand to the top of his head. A fistful of blood covered his palm. A blunt force of some sort had gashed his scalp.

A crimson stream flowed among several soldiers lying prostrate around him. Mangled bodies torn and twitching, and, in a few cases, dismembered.

Where was Lucas?

Suddenly, he remembered. He was in Port Republic, Virginia. The Stonewall Brigade had engaged the blue-clad army that had invaded the precious Vale of Shenandoah.

Private Jonathan "Woody" Woodard recalled mere shadows of the dance between rivals, but he shuddered at the visual aftermath. He finally found the source of the peculiar light...a shiny object that lay between the bodies of a Yank and a fellow Confederate. The enemies faced each other locked in an eerie death stare. They appeared to have killed one another in the same instant.

Despite his mental fog, words filtered through the doorway

of his memory: "And God said, let there be lights in the firmament of the heaven to divide the day from the night; and let them be for signs..."

As Woody stooped down between the bodies, the pressure in his head overwhelmed him. Wobbly, he managed to pick up the article whose bright gleam had beckoned him from across the field of bodies. The ornate gold cover fit in the palm of his hand. He had never seen such an elaborate piece. Was it European? The top had a decorative design of foliage and flowers. He balanced himself and opened the cover to reveal an ambrotype of a child. Before he could examine the image, his vision began to dissolve.

A familiar voice rang out from behind. And then everything around him turned black as a raven.

Two

War's Fury

Private Lucas Halverston broke Woody's fall to the ground. After securing him, he retrieved a dead soldier's haversack and gently placed it under Woody's head. Seconds later, Woody came to, his confused gaze settling on Lucas's face.

These were swollen, sorrowful eyes staring back at him, drowning in a sea of grief, surrounded by new wrinkles and dirt-caked, gritty brows. Lucas had tried to free Woody from the gloominess that gripped him, but he had made little progress over the last few weeks. The death and destruction had wreaked havoc on Woody's soul, and the nightmares had become so intense that restful sleep was near impossible. Not so for him. Woody often marveled at how Lucas could sleep through the crackling bursts of a Virginia thunderstorm.

Lucas loved his friend, but being a man of few words and little sentimentality, he had never said as much. Woody, on the other hand, was effusive in his affection for him. Lucas wanted to reach inside and vanquish Woody's demons by brute force, to end his agonizing, slow withdrawal into himself.

Watching after Woody came natural for Lucas, given that they had been best chums since they were tadpoles. Lucas was two years older, larger in height and girth, and filled with more natural fight inside than his peacemaker friend. From the day the war had beckoned them both to Virginia's defense, Woody had performed his duty with valor. The question was, how long before the killing drove him to a place from which he could not return?

"My head's pounding like a sledgehammer on an anvil," Woody said. "I'm real swimmy-headed."

Woody's skin appeared pasty, his face like the porcelain doll sitting on Lucinda's dresser. Lucas's older sister understood him better than anyone in the Halverston household. "If you gaze at the doll long enough," Lucinda proclaimed when he was five, "she will wink and smile at you." The girl's pale-faced plaything had scared him, and Lucinda used this fear to keep him from sneaking into her room. The ploy had worked. He probed Woody's scalp, suppressing a grin that rose from the recollection.

"Needs some stitching," Lucas said. "Lost enough blood to fill a swimming hole. Should live to fight another day."

Woody massaged his temples, a distant stare etched on his face. "My images of this dance are fuzzy. What happened?"

"Think on it, pard…try to remember." After several moments, Woody returned a vacant stare, so Lucas filled in the details.

The brigade had dodged hellfire across the wheat field below a rolling hill. Minié balls had pattered against flesh like hailstones. The Feds had held the high ground and placed their artillery near the Coaling, a charcoal manufactory belonging to the farmer whose land they'd trampled. The big guns had belched grape, canister, and shell, dismembering bodies in their wake. After two failed attempts to win the morning, the Stonewall Brigade was part of a third and final flanking maneuver. They'd reached the top and finally overtaken the Yankee position.

"Is any of this coming back?" Lucas asked.

Woody shook his head.

"You and two of our boys cut down that artillery major. Or at least one of you did. Then along came some bluecoat who pistol-whipped you from behind and scampered off like a cockroach. That's when we turned the cannons against their owners. A sight to behold as they scattered."

Blood still flowed from the laceration on Woody's scalp. As he sat up, his eyeballs rolled back. Lucas eased him back to the ground. He placed a canteen to his pal's mouth, allowing him small sips.

"Take it steady."

"Thanks. I'm parched," Woody said.

He gulped the water, and then coughed. His face twisted into a grimace.

"Didn't I tell you? Go slow," Lucas said. "Need to find something to keep the little that's left in your noggin from falling out."

He scanned the lifeless bodies around them, men clad in blue and gray and different shades of brown and khaki. Finding the perfect donor, he removed the soldier's bloodied shirt. His white body stood out in a sea of morbid colors. Lucas turned away from the corpse and ripped a long strip from the material. He wrapped it around the top of Woody's head and knotted the ends under his chin. A flood saturated the material almost instantly.

"Hey, I can't open my mouth to speak," Woody mumbled through his closed jaw.

Lucas flashed a knowing smile. "You're a chattering fool. Excessive jawing leads to ruin. Do less talking, more listening to me. Won't hurt you none."

"Yeah, yeah."

Lucas couldn't help himself when it came to watching over Woody, the younger brother he'd never had. As a kid, the Woodard farm was a quiet perch to escape the raucous, clucking cries of his three older sisters. When he finished his chores and they fawned over him like a plaything, he would wander over to Woody's place, where Mrs. Woodard never failed to serve up a generous slice of whatever fruit pie sat on the kitchen counter. As the eldest, Lucas took it upon himself to offer sage advice to his longtime friend. Some Woody chose to take, some not so much.

Case in point: Woody's pending marriage to Betsy Edmonds. Lucas thought her spoiled, impatient, and quick-tempered, and held nothing back in speaking his mind about her. "Don't marry that girl," he'd advised more than once.

He stood an inch taller than Woody and carried an additional twenty pounds. With the strength of an ox, he lumbered at the same pace as one. Or so Woody teased him. Woody also ribbed him about his large, crooked nose, broken more than once in neighborhood melees before the war.

Woody struggled from his rump to a crouch on his feet. After steadying himself for a moment, he rose, then wavered, and almost fell again. He appeared panic-stricken, searching the ground for something. "Lucas, I found an—"

"Ambrotype," Lucas finished. "It's in your haversack. We better start gathering useful items from the field. We won the day, but them bluebellies might come back with a-hankerin' for another dance."

Woody finally made it to his feet. They parted, but Lucas peered over his shoulder several times to make sure his friend remained upright. He thought to stay together, but he didn't want to hover. "See you back in this spot in one hour," Lucas shouted. Woody nodded and continued on.

Protecting Woody became more difficult with each engagement in the recent Shenandoah Valley campaign. As their comrades in Botts Greys started falling, the odds increased that one or both of them would be cut down.

* * *

The picture mesmerized Woody. The subject's innocence acted as a salve against the ugliness of man's savage deeds. Which of the two dead adversaries had dropped this precious cargo? One of the soldiers must have carried the case in his haversack until, during his final violent struggle, it tumbled to the ground.

Woody recalled the Rebel's name, Henry Prescott, but they had never spoken. The bluebelly…? Despite Woody's diminished capacity, common sense had not spilled from his split head. Soon the Union soldier's remains would be dumped into a mass grave, burying his identity forever. Woody turned and increased his pace toward the holding pen where the prisoners had been gathered.

The fog of battle was dissipating, but still the soldiers milling about on the field looked like ghosts. It was hauntingly quiet, save but a few utterances here and there, and the moans of the injured yet to be removed from the field. The incessant ringing in his ears returned. With his Springfield aimed at their backs, Woody walked two captives over to the corpses.

"Do either of you recognize this man?" He pointed to the dead bluecoat.

One shook his head. The other moved forward for a closer look.

"Yeah...but we only got to talking a day or so ago. I think his last name is Braun...or something like that. From Cincinnati…or thereabouts."

"First name?" The man thought for a moment but came up short. Woody returned the prisoners and moved on.

He scanned the field. Boots. Pistols. Canteens. Fry pans. Plenty of items to make a soldier's life easier, right under his nose for the taking. Instead he wandered aimlessly, while his brain pieced together little snippets of the battle. The chaos in the killing fields of Port Republic had subsided. But the explosions and small arms fire, the high-pitched yell of the charging Confederates, still reverberated in Woody's ears like the shrill sound of cicadas at dusk. If the ringing never stopped, he thought he might go mad.

On this horrendous day, the worst in his year with the infamous Stonewall Brigade, he surely must be drifting on foreign soil. This could not be his beloved Shenandoah Valley. He imagined himself stuck in some far-off place, a patch of dirt that any breathing thing would tremble to walk upon. Yet, a mere five-day march away—or was it a universe from there?—sat his farm.

The air grew thick with the intolerable fetor of bodies in the first stages of rotting. On top of that, the stench of his own body odor, generated by the miles he'd marched and the battles he'd fought, made him bilious. He couldn't remember the last time he'd bathed. His light brown hair lay matted on his head, the strands fused together by grime. Beads of sweat chased the trickle of blood still seeping from his head.

All six feet and 170-pounds of him ached, and his

overburdened lower back screamed for relief. Toting essentials for survival, his ten-pound Springfield rifle and another twenty-five pounds around his waist and shoulders, didn't help matters. Ammunition. Food. Water. First-aid gear. His haversack carried personal items, like his bible, pipe, diary, and pen and paper to write home. And the extra cartridges stuffed in his pockets. He'd be hard pressed to lighten his load.

Woody plodded ahead, still in shock, his conscience wrought with guilt over his part in the butchery. Nothing would be the same after this madness, regardless of the victors. Nothing in this rich and beautiful valley, nothing in his way of life, and nothing in his head and heart. Evil spilled its wrath this day, like so many other days. Although his family didn't own slaves, did his unwillingness to stand against the practice damn him? He shuddered to think.

Muffled whispers rose from the ground. He surveyed the space around him until he found the source. The man's lips moved, and Woody leaned close to hear. "Wa...water...please."

The Union soldier's mortal injury, a bayonet thrust to the stomach, made Woody retch. He knelt, unsteady. The heavy bleeding from his wound had slowed, but the inside of his head still whirled. He unscrewed the cap on his canteen.

"Here, Yank." Like Woody earlier, the soldier choked as he gulped the water. "Whoa. Take sips."

The bluebelly struggled to speak, but Woody couldn't understand the words. He leaned forward and put his ear close to the fellow's mouth. The dying soldier choked out his words. "Th...anks...Johnny...I..."

"You're gonna be okay." A lie. "Say it with me. Our father, who art in heaven, hallowed..."

The Yankee attempted to say the prayer. Most men from the North and South had recited the orison as children, perhaps the first real appeal for divine guidance that their mamas and papas taught them. The man coughed.

"...hal...lowed...name...kingd..."

Woody agonized over this death knell. Men meeting their maker in large numbers came as part of the calamitous business of war. He'd suffered no illusions when he enlisted—men would die around him. Maybe his time would come up, but more disturbing than his own demise was the immense physical and emotional suffering he witnessed—the unhurried grappling with destiny and their visceral fear of the unknown.

But this soldier's eyes revealed something different. An unusual peace descended upon him.

Lord, let the end come now.

Silence. He stopped his prayer as the man's pupils widened into a blank stare. "I'm sorry, Billy." He ran his hand over the soldier's open eyes, shutting out the mayhem threatening to disrupt his eternal rest.

This man had somehow embraced his journey. In repose, his face conveyed a mysterious grace that Woody understood but had forgotten in war's devastating aftermath. He had seen the disturbance in death's black scowl, the emptiness on the faces of so many departed men. But this dead soldier's mouth had curled into a knowing smile. Whether soothed by the prayer, or given happy visions of better times, or welcomed by someone on the other side—in the end, this fighter experienced a good passage.

Woody raised his eyes to the heavens. "Both camps claim your favor. But how can you be on either side?"

After a change of heart, Virginia had left the United States, clothed in her righteousness. Woody had gone with her, prepared to turn ferocious against any man who endangered his homeland or sought to harm his family. Over time and after several clashes, his resolve to form a new country melted like a candle dripping into an unformed pile of wax.

He lamented out loud again. "Where are you?" Maybe he was deluded. Had God turned away, leaving these armies to their own destruction?

He sought a sign—any sign—to assure him that heaven approved of their righteous actions. He listened for an answer—a thunderous announcement, a still small voice, or some cosmic sign from creation. Any response to his lamentation would do, but the silence was deafening. The killing had emptied his spiritual storehouse.

The haze of battle now had cleared enough for him to recall a haunting detail about the charge on the Coaling. Just before the void engulfed him, Woody had glanced to his right and there he was. The phantom soldier with no facial features…the same apparition who haunted his dreams had appeared in Woody's waking hours.

Running beside him. Taunting him. Beckoning him forth. A chill ran down Woody's backbone.

Compelled by something he didn't understand, Woody dug into his haversack for the gold case. The object called out to him again with a sweet voice of compassion. He gazed at the image until an almost supernatural calm descended upon him, vanquishing his fear and grief, taming his restless spirit.

The young girl's innocent face soothed him.

His mama always said: Answers often come in small packages.

Three

Homeward

The surgeons had an easy time stitching Woody's scalp back together.

When he thought nobody would notice, Woody slipped back into the nearby woods, away from the ranks. He found a tree and brought his back to rest against the thick trunk, easing himself to the ground.

His Springfield lay beside him, ready to be discharged if peril approached. Again he pulled the photograph from his haversack and stared. The devastation of Port Republic ebbed away as he gazed at her likeness.

Her hair fell to bare shoulders, curling into ringlets. She wore a frilly hoop dress. Round cheeks—hand-colored pink—and a delicate mouth cast a sweet softness to her features. What was her name? She reminded him of a Bonnie he'd once met. Maybe her name was Alice. He breathed in this moment of connection and mused. For now, she was the unnamed girl.

The lass sat on the arm of an ornate chair upholstered in a fine brocade fabric. Her right hand clutched the wooden frame of the seat, and her left hand spilled onto her lap. The photographer had captured her in a haunting pose. Eyes that emoted a loss of innocence—perhaps reflecting an absent father.

Or someone else she loved, gone for a long stretch of time.

The image washed over him. What captivated him so?

Other men carried personal items that lent them solace. Even Abner Gooch, the hard-nosed sergeant that led his unit into battle, showed his soft spot. He read a letter from his seven-year-old daughter whenever the brigade took a break from its incessant marches. The night before Woody left Shepherdstown to enlist with Botts Greys, he asked Betsy if she might snip off a lock of her hair. He'd vowed to carry the golden curl in his haversack until he returned home or a stray missile cut him down. Either way, it would bring him comfort to hold a small part of her. She'd rolled her eyes, and that ended the discussion. At least he had his Bible.

Letters. Locks of hair. Photographs. These and other mementos served as important reminders of home for a homesick soldier. Links to a more normal time when the world made sense. But the girl's image struck Woody in a deeper, more profound way. It was as if they needed each other. As if she held the key to his sanity, his entire future. And having been there when her father fell, whether Confederate or Yankee, Woody possessed the power to bring peace and closure to her family. A softening of the sorrow and emptiness that she would carry for the remainder of her life. The child had lost her daddy much too soon.

A growl from his belly broke the moments of contemplation. Even a tasteless hardtack or stick of jerky would be a welcomed meal. Digging into his haversack, he found the recent letter from his mama, but nothing to quell his hunger pains. He took a gulp of water from his canteen and thought to rest his eyes for just a few moments. Hopefully the demons that prowled in his restless slumbers would leave him be.

Dreams, and more often nightmares, came to him with great clarity these days.

* * *

They talked while moseying hand-in-hand through the wheat fields of the Woodard farm. A mild breeze created the rustling sound over the stalks as all the ears bowed in reverence to the breath of God. The rich, dry, nutty aroma always stimulated memories of harvests gone by.

Betsy stopped and turned her bejeweled eyes toward his. She parted her full lips, a provocative signal. Woody took the invitation to move closer. Placing his hand under her chin, he lifted her face. As his mouth began to brush over hers heaven died a premature death. A swift kick to the bottom of his foot jarred him from his dreamscape back into the real world. Lucas stood over him. How long had he been out?

"Ought not to creep up on a man like that," Woody said. "Might receive a lead ball through your heart someday."

"You shouldn't sneak off the field like a Virginia fox squirrel. The brigade's gonna march into Browns Gap, up into the Blue Ridge. Gonna set a while until things cool down in the valley. What are you doing here, you fool?"

"Do you have any jerky in your sack?" Woody asked.

"Yeah." Lucas dug into his haversack and pulled out a small portion. "Here ya go."

Woody ripped off a mouthful and commenced to chew. The flavor of the beef satisfied his pang. Lucas glared at him, waiting for some explanation. Woody pulled the letter from his haversack. The desperate appeal from his mama had arrived three days before and weighed heavily on his mind. Finding the photograph had clinched his decision. He would take his leave from the ranks to return home for a period of time. Lucas would not be happy.

"Pard...? Are you going somewhere?"

Woody handed the correspondence to his friend and took another bite. He was famished, having emptied his stomach on the trampled wheat.

Lucas perused the message with growing concern written in his eyes. Then he passed the correspondence back. "Going home, aren't you? And without telling me?"

"Don't try to stop me, Luke. The decision's made. The wheat is overdue for harvest. With Daddy having broken his leg and my brother Robert also engaged in the fight, my mama has nobody to work the fields."

Lucas nodded. He could understand the dilemma. These were like second parents to him.

Plenty of men left the battlefield for the same reason and did not suffer being called deserters. Another purpose drove him though. He needed to clear his mind of all the killing and destruction of property. Despite the danger involved, he decided that after the harvest he would journey to Southern Ohio. With any luck, he might find the girl and soon after rejoin the Stonewall Brigade. He didn't share that part with his friend. Lucas would never understand.

He didn't even understand.

"Yep...you gotta go. Don't worry. I'll cover for you with command and let you know how it all shakes out. Try to have you counted as missing for now. Look for a letter from me in the next few weeks."

The journey wouldn't be easy. He'd need to move quickly through the forest and hope to avoid any blue-coated stragglers. The last thing he needed was to dangle on the receiving end of a Northerner's bayonet. He would stop to hunt his dinner and find the closest swimming hole along the way to scrub the dried blood and grime from his body. Then try to get some much-needed sleep. He would travel the Shenandoah back roads—five days walk due north to Shepherdstown, he figured.

"Rain appears to be following us," Woody said, uncertain of when he might see his friend again. "Try not to let it soak you."

Lucas just nodded. Parting words were not necessary. Their eyes said it all.

They shook hands and headed in opposite directions.

Four

Rebecca

Northern Kentucky
June 1862

Rebecca Johnston watched from the adjacent seat as her mentor, former slave John Parker, navigated his flat-bottomed boat the short distance across the Ohio River to the northern shores of Kentucky—a border slave state. While Kentucky had chosen to remain in the Union, owning coloreds was as legal as owning horses.

Many times she had conducted Underground Railroad passengers from her Red Oak farm to havens in the north. A slave would be smuggled to her house for a day or two, and then transported to the next safe haven. This night would be different. Tonight, for the first time, she accompanied John across the Ohio River into Kentucky on a clandestine mission. She and John would escort a Negro named Israel from the tobacco plantation that had been his home since childhood, across the river, and onto the invisible train.

At first, John had implored her to forget the crazy idea. "You'll slow me down and jeopardize the mission, not to mention our lives. This work is not meant for a woman."

"Listen to you," she had responded. "What about Harriet Tubman?"

Scottish to the core, Rebecca's stubborn will prevailed. This would be her first escort. As long as her husband, George, faced grim odds of survival in the Union army, she would continue the holy work of deliverance begun decades before. To her dismay, the number of riders trickled as the war dragged on longer than anyone had expected. The weeks turned into never-ending months with no end in sight.

She pined for her beloved. *Come home to me soon, George.*

Following John, Rebecca jumped into the knee-deep cold water, her soaked pants sending an immediate shiver up her spine. She and John pulled the craft onto the shoreline and they began the journey inland on foot. As Rebecca pushed herself to keep John's pace through a wooded marsh filled with thick underbrush, she pictured the hardships Israel and other slaves faced. Long hours of backbreaking work in the fields. Living in crude quarters, subject to bad weather and disease. Family members being sold off. Whippings. Slavery may have been judged legal in the southern states that seceded, and even in some that didn't, but she would never abide such an unjust, abhorrent institution. Lawful or not.

The principles against human ownership were worth dying for. In her weaker moments, George's face flashed before her. What if death wrestled him away and passed over her? Life without him might destroy her. The waiting, the not knowing if her brave crusader would return, had been chiseling away her faith. So she conducted the railroad to stay strong and relevant. To be whole for George when he came home.

Would he be the same man?

A flickering lantern lifted the black veil of night that obscured the path ahead, leading them over the hilly terrain and through muddy marshlands, some two miles into Mason County. A possible collision with death awaited, as did a brave slave named Israel. The parallels with an escape in long-ago Egypt piqued her curiosity about the man. The next traveler on a symbolic railroad with no tracks or cars would be standing in the shadows of a tobacco estate, behind the owner's squalid attempts to provide shelter for his workers.

Israel awaited a deliverer, his personal Moses. A freedman named John Parker would lead Israel to a different promised land.

John, owner of the local foundry and one of Ripley's wealthiest citizens, quickened the pace. He checked the unforgiving taskmaster in his pocket. "Making good time so far," he announced over his shoulder. Rebecca pushed herself to keep up. The escape plan had worked for hundreds of coloreds who'd fled their masters with John at their side. Some were close calls, but he had never lost a passenger.

First, they had spotted the beacon from high atop the hill. It signaled no activity on the waterfront or the city streets…a good sign. Second, they rowed to the Kentucky side. The third step was in progress: secure the passenger from the clutches of a tyrannical slaveholder named Franklin Wills. Their final task would be to lead Israel up the one hundred steps from the streets of Ripley to the small farmhouse of Presbyterian Minister John Rankin, a vocal abolitionist. A safe house suspected for years to be a hiding place for runaways.

Rankin, now sixty-nine, and his sons joined with John and Rebecca and other conductors before them to usher the railroad passengers to places where the citizenry frowned upon slavery. To Northern Ohio and Canada.

This was all done under the cover of darkness. To their advantage, no towns existed between the river and Maysville, Kentucky, the county seat to the southeast.

They continued at a brisk pace until John lifted his hand. Finally, a break. He passed a canteen to Rebecca, who gulped some sweet relief.

"Better save some for later," John said.

"Sorry."

When she passed it back, John replaced the cap without taking a drink. Instead he opened his special timepiece again, a birthday present from a young abolitionist couple in the sleepy town of Red Oak, north of Ripley. He gazed up at her, and a nod of mutual affection passed between them.

"Seems like yesterday," she said. "Cincinnati became heaven for a few days. Then George's leave ended. On the last day that pocket watch reached out to us through the store window. We spoke your name at the same instant."

"Whenever I check the time, I'm reminded of you."

John announced the arrival of midnight. They were right on schedule.

From the perimeter, they walked through acres of recently planted tobacco fields, fresh with the scent of turned soil and fertilizer. They tiptoed to the nearby barns and peeked into one. Air-cured hanging leaves from the previous crop left an earthy smell, which was tinged with sweet memories of George smoking his pipe on the porch, a white cloud snaking through the night air.

Several crude dwellings, no doubt the slave quarters, sat clustered two hundred yards away from the main house. On the opposite side stood bunkhouses for the hired hands. John and Rebecca crept forward, careful to avoid the crackling of dead ground cover. John ducked behind trees and around some cabins, Rebecca trailing close behind.

A shadowy figure behind one building stepped forward. He wore a brownish osnaburg shirt and cotton trousers. John addressed the man in hushed tones.

"Are you Israel?"

"Yessir. You Mr. Parker?"

He nodded. "This is Mrs. Rebecca Johnston."

"Glad to meet you," she said.

"My pleasure, Mrs. Johnston. Thank you for your assistance."

Israel's hair was cropped, his body chiseled. When he shook hands with John, Israel winced and then revealed the raw blister on his right palm.

"Ouch," John said. "Are you a smithy or carpenter?"

"A smithy. I got calloused hands, and I wear the proper gloves. Somehow this rascal sneaked up on me."

Rebecca had grasped much from John's powers of observation. With special skills, Israel would be valuable property to Wills, a possession worth fighting to reacquire. Owners often leased such laborers to other plantations as a lucrative side business. By morning, Ripley would be awash in a slave master's wrath.

Broad shouldered, Israel towered over Rebecca. She put his

age at around twenty-five. His voice sounded fru strong in a pleasant way. The feature that captur gentle eyes—half-crying, half-laughing at the sa spoke of both broken dreams and new possibilities. colored face was etched beyond his years.

"We need to reach the river undetected and deliver you the first stop in Ripley before dawn," Rebecca said. "Are you ready?"

"Not quite." Not the answer Rebecca anticipated.

A dog barked—once, and then again. They froze, hoping this would be the last of the canine chatter. The whinny of a horse echoed into the night and rode the wind high above the treetops. Apparently, nobody stirred inside the bunkhouses, a short walk from the outbuilding that housed the animals. Rebecca breathed deep, waiting for watchful men to emerge with pistols and rifles in hand. She'd never been the target of some trigger-happy plantation overseer, and she didn't want to start tonight.

All three of them held still. Twenty seconds. Forty. Two minutes. Precious silence. Relieved, but still alarmed, Rebecca faced Israel to convey the urgency of the matter.

"Perhaps you misunderstood, Israel. We must leave—now."

Rebecca and her mentor walked away, expecting Israel to follow. When she turned around, she watched the slave rush behind the cabin. She braced for a cacophony of animal protests, followed by an army of determined men who would shoot on sight. An extra minute might mean the difference between getting to the skiff and rowing unharmed to the opposite shore, or being filled with lead. Or even worse: becoming an early-morning breakfast for a pack of vicious bloodhounds.

Israel didn't understand the gravity of their situation. Bullets or a canine jaw—either would result in the same outcome.

John paced. "Worst-case scenario, if he doesn't show up, we—"

Rebecca's quick glance over his shoulder caused John to pivot. There stood Israel beside a young woman, her protruding belly evidence of an unborn child. The baby would soon trade its cocoon for a new adventure in the outside world, much like the parents-to-be.

'Mr. Parker and Mrs. Johnston…meet Fannie," Israel said. ..e mother of my child. We go together, with you or without ou."

Side by side, Israel towered over Fannie. A wrap covered her head, leaving a round caramel face that looked soft and smooth, full of childhood innocence. Wearing a calico gown and fine linen apron, she probably worked as a house servant.

John turned to face them, the certainty of his calling written on the pages of his own long-ago escape from bondage. "Let's go," he said. "We're about to get Mr. Wills's dander up."

Fannie hugged him. "Mr. Pahker, you our brave liberator—gonna carry us to a promised land. You our Moses."

John led the way. As they reached the outskirts of the plantation, one of the hounds began to bark. The yelps turned to howls that could raise the dead. The other dogs deciphered the first hound's call to arms and passed the urgent message to others. Horses neighed adding to the discordant mix of voices.

This time, instead of floating away in the breeze, the disturbance swirled like a dust storm, bobbing into each structure, searching for ears to tickle. A full-scale alert had begun. Men bellowed into the night air. They would first check the shacks to determine if a slave had made a run, giving the rescue party a much-needed head start.

John pulled out his pistols and urged the couple on, waiting for them to move in front of him. "Hurry."

They ran as John barked out directions. They had to reach the skiff before the snarling dogs and row out beyond the range of the farmers' weapons. Fannie tripped, and Rebecca wrapped an arm around her lower back and urged her forward.

A little less than a half-mile of water separated the two banks of the Ohio. The desperate pursuers would find a way to track them. Early in the morning they would continue the search in Ripley and beyond, relentless in their mission. Unless, of course, the hounds succeeded in cutting short their escape. Fannie stopped, struggling to catch a complete breath.

"Oo, Lawdy. This child wantin' to come into this world."

"Breathe." Israel modeled slow, deep breaths.

"If I can rest a short while," Fannie said.

"Are…you...okay, Miss Fannie?" Also winded, Rebecca

could hardly speak.

"I'm fine, Miss Rebecca, Mista Pahker." She placed both hands over her middle and smiled. "But this baby be jumpin' and rollin'. Israel, come feel your baby's big feet. Gonna be a boy, sure as we bein' delivered ourselves."

Rebecca marked their location by the cluster of trees in front of them, the spot where she and John stopped for water on their way to the plantation. The halfway point. John lifted the lantern higher to check his timepiece. "Just a moment's rest," he said. "Best take some water too."

Israel placed his hand on Fannie's belly. His eyes opened wide with each movement. Rebecca pushed back a twinge of envy. Before George left, they had spoken about having children, but decided it would be prudent to wait for his return. Would she ever become a mother?

In one heave of her chest, dreams of having a family tumbled to the ground. She picked them up, one by one, and stuffed them back into her heart. How she longed to hold George at that moment.

"Miss Rebecca…?" Concern leapt from Fannie's eyes.

"Oh, it's nothing…I'm fine."

John's attention shifted to somewhere in the distance. "Do you hear something?" They listened. Nothing. They focused again, and this time the faint sounds of barking and cursing men drew closer. "Keep on moving, Miss Fannie. We're almost upon the shore."

They started off again, but soon Fannie stopped in her tracks. Moans escaped through her labored breaths. Israel's calm turned into panic. "Fannie, honey. What's wrong?"

A stream of water ran down her legs.

Five

Labor

The peril behind them had legs. And sharp teeth. John ran ahead, as Rebecca and Israel wrapped arms around Fannie to keep her upright and moving.

"Almost there," Rebecca said. "Stay strong, Fannie."

Fannie entered labor as the hellish hounds snarled and slobbered and the foul encouragements from their masters got louder. With each stride, Rebecca imagined the worst. Given the opportunity, these desperate pursuers would shoot her and John where they stood, and cart Israel and Fannie back to the plantation. Israel's back would be laid open, and the cruel overseer would admire his butchery like a prime cut of beef. Fannie and the infant would be sent up the Ohio, never to be seen again.

They guided her across the swamps and over the remaining hills. Fannie lost her balance, but they kept her from falling into the brackish water. The pace and Fannie's added weight on Rebecca's shoulders took their toll, but she ignored the pain and kept going.

Extreme consequences nipped at their heels. Fannie's determination and courage gave Rebecca the strength to continue. Moments later, the waters of the Ohio stretched before them.

"There's the river, honey," Israel said.

"Gonna live…our…own lives." She gasped between breaths and stopped, unable to continue under her power.

"No massah be over us," Israel responded, as he scooped her into his arms and slogged toward the water.

"O Lawd, river's a blessed vision to behold."

"A few more steps now," Rebecca said, uncertain whether her own bursting lungs and cramped legs could withstand another inch. The gentle river current petted the shore, lifting a sweet melody to her ears. A pair of red black-masked northern cardinals perched on a nearby hackberry tree and welcomed their arrival with a song.

John heaved his skiff onto the shallow waters as the fugitive slave catchers emerged from the trees. Savage hounds barked and snarled like crazy, rabid wolves, tugging on their leashes with one purpose—to break bones and tear flesh.

"Hurry now," Rebecca said. "Hell's wrath is upon us."

They all boarded. Fannie wrapped her arms around her protruding belly, like a bald eagle sitting on her clutch. As John rowed, the volley of lead plopped into the water. By a miracle or just plain bad aim, nothing hit the skiff or its passengers.

"Duck." John drew his Colt pistol and discharged several bullets, aiming wide. "Don't mean to kill anyone this day, just to slow them a bit."

The gunfire did the trick, as the pursuers dropped to the ground for cover.

John hauled the oars through the water.

The henchmen reached the riverbank as the craft glided away, almost beyond their reach. Angered, the slave catchers screamed and shook their fists. To these misguided souls, she and John were guilty of a high crime. Israel and Fannie amounted to nothing more than horses stolen from a barn or someone's fine silverware snatched from a kitchen. But their owners would stop at nothing to get them back.

Depravity found its home in such misguided thinking.

The final shots fell short and wide of the vessel.

One man screamed a disturbing taunt. "We're comin' for you, Israel, and your whore. No matter where you roam, we'll find you. One day your bastard child and its mama will disappear into the night, and you'll never find 'em."

This dire prophecy sank its teeth in their hope. Israel's eyes grew wide in the dark night. "Hogwash," Rebecca said. "They're a bunch of blowhards."

But the taunt disturbed her too. This was a promise, not an empty threat. These innocent people might be hounded by wretched men, forced to look over their shoulders for a long time to come. Even after this whole bloody mess of a war ended and slavery was pronounced dead. Would this abomination, this plague, ever be exterminated?

Liquid panic moistened her forehead. She tried to banish the tension of the chase from her mind. She was no good to anyone in a fright.

Halfway across the river, John's arms and shoulders cramped, so Israel helmed the skiff. The band of thugs retreated, but nightmares like these always returned.

Angry for losing their charges, they would likely cross the river at dawn and barrel their way into town, drunken and itching for a fight. A door-to-door search would be conducted, and when the searchers found no sign of Israel and Fannie, they would work their way northward. Several such inquisitions had been conducted at the doorstep of her own farm, always with the same outcome. Her passengers would have moved on to the next stop along the line, undetected.

Neither John nor Rebecca could be identified as the perpetrators of this improbable escapade. Although tagged as a slave stealer, John had never been seized red-handed. Not yet, anyway.

This had not been a smooth rescue.

Six

One Hundred Steps

This had been the strangest, most dangerous of John's rescues yet, and Rebecca had heard some amazing stories.

Approaching the shore, they reviewed the plan, which so far worked as well as a bent shotgun barrel. They'd be forced to awaken Margaret Putnam, the midwife, and take her to the Rankin house to deliver the baby. Margaret was sympathetic to the plight of slaves. Unfortunately, her fire for emancipation and midwifery had smoldered with her advancing age.

John bemoaned this turn of events. "This will widen the circle of involvement in our little adventure."

"Unavoidable." But a doomsday scenario haunted Rebecca. The sun waited for no one, and babies could be just as stubborn. What if the searchers reached the Rankin place in the middle of the delivery? As they came to the shore two men stepped from the shadows. Surprised by the extra person, the operatives swung into action at John's direction.

"Otto, hide the skiff," John said. "David, take Miss Fannie and Israel to the house. Carry her up the steps if you must. We'll be along shortly."

The men moved to do his bidding.

John called out, "David." He stopped and turned back to his

mentor. "Tell Jean to expect visitors sometime after daybreak, men who'll be riled up and unreceptive to social niceties. She'll know what to do."

* * *

Ripley, Ohio

Rebecca followed as John moved along Front Street with the stealth of a hungry cat.

In a few hours the first streams of light would color the horizon. That spelled danger. Even now, the slightest noise might draw the wrong citizens into the streets, citizens looking for any reason to pick a fight. Ripley experienced many such nighttime disturbances. Rebecca and John's discovery in town could spell doom for the Negro family on the run.

She got a silvery peek at some of the town's most elegant homes, which adorned five blocks near the waterfront. They passed John's own two-story brick house, where his family was tucked within the safety of its walls. Moving in the shadows, they avoided the street lamps installed by Ripley Gas Light & Coke Company, which made Ripley the first Ohio town to be illuminated at night, a civic achievement lauded by most citizens.

But on this night, the cloak of darkness was their friend.

John rapped the door of Margaret Putnam, the midwife.

"Shh." Rebecca looked to the left and the right at the neighbors' houses, waiting for a light to flicker through a window, a person to peek outside.

"You know Margaret—hard of hearing," John said. He knocked again. This time the disturbance created a stirring inside the house.

The door opened a crack. A woman wearing a lace-trimmed nightcap and holding a candle poked her wrinkled face into the gap. Margaret, widowed the year before, lived alone.

"Who is it?"

"John Parker and Rebecca Johnston."

"John?"

"Can you dress quickly?" John asked. "Your services are needed."

"Land sakes, it's early, and I'm old. Why can't these women labor in the light of day?"

"Come, now. The train's a-waitin'."

"Oh…stay there. I'll be right back." The door closed.

Rebecca smiled. "That did the trick."

They waited on the stoop for what felt like hours as Rebecca scanned the nearby homes, certain that at any moment, someone would come out, point a finger, start accusing them of all the sins they'd committed. *Please hurry!*

Finally, Margaret returned to the porch and followed them, shuffling her way to the hundred steps that led to the Rankin house, high on a hill. When they arrived, Margaret lifted her head to gaze up the steep stairway. Resigned to the task, she sighed and lifted a foot to begin the long ascent. Halfway up, the midwife stopped, her breathing heavy.

"Sorry, but the years have weakened my legs and creased my face," Margaret said. "The vagaries of growing old. Hold tight to your youth, for time intends to wrestle it from you."

Yes, yes, Rebecca thought. Wise words, but must they dally? The air was tinged with a woodsy fragrance from the trees and underbrush lining the pathway. The earliest risers chirped away, unaware of the human drama being played out. At the top, they stopped again so the midwife could recover from the climb.

"You best go inside," Rebecca said. "A baby is anxious to make your acquaintance. The dawn is soon to come and men of ill will would love to ruin the joyous introductions."

John led the midwife to the mother-to-be. Rebecca remained outside, gazing toward the eastward horizon where nature's palette swirled in a mixture of orange and yellow and red colors. A new morning, like millions of beginnings before it, promised that life would go on, with all its joys and heartaches. Would this assurance extend to George? After asking God's blessing, she glanced below to the streets of Ripley as the outlines of her buildings began to take shape.

Ripley's population had tripled over the last twenty years. During the day, women shopped at the stores along Front Street. Men toiled in meatpacking plants. Children attended school. But at night, the ugly side of the town made itself known. Frantic screams, the cracking of whips, loud pounding, and pistol shots. Pro-slavery, anti-abolitionist mobs had burned down schools, churches, barns, and homes. Some of Ripley's citizens had found themselves caught in the crosshairs.

Danger crept closer to Rebecca each time she dared to help rescue a life.

* * *

"Again…push," Margaret Putnam said.

The midwife's instructions, and Fannie's cries in response, bled through the closed door. Israel paced. Rebecca tried to calm him, but to no avail.

Margaret carried his world in the palms of her hands. The lives of Fannie and their child hung in the balance and he had no choice but to trust. He pleaded to be at his beloved's side, but Rebecca wouldn't allow it.

"That's just the way with these things, Israel. I'm certain you'd rather not watch the baby slide from Fannie's womb."

So he waited. Rebecca kept vigil with him, along with John Parker and Jean Rankin, the owner of the house. Jean offered her guests something to eat or drink. Each of them declined. Then she tried to distract them with stories about her own babies' births, but they seemed to heighten Israel's anxiety so she stopped.

Rebecca understood the overwhelming sense of helplessness that came when the fate of a loved one was beyond your grasp, and all you could do was wait. Several weeks had passed since she received a letter from George, which was why she'd begged John to let her join in this rescue. Distractions helped.

Israel needed one now. Something other than stories about birthing children.

"John, I'll bet this is another first for you," Rebecca said. "I mean, besides having a woman traipsing along. Israel…John here has done more than six hundred rescues."

"Lawd, have mercy." He turned to John, admiration lighting up his face. The sounds of painful childbirth subsided for the moment. "Please, Mr. Parker, share a story."

"Okay, but first you must promise to call me John."

"Yes, sir…I mean, John."

"Once, I entered the house of a Kentucky slaveholder to snatch the infant of a couple who hid in a cornfield. Waiting for a miracle, just like you, Israel. Every night the cruel man had taken their little one to discourage them from trying to flee. His wife put the baby to sleep at the foot of their bed as if the child belonged to her."

Israel stared at him, rapt.

"Quiet as a mouse, I secured the child and fled the main house. We hightailed it across the fields, the lead balls flying behind us. The scoundrels made chase with their fanged beasts leading them. But like tonight, Providence placed us beyond their reach."

Israel nodded. "The masters can be cruel. Like Mr. Franklin Wills, thinking he's gonna separate my family—sell Fannie and our baby down the river. Him figurin' I'd just lay down and say, 'Yes, Massah. You go on'."

"Those days are behind you," John said.

Israel stared at this new mentor. "I'm not havin' any of that nonsense no more. Thanks to you and your friends." He made eye contact with Rebecca and then Jean, one at a time.

Fannie cried out again. Israel needed another distraction.

"Tell him some of your story, John," Rebecca said. "Tell him why you risked your life to help him and Fannie."

The moans grew louder, but Israel's eyes remained glued on the storyteller as the events of 1835 rolled out of him.

At eight years old, John had been ripped from his mama's arms by an overseer and dragged away. "I can still hear her voice…'sweet boy, keep your head high, for I will be with you.' Confusion and anxiety gripped me, but I tried to be a man like my mama told me. We walked more than a hundred miles from Norfolk to Richmond. A kind old man chained next to me tried to…"

He stopped. A tear formed at the edge of his eye, glistening in the lamplight. He heaved a sigh and continued.

"One night, the old timer comforted me when I wept. For that act of compassion, he received many lashes from the overseer's whip. I thought they'd never stop. The man lay dying, his back torn to shreds, and all for what? Because he'd been kind to me. They sold me to another slave trader, and I walked eight hundred miles to Mobile with four hundred other coloreds."

John decided he would create a better life—one with liberty. He worked odd jobs, scraped together eighteen hundred dollars, and bought his independence.

As John finished the story, he stood and threw his shoulders back in one determined motion. Rebecca had never witnessed such an emotional display from him. Apart from the subdued moans coming from the bedroom, the room was quiet.

John approached Israel. "It's time for me to leave you now."

Israel pleaded for him to stay a while longer. "Must you go?"

"My presence here might raise the suspicions of some townsfolk if the slave hunters from the Wills plantation make inquiries." He offered a relaxed smile, as if all were well.

"Besides, the sun's rising and my Miranda will have a fit if I'm not home soon. Israel, I'm confident you will be a wonderful father. This I promise: You and I will meet again someday in a different place, at a better time. Godspeed."

Israel stepped forward, his hands awkwardly reaching up, and then dropping to his side. John placed his hand on Israel's shoulder like an older brother.

Israel promised John that he would recount this story to anyone who would sit long enough to listen. Generations of his family would retell the tale that unfolded across the Ohio River that morning.

Through the walls, Fannie's cries echoed. She wailed, "You gonna come now, right into this morning."

Unable to contain himself, Israel burst into the room, Rebecca right behind him trying to intercede.

"What you doin' in here?" Fannie breathed deep and gritted her teeth. Pain contorted her face, and the veins in her temples popped out as she squatted and pushed.

"Best take your leave," Margaret said.

Israel hesitated. "Now!" Fannie screamed.

He froze, startled by the outburst. Rebecca shuffled him backwards toward the door. She glanced at Margaret, who was positioned to catch the infant when it emerged. Margaret looked haggard from the difficult delivery. What else could she do but continue to coach and encourage Fannie? Rebecca lifted a silent prayer as she closed the door.

Thirty minutes later, Israel became more disheartened. The groans sounded more intense, and Margaret's instructions became increasingly worrisome. If the riffraff from Kentucky paid a visit now, all would be lost.

Seven

Melancholia

Storm clouds continued to gather as Woody bathed stark naked in a murky pond, dead center in an open pasture.

A few hours had passed since the Port Republic battle. Thankfully the ringing in his ears had stopped, but a pensive mood gripped him. He wished he could shake off the emotional wounds he sustained in battle like Lucas, but he had accepted that he was made differently. The pond's cold water shocked his system at first but turned tolerable as he scrubbed his chest and arms with the chunk of lye his mama had sent weeks ago.

The worth of that cleanser surpassed precious metals at that moment. Gold could not remove the stench from his body or the vermin nesting in his hair. He'd been knee-deep in Virginia's sacred soil for the longest time. Before the battle, Lucas had called him a walking pen of pig manure. In fairness, his partner agreed his own stench matched Woody's on most days.

Woody had first used the lye to wash his rags, which lay on the bank. A new outfit would bring him the simplest of joys. For now, ridding his tattered clothes of the blood spilled by countless men and the sweat from marching thousands of miles would be enough.

The war had driven the schoolboy out of him, replacing

naiveté with the nasty business of inflicting the worst kind of misery upon others. On top of that, the bad food and stretches of no food at all robbed him of body fat and then muscle. Long marches. Diseases. All combined to hammer the joy from his days. Not too long ago, he and Lucas would hunt and swim and skip rocks in the summertime after clearing the fields and finishing their chores. Life was carefree.

Now a deep melancholia wrapped its tentacles around his spirit, threatening to squeeze away the final echoes of happiness.

Water brought to mind treasured memories...and some frightening experiences. As Woody submerged to rinse the soap from his hair, he soared across the canyons of time to another body of water that almost took his life. As he relived the harrowing underwater event, he panicked and couldn't surface for air.

He and Lucas had been fishing for hours along the nearby shore of the Potomac River. Seeking cover from the blazing sun, he pulled off his shirt and dove head first into the water.

The momentary relief gave way to searing pain. Try as he might, he couldn't find the surface. Couldn't even move. The last bit of air in his lungs bubbled upward, mixing with a meandering trail of red. Bewildered, his last thought was...*I'm going to die.* A moment before his conscious mind ebbed away, a heavenly presence drew him upward to meet his maker. Or so he thought. Seconds later, lying facedown on the ground, he coughed up several mouthfuls of water until traces of life-giving oxygen reawakened his brain. He rolled over to gaze on the face of an angel. Lucas always showed up at the right moment.

As that memory faded, Woody forced himself to the pond's surface. He shook his head and blew enough water from his nose to douse a roaring campfire. Part of him would have been happy to sink to the silted bottom and stay.

Dazed by the sheer power of this remembrance, Woody's attention was drawn to a quick movement at the edge of the nearby woods. Earlier he had spotted something at the same location. A grazing stag, he'd thought at first. Now he wasn't so sure.

* * *

Woody found a spot between two trees where he pitched a lean-to using a rectangular piece of canvas. He gathered firewood and created a pit bounded by rocks and wood that he hoped would protect his fire.

The high-pitched daytime call of the cicadas gave way to the chorus of tree crickets and katydids, filling Woody's ears in the first few hours of darkness. He delighted in the sights and sounds of the valley, warmed by the crackling flames. A light rain began to fall, accompanied by a breeze.

Back home, the songs of the small vireos and thrushes would lull him to sleep in his hammock after the sky's yellow orb receded in the west. On the porch after dinner, he and his father would enjoy a smoke and listen for the calls of the whip-poor-wills who flew at night, hunted and ate during the day, and slept in-between. At campfires, the chirps of the sparrows moved about in the dark to avoid larger birds of prey, assuring him all was well in his world.

He'd made a habit of studying them all in his younger, more carefree days.

The rabbits he hunted earlier for dinner had eased his hunger, but sleep still eluded him. As he lay beneath his blanket, he pictured Lucas bivouacked with the Stonewall Brigade somewhere along Browns Gap, no doubt blowing a Georgia tornado through his mouth with every breath. Now that they were separated, he missed the racket. How did Lucas rest so easily?

Woody rose and added fuel to the smoldering fire, which filled the air with hisses and flaming pops. The clouds temporarily gave way to glittering stars and a half-moon that shined the Creator's light through the sparsely wooded area where he camped. The new wood ignited with sparks, then burst forth with flames that danced upwards and outwards like couples doing a Virginia reel. A gust of wind captured the spewing smoke and returned it to the fire starter.

He coughed and took a swig of water. After relighting his pipe, he pulled the ambrotype from his haversack and stared at the girl's likeness for a spell. Before long, his eyelids became heavy, as if silver dollars lay on top, drawing them downward.

The case tumbled to the ground as he succumbed to his body's need.

* * *

The long march tired him. Not on some hot, dusty trail or familiar muddy mountain pass. Rather, Woody trudged on a deep, dark stairway, circling again and again into a pit.

A faceless soldier—Confederate or bluecoat, he couldn't tell which—led the way. Chains shackled his wrists and feet like a plantation slave. He glanced up. The unnamed girl stood at the top of the stairway. She tried to warn him of some approaching danger. How strange. She spoke with the timbre of a man's voice. The voice, and a snapping branch, woke him. He reached for his Springfield.

"Leave it be, Johnny Reb," the Union soldier said, inching forward. "Got no beef with you tonight. A warm fire and a portion of what's left on the bones of them-there rabbits. That's all I'm interested in."

The interloper slinked into camp, his rifle lifted, the bayonet affixed. A heavy residue darkened his face and dimmed the blue color in his coat. The man's kepi sat crooked on his shaggy head. An artillery gunner? Maybe a deserter from Port Republic. The soldier shifted his attention to the ground, and Woody followed his gaze to see the gold case lying in the dirt. In the time he'd slept, the clouds had released the burden they could no longer carry.

Woody stood, his arms raised above his head. His heart thwacked the inside of his chest and his mind blanked out. The intruder lowered his weapon and pulled a pistol from his pants. He waved the gun toward the tree, a signal for Woody to sit back down under the lean-to where he'd been dreaming moments ago.

The bluecoat picked up Woody's Springfield and leaned it against a tree several paces away. Then he sat by the fire, his pistol still leveled. The rain had soaked his clothes, but he seemed unfazed. The man was small in stature, maybe five foot six, and older than most Union soldiers. Maybe in his mid-thirties. Perhaps a big-city man caught up in the frenzy of combat like him. In another life, they might have been friends.

The wanderer gazed at the rabbit meat hanging above the flames. "I'd be real thankful to lower this-here firearm and have a bite of them hares on the skewer. Been frightfully hungry since this morning."

The man set the pistol on his lap.

Woody gave him a nod, and the man wrenched a leg from the carcass. "Thank you kindly," the Yank said and sank his teeth into the sizzling meat. As he chewed, Woody tried to determine his next move. The man pulled off another leg and continued eating, his eyes now concentrated on the gold case.

"Saw you staring at whatever's inside, back in the woods after the battle and here by the campfire." The stranger toggled the hot meat from one side of his mouth to the other. "Almost like some kind of magic hypnotized you."

"None of your concern," Woody said. "You been following me since we beat your pants off back at Port Republic. Why?"

"Might say we both skipped the field."

Woody took exception with his statement. Although technically true, hardly a man would quibble with his reasons for skedaddling. Besides, he'd done his duty until his side claimed the day. What possessed this Yank to leave and follow him through the forest? He doubted the man's intentions were honorable. The pistol in his lap proved that.

"How's your head?" the man asked. "I whopped you mighty hard when you reached the Coaling?"

Woody stared at him, dumbfounded. What was this bluebelly's aim?

"Don't recollect?" the stranger asked. "I sure remember you. Can't be certain, but I think it may have been you who killed one'a our best officers. Three of you Rebs fired at once. Almost blew the man clean out of his boots. That's when I knocked you senseless and ran off. Yes, sir...a real straight shooter, that officer. Not that I liked him much."

Woody took a heavy breath. How many brave men had he slain in battle? Men with wives and daughters like the girl in the photograph. Brothers he had no personal argument with, but who would deal the same fatal blow against him if given the chance.

"What was his name?" Woody asked.

"Major George Johnston."

"From where?"

"Small town on the north shore of the Ohio," the soldier said. "Place called Ripley Oaks. Or something like that."

Woody experienced a tinge of remorse, even though it was possible he had not delivered the fatal blow. Someone in this Ripley town would soon be mourning the loss.

"Seems you got some regrets," the Yank said with a condescending smile.

Woody's impatience bubbled over. "You've finished eating, mister. Best you be heading out now."

"Thinkin' I will. Mighty fine meal. B'fore I do…why don't you just hand me the case?"

"Can't do that," Woody said.

"The lead pills in this-here New Army Colt say different."

He raised the pistol and cocked its trigger. A roaring thunderbolt followed.

Eight

Brother Against Brother

Woody didn't want to hand over the case, but he wasn't going to die for it, either. He held it out, and the man snatched it.

"What's your name?" Woody asked.

"Charlie Crane." He gazed at the photograph.

"Well, sir, that image carries a personal meaning for me. The girl sustains me. Being a soldier yourself, I'm sure you understand. I'd be obliged if you hand back the case."

"This your sister or something?" the bemused man asked. "I got an older sister back home. More trouble than she's worth." He pulled a glass flask from his pocket and guzzled some of its contents. The fire began to dwindle, so Woody stood to feed it again. Charlie waved his six-shooter, and Woody sat to let the flames run their course.

Charlie shook his bottle. "This bark juice will keep you warm enough."

For lack of a better plan, Woody grasped the vessel and took a chug.

"Hey, Johnny...take 'er easy. Leave some for me."

The deep draw made Woody gag.

Charlie laughed as he inspected the gold case. "Wonder if this is the real thing. Might take her to a pawnshop and fetch me some U.S. dollars. Whad'ya think she'll bring? The container, I mean. Not the girl."

Charlie quaffed again from the flask. The drunker Charlie became, the greater the chance of Woody escaping injury, so he stuck his hand out for another drink. With any luck, the alcohol would send Charlie stumbling back into the dark with no harm done. Brother against brother back at Port Republic, and in all the battles up and down the Shenandoah, left Woody's soul yearning for peace and rest.

Charlie passed the drink over and Woody tipped the bottle, allowing only a trace of the liquor to pass his lips. "Who's waiting for you back home, Charlie? Got a girl? Your folks?"

The stranger's demeanor turned sober. "Daddy's a drunkard. Ran out on me and my sister and our addled mama five years ago. She needed a lot of looking after. Sis was useless, like I said, so old Charles here took on most the burden. After a while I did like my father and ran off. Didn't look back, neither."

Charlie took a gulp. Liquid courage dribbled down one side of his mouth. His gaze turned empty, like the man inside vacated his physical shell and wandered away. Woody stood up in a deliberate fashion, one hand raised and the other pointing to the last bit of firewood.

"The chill out here is growing. Do you mind if I...?" The request brought Charlie back from wherever he'd slipped off to. This time, he nodded his approval.

The rain danced through the treetops.

"Never took much time for women," Charlie said.

The admission made him sound…forlorn?

"A hard-luck story buried in there?" Woody asked.

"Enough of this blubbering." The man's mood lightened. "Know what, Johnny? Here's what I'm thinking. This little item comes with me when I leave."

Woody slapped his knee with feigned amusement and took another slug. He swiped his arm across his mouth to catch the dribbles. One thing struck him with certainty: This man intended to lay him under before moving on. In the event of a fair fight, Woody figured he'd hold the advantage, being larger and heavier. But staring down the barrel of a pistol was anything but fair.

"Sure, Charlie. A heartfelt gift from me to you. Let's take another swig to seal the gesture." They shared the last of the inebriant, with Charlie drinking most of it.

"No sense wasting any." Charlie lifted the bottle high, the opening pointed toward his mouth. The last three drops fell to his extended tongue. He hurled the flask into the trees. "All gone. And things was starting to get fun."

Woody had not figured out how to turn this dire predicament to his favor.

"Well now, Johnny...hah! I don't know your real name. No matter. You traitors are all Johnny to me. Adieu...parting is sweet sorrow, or some such nonsense. I need to be heading out now, so thank you for this gift."

As he rose, Charlie stumbled backwards and fell.

The pistol slipped from his lap, and Woody grabbed it, sure and steady, ready to fire.

Charlie righted himself and then looked up. His eyes widened at the sight.

Woody kept the handgun aimed and prayed there would be no taking of life this night. Charlie's next move would determine that.

"By some fluke," Woody said, "I am a Johnny. Jonathan Woodard, to be precise. Or Woody to my friends, but that doesn't include you. Now pass the case back to me, nice and slow like. Be a right shame for one of these hornets in your gun to sting you. Like I said, the photograph's important to me. Don't mean to lose it to the likes of some deserting Billy Yank looking for a quick dollar."

"Sure, sure...Woody."

As the man handed over the case, it tumbled to Woody's boots and into a small puddle of rainwater. He lowered himself ever so slowly, glancing downward for an instant. Time enough for Charlie to unsheathe a dagger from his ankle and slash Woody's arm. One shot rang out before the pistol tumbled several feet away.

The blade had torn through Woody's jacket and sliced his right forearm. Blood flowed to his hand, as he reached to grab the Yank's wrist before he could strike a crippling blow.

They wrestled each other to the ground. Charlie pinned

Woody below him, grunting as he struggled to drive the dagger through his opponent's heart. Charlie was stronger than Woody had anticipated. The Yankee's face turned red and the veins in his neck bulged—an otherworldly resemblance to the foes seeking to kill him in his nightmares. The tip of the blade penetrated Woody's clothing and threatened to tear into his chest. As Woody braced for the searing hot pain of a plunging knife, Charlie's strength began to falter. The Yank mustered one last push.

A stream of blood trickled from Charlie's chest down to Woody's face. The one stray bullet had somehow found its mark. Charlie smiled as his body went limp. Woody pushed him to the side.

Woody lay still, panting, his chest heaving. Tears of gratitude formed at the edges of his eyes. Then he looked over at Charlie's lifeless body and became angry. All he wanted was to avoid killing, and not even a day off the battlefield he had done it again.

"Why, God?" he cried out.

Why hadn't they parted company without inflicting violence? Woody picked up the gold case and glanced at the girl. This time she offered no consolation.

* * *

The bayonet on Woody's Springfield served as a digging implement. The stinging rain had hammered the ground beneath the trees, helping him to hew a shallow grave. Dragging the body over, he laid Charlie in the hole and dropped his old Springfield over the corpse. Charlie's newer rifle and revolver would prove useful for the rest of Woody's journey home.

After saying a few words and a prayer, Woody pushed the dirt back into the hole as best he could without a shovel. He topped the mound with branches and leaves to prevent any wild animals from disturbing the remains.

The hour grew late, and he would not find rest after this encounter. He broke camp and traveled north. Sadness streamed down his face, mixing with heaven's teardrops. The madness he'd sought to escape had somehow found a way to follow him off the battlefield.

The howl of a Virginia gray wolf cut through the night air and over the wooded hills. A second plaintive cry followed, the pitch sounding both admirable and abhorrent. Woody had known these predators to wander off the mountain and savagely reduce flocks of sheep in the valley.

Man struck him as similar in some ways, able to wantonly kill. War had introduced Woody to the darker side of his species, and he mourned for man's fallen nature.

For now, he would hold tight to the unnamed girl and the comfort he derived from the Scriptures. Charlie's interference emboldened Woody to search for the girl after the harvest.

Nine

In Hiding

Ripley, Ohio

The silence from the bedroom threw Israel into another panic, but Rebecca heard the faint whimpers of protest from one of the earth's newest inhabitants. Margaret emerged from the bedroom with a newborn swaddled in a blanket.

"Here's your son, Israel." She started to hand the infant to him, but he backed away.

"I don't know how."

"Here, allow me show you." Rebecca stepped forward to take the infant. "You cradle the baby with your left forearm and hand…like this. Now you try."

Still hesitant, Israel held his son. A good man and woman had been blessed with a healthy child. The joy that filled the room crowded out the uncertainty and strife that ran wild beyond these walls. For moments like this, Rebecca put her own circumstances aside and reveled in the miracle of a new life.

A smile as wide as a quarter moon burst forth on Israel's face. "Is he normal? Does he have...?"

The midwife opened the top of the cloth. "He has all his fingers and toes," Margaret said. "He's perfect."

"This is a big boy," Israel said. "Maybe ten pounds. How's Fannie?"

"She's fine," the midwife said. "You may bring your baby back to her, but stay only a moment. Rest is what she needs now. Soon enough, we'll need to hide you."

"Please come, Miss Rebecca," Israel said.

They walked into the quiet bedroom, the newborn held close to his chest. Fannie, weakened and tired but peaceful and content, opened her eyes to this glorious picture and smiled. Israel handed the baby to Rebecca and sat on the side of the bed, stroking Fannie's forehead.

"You okay, Fannie? I been sick with worry."

"The hurtin' was something terrible. But now..." The joy of a new mother told the rest of the story.

He retrieved the baby. With eyes closed Israel said, "Honey...meet Parker Rankin, our son. I mean, if you agree with the name." One eye opened, awaiting her response.

"Hello, Parker," Fannie said. "Welcome to the world."

He sighed and laid Parker at her breast. After a few stops and starts, the baby suckled. Fannie hummed a lullaby, and before long, she and her child fell fast asleep.

Peace filled the room. For these precious few minutes, Rebecca ignored the violent storm that brewed outside.

* * *

Soon after young Parker came into the world, Jean and Rebecca walked the family to the barn on the west side of the house. The loft was filled with hay, the floor strewn with tools. Chopped wood was stacked in a mound to one side. The horses snorted in their stalls when the humans arrived.

Jean led the family to an isolated spot where horse blankets and other equipment lay. Moving the items aside, she pulled open a trap door that led to a clandestine sanctuary, a small space where coloreds who thirsted for freedom could take refuge.

Resolute, Israel climbed down to evaluate the hideout. The new mother rocked side to side with little Parker sound asleep, snuggled in her arms. Beads of sweat dropped to her eyes, which blinked rapidly. "O Lawd, be with my baby."

"This is a cramped space," Rebecca said, "but you'll only be down there for a short time. Hopefully just a few hours."

Who wouldn't be anxious, locked up with a newborn yards away from slave catchers who would slap them in chains? Incensed by the injustice, Rebecca struggled for a way to assuage Fannie's distress.

That proved unnecessary as the new mother lifted her head and stood tall. Apprehension gave way to newfound courage. "Many as ten of us livin' in one'a them slave cabins on the plantation, and we still did the cookin', cleanin' and other chores," Fannie said. "Gonna manage here too. Only thing, my Israel hungers for freedom. To build a life where he no longer hidin' from men out to rob his family of respect."

"How long, Miss Rebecca?" Israel asked from the space.

"Those ruffians will likely show up some time before noon, after they liquor up. When they find nothing, they'll keep eyes on the farm during the night. But don't worry. We have a decoy to throw them off track. Y'all will be on your way to the next station around midnight."

Jean handed him a small oil-burning lantern and food and water. Several folded blankets lay stacked in one corner. "The air holes will provide you with plenty of oxygen."

Jean's assurances always calmed Rebecca. In her late sixties, Jean had brought thirteen children into the world, all of who joined their parents in fighting slavery as adults. Beneath the white bonnet that covered most of Jean's parted hair was a soft rounded face and wise eyes. When pursed, her thin lips revealed the strong and determined woman that Rebecca so admired. Israel saw only her soft side and he too seemed calm.

"Air's not bad. A tad musty, but we'll be fine."

Fannie climbed down into the space while Israel held the baby. Once settled on a bed of straw, she brought the boy to her chest. Rebecca stooped halfway down and caught the lantern's shimmers against the mother and baby. Israel approached the secret door where Rebecca and Jean waited for a final word.

"Be strong," Jean said. "In no time, we'll be back to release you."

Rebecca held out one hand, which Israel grasped reaching

up. Israel blew out his cheeks, and his eyes stared beyond them for a moment.

"Hope I can be a good father." He released Rebecca's hand and glanced at Jean. "While we're down here, we'll be praying no harm comes to this house."

The Lord had been merciful. Not a soul had been lost. With his help, that would be the case tonight. Jean told them to maintain silence as she lowered the door. The two women stood in the same place for several moments while Jean prayed God's protection over the new Rankin family. The responsibility for their safety weighed heavily on Rebecca. She and John had set out to free one man and ended up fleeing with three people, including an innocent fetus whose future depended on their success. They had avoided disaster so far, but Rebecca feared that their luck might run out. She laid it in God's hands.

As they turned to cover the trap door with the tools, Rebecca grabbed Jean's arm. A faint but unmistakable song came from the hideaway.

"Swing low, sweet chariot."

Both women understood the symbolism of those words, the chariot being the engine powering this figurative railroad. Field workers on farms throughout the South had sung the call and response chant, their taskmasters being none the wiser. With a smooth, resonate baritone, Israel called out the first code words again. This time louder, almost so they might hear and perhaps be encouraged by the family's high spirits.

"Swing low, sweet chariot."

To which Fannie answered. "A-comin' for ta carry me home."

They repeated the verse. The next words in the spiritual referred to Ripley and the people of the Underground Railroad. This band of angels swooped over the Ohio to transport those in need to their new home…to freedom.

"I looked over Jordan, and what did I see."

Jean began to speak of a time when young children like Parker Rankin would not know of human bondage, of hiding in shallow holes to avoid detection by men with chains and whips.

Rebecca raised a finger to her lips. "Ssh…listen." She stomped twice on the trap door and the singing stopped. Jean camouflaged the location and the two women hurriedly made their way back to the house.

Multiple horses galloping and neighing came to an abrupt halt outside, as men barked out orders to each other. Rebecca couldn't understand the words. She peeked through the curtains and saw three men on their way to the door. A moment later, one man pounded with the strength of a gorilla.

"Let me handle this, Rebecca."

Jean moved like a turtle, in no hurry to answer their rudeness. She ambled to the kitchen and moved the coffee pot from one burner to another. On the way back, she straightened knick-knacks that were not out of place and picked up several items only to return them to the same locations. Meanwhile, the man at the door knocked again so hard, the walls in the entryway around the door began to crack.

Pulling the curtain back to expose her presence, Jean feigned surprise and smiled, ignoring the man's seething anger. The tension in his bulging neck, his clenched mouth, and his lowered eyebrows finally brought her to the doorknob. Still she delayed.

If these animals broke through the door, they would find nothing amiss. No bloody rags or water basin, no afterbirth that chased little Parker into the early morning. When she decided the purposeful stall tactic had gone on long enough, she eased the door open. Three fully armed, unsavory characters stood before her. The apparent leader growled as droplets of sweat dripped down his twisted face.

"About time," the man said.

Rebecca stepped forward. "Why, top of the marnin' to ya."

One man belched and spewed the unpleasant odor of digested beer. When the apparent boss came closer, his body stench overpowered her. The rotund man, his bewhiskered face marked with pocks, scowled his displeasure. A long scar extended from under his eye patch, down his left cheek to below the side of his mouth. Spittle seeped to his chin.

None of them bothered with the courtesy of removing their hats. Rebecca laid her sunny disposition on thick. "What can we do for you gentlemen on this beautiful Ohio morn?"

The unkempt, scarred man answered, every word laced with contempt. "Across the water, over yonder in Ken'tuck, things ain't so perfect. Last night, our boss lost some merchandize to thievin' no-accounts. Brung the papers to show you."

A second man chimed in, talking about a woman spotted with the raiding party. "Might'a had red hair—like yours." He came to within three inches of Rebecca's nose. She fought the need to turn away from his disgusting breath and his lustful leer.

"You wouldn't happen to be acquainted with a female culprit lookin' like that, now would ya?"

The leader removed documents from his coat pocket and tried to hand them over, but Rebecca ignored him. She expressed outrage at the prospect of petty criminals in her neighborhood. "Land sakes, the state of our community becomes more unfathomable every day. People not respecting the property rights of others or the rule of law."

When the leader began to speak, Jean interrupted him.

"May I ask, sir, what did they take? A family heirloom, or perhaps an expensive painting? Like my reverend husband says, people need to examine their wicked ways. To repent of their sins and such." The mischievous grin on Jean's face did not go unnoticed by the men. "Seems like someone should in these difficult times—repent, I mean, what with this war to decide if it's right to own other people. Don't y'all agree?"

The leader ignored Jean's taunt and turned to Rebecca. "I'd advise you against trying to lead us astray. Two of our Negroes ran with another colored and a white woman. What do you know about it?" His eyes closed to slits as he studied her. "My tolerance is wearing thin, so confess the robbery."

Rebecca glared at him. She was about to speak when Jean uttered a defiant, one-word retort. "Nonsense."

The man's face turned bright red and slid into a scowl. "Who might you be, anyway?"

"The owner of this house. And I want you to leave."

He slammed his fist against the door again, causing both women to flinch.

"Truth is, I'm getting' real sour on you Lincolnites. You don't want a row with us, I can promise you. Now where's the man of this house? I'll speak with him now."

"He's in Cincinnati on business," Jean said. "And I believe we're done here."

As Jean began to close the door, the spokesman, who carried a rifle, two six-shooters, and a large knife, put his foot down at the threshold. He shoved the door open and entered the house. The others followed. Rebecca reached for Jean's hand.

"Gonna stay a spell," the man said. "Check around before we move out. We wouldn't want you two lovely ladies to be in any danger." The men began to search the house. "You got some hidden chamber here?"

Rebecca's fury bubbled up, but she did not expose it. The Rankin house had long been suspected as a railroad stop for hundreds of coloreds fleeing slavery over the years. Other men in pursuit of escapees had made similar stops here but always came up empty-handed. She thought it best not to provoke them further.

The intruders inspected every room, but they found nothing. The leader came close to Rebecca, deepening her revulsion. Inside this malicious man, an innocent little boy remained locked away, bound by chains of hatred even stronger than the manacles he sought to slap on Israel's wrists. What happened in his life that made him this way? She mourned the lad lost inside the shell…until Israel's image crushed her sympathy.

Rather than shrink back, she stood tall, emboldened by the picture of Israel's family in her mind and their courage to face any danger.

The head coward turned to one of his hired guns and barked an order to check the barn. Rebecca gave Jean a tight-lipped smile. The secret belonged to them, and now they must rely on that band of angels encircling the concealed hideaway. The women took seats on a couch in the parlor and remained silent. The leader and the other ruffian shuffled into the kitchen and then returned to the parlor with peaches in their hands. Rebecca stared at the grandfather clock, anticipating each movement of the minute hand. After twelve minutes, the third man returned, shaking his head. Rebecca exhaled.

The leader squared off with Jean. He tossed the peach pit to the floor.

"Tell your husband that we're watching. He will pay if he's had a hand in this business."

She remained silent. They turned and left and didn't bother

to close the door.

Ten

The Ruse

Ripley, Ohio

At 10 p.m. that night, Rebecca and Jean emerged from the house and headed toward the barn. Young David Crabbe, a member of the American Anti-Slavery Society who had assisted in the rescue earlier, followed close behind. They moved at a casual pace to avoid arousing the suspicions of anyone who might be watching.

"Wait, Jean," Rebecca said.

She ambled to the edge of the hill. The view of Ripley and the Ohio River from this vantage point always captivated her. On a clear night, the twinkling stars and soft beams of moonlight that floated to the earth made the waters shimmer. A restless star streaked across the expanse of sky, chasing some elusive goal never to be achieved. The tiny light with a tail appeared to crash far away into the earth. Several gaslights illumined the empty streets of Ripley below. A calm ruled over the town, but that didn't mean that the men from Kentucky were not on the prowl.

As all three of them gazed downward, Rebecca was mindful that Israel and his family had remained in their hideaway all day.

But a grand deception would soon be launched, and if all went according to plan, the family would soon be transported to Rebecca's house in Red Oak, five miles to the north. Earlier, Jean had sent a message to friends up the railroad line who would conduct Fannie, Israel, and little Parker northward after their stay at Rebecca's farm.

Jean predicted the hunters would return to spy on her house, but she couldn't be certain when. They might have had eyes on the farm since they stormed off that morning. There was no way to know. The only way to lessen the risk was to draw the Kentucky men away from the surrounding area with a decoy—the task that lay before Rebecca and David.

"Okay, you two," Jean said. "It's time."

They entered the barn. Moments later, a two-horse wagon carrying peaches rolled through the door and stopped. David drove the rig, and Rebecca sat by his side. Jean shut the barn door and walked up to the wagon.

"This is it," Rebecca said looking down at her mentor. She heaved a nervous sigh and clasped her fingers together to stop her hands from trembling.

"Godspeed," Jean said.

The wagon lurched forward toward the road leading to Cincinnati. Rebecca held the lantern to light the way, as David drove the team, slow and steady. The ride was uneventful, and despite David's attempts at conversation, few words were exchanged between them. After thirty minutes, Rebecca became concerned that their plan of distraction had not worked.

She had given up. "David, maybe we should turn around and—"

The sound of galloping horses interrupted her. The slave catchers reached their location and forced David to stop the wagon. The ruffians trained their guns on him.

The portly man with the facial scar glared at Rebecca, stroking his chin. He pulled his horse close to her side.

"Well, well…look at this, boys. You're the red-haired lass from this morning, back at the farmhouse. Fancy meeting you again. Better keep your sassing to yourself this time or I'll put a hole in that pretty head of yourn." He pulled his mount over to David's side. "Don't consider any foolish moves that'll get you kilt tonight, lad."

Rebecca glanced at the blanket beside her, calculating how quickly she could grip the pistol underneath. She wouldn't hesitate to protect herself. Outgunned three to one, she figured to take at least one of them down before they got David and her. Her husband George had taught her to be an expert marksman and quick on the draw. And then there was Quentin. If any shooting occurred, he would even the odds. His job was to ride behind to ensure the slave catchers had pursued the wagon, then ride back to collect Israel's family and move them to Rebecca's farm. That is—if all went according to plan.

"Don't mean to sass no one," Rebecca said. "Just getting a quick ride to a house where some family friends have taken ill."

She and David raised their hands in a gesture of obedience.

"Don't shoot me, please," David said. "I got no valuables, except this clock my grand pappy done left me." He pulled the timepiece out of his pocket.

"We're not interested in your dead granddaddy or his old hand-me-downs," the leader said. "We come to claim our property. I'm betting they're under all this fruit."

"No sir," David said. "I'm delivering this haul to market in Cincinnati. Reverend Rankin went ahead and waits for me so he can do his business. Like Miss Rebecca said, she just hitched a ride to visit sick friends. Nothing in back but what I'm a-haulin', and maybe a few bugs and such."

The leader jutted his chin toward the bed. "Charlie and Jess, check it."

The other two men holstered their irons and dismounted. The ringleader held a gun on David while the others threw the wagon's contents to the ground. When they'd emptied one side about half way and hadn't discovered an enclosed space, they went around to the other side. They tossed enough fruit to satisfy themselves. No escaped slaves, but both men selected a peach.

"Didn't I tell you so?" David said. "Ain't nothing and nobody on this journey but me, the lady here, and the load we're hauling."

"You was right. Continue along the road, a'fore this becomes the last haul you ever make."

The ruse worked. "And what about all the peaches you boys scattered?" Rebecca said.

The crew remounted, turned their horses, and galloped off into the night. The man she spied earlier lurking in the shadows had gained a significant jump. Quentin had set the next step into motion.

David turned the lighter rig around and headed toward Ripley, this time at a quicker trot. A couple of miles ahead they would transition to a less-traveled road that connected to the main thoroughfare between Ripley and Red Oak, five miles to the north.

At the junction, they would intercept another wagon filled with hay.

Eleven

Phase Two

Red Oak, Ohio

Dawn would not break for a few hours. Rebecca clutched the seat of the wagon to keep from being jostled as David drove the team as fast as the narrow roadway allowed.

She could hardly believe the events of the last few hours. Behind the actions of these determined men was a Kentucky plantation owner who paid money to own individuals and families who were forced to work in his fields. Did he have a family of his own? How did he treat his slaves?

The first-hand experiences from her youth began to escape the hidden box where she had long kept them under lock and key. During the summers, Rebecca had spent weeks at a time visiting cousins near Charlotte. She visited several plantations, some owned by people who treated their field hands kindly. But she had also witnessed deprivation and cruelty. Later, she discovered that the most heartless of men violated some of the women, which seared her hatred for this vile institution.

Suddenly, the wagon hit a dip in the road that lifted her and David inches off their seats. "Sorry…snuck up on me," David said with a smile. The jostle brought Rebecca back to the matter at hand—how to keep Israel's family secure for their journey northward.

Twenty-four hours from now she would say goodbye. The family would be conducted into the next county and then north to a trail of safe houses stretching from Cleveland to Canada. The slave catchers would be hard-pressed to find them, but this kind of chase sometimes left long footprints. Pursuers had been known to move heaven and earth to recapture freedmen like Israel and send them back south.

The first part of the ruse had worked, but the next maneuver at the Rankin house would prove more dangerous. The misfits would likely return and continue monitoring for suspicious activity. The family must be moved—now.

Unfamiliar with this route, Rebecca fidgeted in her seat, turning her wedding ring in full circles on her finger. "How much longer until we find the wider road?"

David glanced her way and grinned. "Miss Rebecca, try not to worry. All will be well."

Distracted by this strange evening's turn of events, Rebecca had done little to return David's cordial attempts at conversation, and she felt badly. Small in stature, David possessed a giant heart of concern for the welfare of others. He had landed a job in John Parker's foundry after his father joined the Union Army the year before. Now sixteen, David's work ethic exceeded that of some men twice his age, or so John often bragged.

"Yes, David, you're right. Everything will work out fine."

"A couple more turns, another short stretch, and we'll arrive. Let's hope Quentin's part came off as planned."

A few minutes later, David steered the rig onto the thoroughfare that Quentin would take to her farm. He pulled over and parked while she scanned the road in both directions.

"Nothing yet." The knot in her stomach made it impossible to sit any longer, so she climbed down and began to pace. If the plantation hands had somehow intercepted Quentin's wagon and the precious cargo it carried, all would be lost.

Rebecca counted the endless minutes. Just when she began to lose heart, the unmistakable clatter of horse hooves signaled someone's arrival. She held her breath until the faint outlines of a wagon appeared. *Thank you, Lord.* Waves of relief rippled down her spine as Quentin pulled up next to them.

"Quentin."

"Hello, David. Mrs. Johnston, nice to see you again."

"Always a pleasure," she said. "Our cargo?"

He pointed to the right side of the bed. "Miss Fannie is inside the box, and Israel's lying under the hay with Parker."

She moved closer. "Can you hear me, Israel?"

"Yess'm."

"Stay quiet for a while longer. Almost there."

Quentin quickly recounted his wild ride. Hidden away at Jean's farmhouse, he'd followed the wagon filled with fruit and the riders who trailed them. He hid as the angry men tossed the peaches from the wagon. Before they'd finished, Quentin retreated to where he'd tied off his mount, and scooted the horse into a gallop back to the Rankin house.

"When I arrived ahead of them, I told Mrs. Rankin they'd followed the decoy wagon. Once they realized we bamboozled them, I knew they'd be right behind me. Twenty minutes, tops. So we hurried our friends into this-here rig and made our way slowly…so's not to call attention to ourselves. Sorry for the wait."

Rebecca climbed aboard the wagon with Quentin. They continued toward her farm. David returned to salvage the abandoned peaches.

The fruit would bring David a good price in Cincinnati's markets. Fair payment for his hazardous duty.

* * *

After they'd traveled more than a mile, Quentin poked through the wall of silence. "Any word from George?"

He meant well, but the topic was difficult to discuss. "I don't want to imagine what my George is going through."

He slapped the reins down to quicken the team's pace.

George had cleared several of the sixty acres surrounding their farmhouse in Red Oak before he left and dedicated most of the plowed field to subsistence crops. A few acres remained open, set aside for their experiment—a commercial size sorghum cane crop and a larger mill to produce sugar and syrup. The first harvest had turned a profit, but war interrupted the expansion, and they put a hold on their dreams.

Conducting with the Rankins and John Parker and close involvement with the Red Oak Presbyterian Church distracted her from an uncertain future. Could she recover if anything happened to her beloved? The question burned a hole in her spirit. She wouldn't burden Jean or anyone else with her anxieties. Trouble visited everyone in these violent, unforeseeable times. She needed to stay brave and independent to survive. That's what George would tell her.

Quentin said, "How are you doing around the spread? Do you need help?"

Yes.

But she would never admit it. George would call her prideful and independent. To ask for and take assistance came hard for her. Fences, among other things, needed repair, and she couldn't keep up with the planting. The daily work, like milking the cows, feeding chickens, and collecting eggs overwhelmed her. She had finished sowing the next sorghum crop two days before, but only because her father had insisted on helping.

"Oh, I'm fine. Thanks. Like your farm, there's a lot of picking and feeding. Most days I turn fruit into preserves and mend quite a bit. The next time I need a hand, I'll call on you."

They continued north. The call of a mockingbird reverberated through the trees and faded into the night unanswered. Loneliness was not just a human condition.

When they arrived at her farm, Quentin drove the wagon into the barn and dismounted. "I'll unhitch the team and take my leave."

A hand rose through the hay and brushed away the strands. An arm emerged, followed by Israel's head. He sat up with baby Parker in his other hand and gave him to Rebecca. She cooed, and Parker responded with the smile that flickers on a baby's lips. A ray of sunshine. She raised his bottom to her nose.

"Whew...serious business." After Israel jumped to the ground, Rebecca handed the baby back to him.

Walking over to the compartment, Israel called out to Fannie. "Come on out, honey." Rebecca moved straw away from the box as Fannie appeared. Israel and the baby met her with a hug. "The boy needs a changing."

"Come, I have some diapers inside," Rebecca said. "New mothers often visit, so I keep some on hand. Settle into your quarters while I clean his little rear. Then I'll rustle up some food."

They climbed the four wooden steps leading to a portico extending the width of the colonial-style, two-story farmhouse. The siding around the house needed whitewashing, one of those tasks that got pushed off because of the war. For a moment, she pictured George on the porch at sunset, sipping lemonade after a day of toiling in the fields. She sighed as the vision melted into many wonderful yesterdays. The porch's roofline, supported by ornate posts, dove back to the middle of the house. Two four-paned windows flanked the front door, with another two on the second floor.

The house, in all its disrepair when they'd bought it, represented their aspirations to build a home on a foundation of rock that would never sink or crumble.

As Rebecca opened the door, her own four-legged child greeted her. The dog panted with excitement. "Meet Yankee," she told her guests. The purebred, cream-coated Irish wolfhound had been her constant companion since George left. They spent countless hours together while George fought to save his country. She spoke, Yankee listened, and both were comforted by their conversations.

She bent down and showered the hound with hugs and scratches. The dog's backside wiggled out of blind devotion, as he slobbered all over his master and almost knocked her over. Any separation made them pine for each other. Thankfully, her daddy looked after Yankee whenever she was away.

Fannie kept her distance while holding the baby.

"Large dog," Israel said, also shying away.

"Yep," Rebecca answered. "Gentle when stroked, fierce when provoked."

He chuckled. "Then I sure don't want to provoke him. Did you make that up?"

"The saying got started centuries ago. These Wolfhounds go all the way back to the time of Jesus. Ancient Irish kings carved this breed on their royal crests, along with the motto I just recited to you. Make yourselves comfortable."

The colors in the couch fabric had faded over time, like the autumn leaves before falling. When she and George got back on their feet, new furniture would rank high on her list of priorities. Two hand-me-down sitting chairs faced the sofa, and a small table rested between them. Like the land, improvements to the decor inside would have to wait until life returned to normal. What would life look like when George returned?

Fannie examined the living space. "This here's a beautiful home, Miss Rebecca. Lord willing, maybe someday we gonna be living in a house like this one."

The comment gave Rebecca pause. Her eyes detected the flaws around her, but Fannie's beheld something grand. This humble woman reminded her to be thankful.

"All things are possible, Fannie. Before we go upstairs, I need to show you something. Israel, please give me a hand with this hutch."

The large wooden structure rested against the sidewall that grew higher with each stair step upward. The wall was papered like the other walls in the room, but as they pulled the hutch away, they saw the paper covering a portion of the staircase wall hung loosely from the floor to about five feet up. Rebecca lifted the wallpaper and revealed a small hidden door. She opened it, and Israel's lighthearted mood turned dim.

"Let's hope we don't have to use it," she said. "But we're going to test it. I will need you both to come downstairs when I call. We'll assume the door was closed and count ten seconds for pulling back the hutch and opening it. You enter the space, and I shove the hutch in place."

"But can you move the piece by yourself?" Israel asked.

"Yes…but let's change Parker's diaper first and then eat. We can do the run-through later."

* * *

Rebecca led them up the creaky stairs to the second floor. Fannie grasped the bannister as she carried her newborn. At the top they turned left to the guest room. The living space, a voluminous cavern compared to the human storage compartment downstairs, held a small bed, a rocker, and a dresser.

Rebecca's bedroom, a few steps down the hallway, overlooked acres of grassland in the distance. "Let me change him in my room," Rebecca said. "The two of you can relax for a few moments."

The rocker creaked as Fannie rolled back and forth. She and Israel hummed a melody that meandered through the hallway and invited Rebecca into the trials and travails and joys of generations of enslaved people who hummed the same spiritual songs. The child stared into space. He had no idea he'd been born with one foot shackled in iron and the other dancing and singing praises to the Almighty.

So much packed into a simple melody. Rebecca rubbed her thumb across the baby's forehead. "I'm partial to your name, Parker Rankin. You are free, like the people you're named after. Your mama and papa dared to insist that you grow up and fly like an eagle. Nobody owns you."

As Rebecca walked toward the guest bedroom with the baby, she stopped to glance in the mirror above her chest of drawers and was mortified. She looked awful, weary and haggard with dark circles under her eyes. Had two days with no sleep and a daring rescue aged her that much? Pulling several clips and pins, she let her hair crash to her shoulders.

She handed Parker to his parents and went downstairs to prepare a meal. The breakfast menu included hot cakes, sausage, and fried potatoes. She fired up the wood-burning antique stove. The long night's activities left her with a voracious appetite.

When breakfast was ready, she climbed the stairs to collect her guests. Baby Parker slept in Fannie's arms, and the new mother cherished the moment too much to lay him down. Israel delivered her food to the room before joining Rebecca at the kitchen table. He cleaned his plate as the oven fire ran its course. "Mighty tasty. Thank you."

"More coffee?"

"If you don't mind."

She took an immediate liking to Israel, more so than most railroad passengers. The man doted on Fannie like George did with her. The colored family would live free like them, and playing a small part in their liberty brought her deep satisfaction.

A mental image of the scoundrel with a facial scar shattered the pleasant moment.

Twelve

Trouble

The next night as the family rolled down the path toward freedom, Rebecca mulled over Israel's parting words about the sorghum mill in her fields. They'd talked about her sorghum crop, and she'd served him some cake sweetened with the sugar substitute the night before. He gushed about how good the dessert tasted, made from a recipe printed in a monthly farm journal called The Cultivator. Maybe when the family settled, he too could buy some land and harvest the sugary canes. The thought should have given her rest.

Instead, she chased sleep for almost two hours. Agitation gave way to a fitful slumber. Suddenly, she sat up in bed, startled. Tears trickled from her eyes. An explosion of some sort? The clock reported the hour—two in the morning. She realized she'd been dreaming, but why was Yankee growling at her bedside?

As her mind cleared, she heard loud knocking at the front door. Stumbling in the dark, she lit the wick in her lamp, threw a shawl over her nightgown, and stepped down the stairs. The squeak midway annoyed her, another repair for George when he returned. *Soon please, my darling.* As she reached for the doorknob, another bang announced her visitors. A handgun lay in the desk drawer at the side of the doorway.

A hunch made her withdraw and cock the pistol. She concealed the weapon in the event those slave trackers had made their way to Red Oak. Yankee bore his teeth but stood dutifully in the shadows, prepared to defend his master and home.

"Identify yourself," she said.

"People with urgent business." The familiar dreaded voice crushed her. Yankee must have sensed her distress. He whimpered and then barked at the door.

She cracked open the door and stared at three men. One wore a patch over his eye, and a long scar stretched halfway down his face. As she suspected, the same wretched Kentuckians stood before her drunker than when their paths crossed earlier on the road. The search for Israel had extended beyond Ripley. She fought to quell the trembling in her hands. If they forced their way in, she'd kill the ringleader before the others subdued her. Yankee would have his way with them, assuming they didn't shoot the dog right off. No need to guess what they would do next.

"What do you want?" she asked.

"I'll be asking the questions. What are you doing here? Thought you had sick friends to care for."

"They made an immediate recovery, thanks be to God. Their son gave me passage home soon after I arrived."

"We been through this twice now," the leader said. "Our time here can go slow or fast, depending on if I think you're lying. Are you hiding our boss's property in there?"

"No one has been this way."

Another outright lie, but one for which she harbored no remorse. For some reason, the men didn't force their way inside like they had at the Rankin house. They left with little fuss, but she expected them to return at some point. Would they ride farther north that night?

As she climbed the stairs, she chided herself for becoming so personally involved with Israel, Fannie, and little Parker—an occupational hazard. She had done all she could for them.

A tornado of disparate, jumbled thoughts whirled through her mind. About Israel's family…about George…about tomorrow and the days to follow. She slid back into bed.

One picture remained frozen in her consciousness: Israel and Fannie being marched south in chains, past her farm. Scarface whipping their backsides, taunting them to walk faster. An ache formed in her stomach, causing her to pull both knees to her chest in despair.

What would happen to baby Parker?

Oh how she needed George now.

Thirteen

Love Scorned

Browns Gap
Blue Ridge Mountains
June 11, 1862

The picture of Woody running through the western edge of the Blue Ridge occupied Lucas's thoughts.

The Stonewall Brigade had moved into Browns Gap, the sheer brutality of Port Republic lingering among many in the ranks. Hunkered down for a rainy night, Lucas pulled out the letter he had hidden from Woody when it arrived several days before. He hesitated, hoping he hadn't made a terrible mistake that day when Woody excused himself to answer nature's call.

As he reflected back, letter in hand, the conversation filled him with guilt.

"Be right back," Woody had said, when the brigade commanders stopped the march for a rest. "Watch out for mail call."

Moments after Woody left, their squad leader came around with a thick stack of letters in his hands. "Woodard," he called out. The sergeant had perused the group of soldiers around them, and after a few seconds of no response, he tucked the correspondence away and started to move on.

Lucas spoke up. "I'll take Woody's." The name on the envelope, Betsy Edmonds, gave him pause. Betrothed to Woody when he left for the war a year before, she failed to write him a single letter. Woody grieved for months over his fiancé's apparent lack of concern, but he clung to the promise that she would wait in Shepherdstown for his return. No matter how long this dreaded war lasted.

Betsy Edmonds had as much patience for waiting as a pesky fly. Somehow Woody could not see the truth about her. Lucas had decided nothing positive would result from Woody receiving this note, so he tucked it into his haversack. When Woody returned, he asked Lucas if he'd missed anything.

"Naw."

Woody studied him for several moments. "You're scratching your nose and sweating like a hog at butchering time. What are you holding back?"

"We had a mail call while you wondered off."

Woody rubbed his hands together. "Anything for me?"

"Nope. Me neither." Woody's bright smile gave way to a long face.

Now, as Woody headed for home, Lucas could no longer shield his friend from the disappointment sure to come. He unsealed the correspondence and read.

> Mr. Woodard,
>
> I hope these words find you healthy in body and mind. This dreadful war continues long beyond anyone's expectations. Remember how we believed the conflict would last a short time as you Virginia boys went marching off? Now we women are all alone, wondering if you'll ever come home. I tried to be patient, but I can wait no longer. During these painful months, someone new has been helping me survive. Thankfully, he is not a soldier. He cares for me and would never leave as you did. Today we decided to be married and leave Virginia. So I am releasing you. We will likely never meet again, so I bid you a final goodbye.
>
> Betsy

Hallow, uncaring words, just as he'd expected. Lucas fumed

at the casual dismissal of such a good man, one to whom she had professed undying love and devotion.

Instead of addressing him as Woody, she'd used his surname. Such blatant disregard for his emotions. This would devastate his sensitive friend. Seething, Lucas ripped the paper to shreds and dumped it on the ground, then covered it with a handful of dirt. For good measure, he stomped the mound with his tattered shoes.

The photograph Woody had found held some kind of spell over him. That much was clear back on the field. Lucas prayed that the image could work some magic when Woody figured out that his lady back home was a shrew.

Fourteen

Black Friday

Red Oak, Ohio
July 4, 1862

A few weeks after bidding farewell to Israel and his family, Rebecca rose before dawn to feed the horses, milk the cows, and collect eggs from the hen house. She lit a wood fire in the stove to bake a batch of cakes using her own sorghum sweetener. The cakes would cheer up four-year-old Nathaniel Smith who lay in bed, recuperating from a nasty cold. The Smiths lived nearby, so Rebecca planned to hitch Agnes to the buckboard and deliver her magic cure to the farm later in the day. Sweet cakes were Miss Rebecca's special medicine for kids.

On the way home, she planned to drop by the Presbyterian Church to attend to final details for the Fourth of July celebration. She looked again at the handbill lying on the kitchen table.

> All are invited to the Independence Day Cookout and Dance on Friday, July 4, at 5 p.m. Join us at Minter's farm for some good fixins. Dance to the best fiddling and banjo playing this side of the Ohio, and sing a salute to our nation's birthday.

Many Southern sympathizers in Ripley and other parts of Ohio would not be paying homage to the Union this day, or any other federal holiday.

Rebecca smiled, recalling how she and George had danced the night away two years before and how they'd dreamed of their future and raising a family. He'd worn a full beard back then. When he finished eating, she giggled at the amount of corn, baked beans, and chicken left behind in his facial hair, but she didn't reveal the source of her amusement. Puzzled, he eventually raised a brow and said with a slight Scottish brogue, "What, m'darling? Do I have a wee bit'a supper in ma bushel?"

She picked out every morsel, and even now she swore his smell lingered in this room, a fragrance that spoke of his personality—gregarious and principled, forgiving to a fault.

The knock on the front door startled her, as friends from the community would not be paying a casual house call this early. Either good news or bad news waited at her doorstep. Most likely the latter. Terrified, she inched toward the door. A frightful possibility dawned on her. The three men she prayed never to lay eyes on again might be waiting on the porch.

Another knock. Soft, patient as a white oak. Nevertheless, as she cracked open the door, the site of Reverend Thomas Matthews made her legs unsteady. His mission could only be a holy one at this hour. She eased the door open, gripping the knob to stay upright until she could brace herself emotionally.

"What are you doing out at such an early hour? I thought I'd see you at the dance committee meeting later today."

His face spoke a thousand sorrowful words with just one frightened glance, and her stomach sank to the floor as he shuffled inside.

"Rebecca, would you sit?" He motioned toward the couch. His eyes shifted away from hers. One hand held a haversack. George's, no doubt. The other shook.

"I will stand."

She held her head up, determined to withstand this devastation with grace, but despair overcame her physical determination. Both knees began to buckle. She fought to keep from passing out. The reverend led her to the couch, where they both sat. Her eyes welled up. Words didn't come.

Reverend Matthews handed her the haversack. She pulled out George's Bible and flipped through it. A letter had been tucked inside. She'd read that later when she was alone. The sack also held his pocket watch, his wedding band, and a photograph of them. She placed each item on the small table in front of the couch.

This moment had played out in her mind countless times before, but she could not have anticipated the shock. She was a widow now. The widow Johnston. The reality crushed her.

After unfolding the simple frame, she stared at the ambrotype, desperate to be back at that moment again, a moment when her George breathed, and smiled, and brushed his hand through her long red hair at night. "He looked so handsome in his uniform," she said, turning the frame so the preacher could see the image. "A special time for us in Cincinnati."

The smallest details of their short visit together surfaced in the image. It was a cool, wonder-filled March day, seven months before. Silent tears trickled to her upper lip, as she heaved a sigh of grief.

The reverend withdrew a kerchief and handed it to her. She dried the flow, but more followed. "Tell me about that day, Rebecca." As if by magic, the walls of her house dissolved as she and George walked the streets of Cincinnati, side by side, her hand tucked in the crook of his arm. A slice of heaven replayed itself with total clarity so she might hold a piece of him and not succumb to the notion that her reason for living had ended.

His mother had taken ill, and he was granted a leave so both of them could go see her. One night she made a miraculous recovery. She awoke the next morning with a smile that outshone the rising sun. With a few days left to celebrate, they decided to take a short trip to Cincinnati, where Wendell Phillips would be giving an anti-slavery speech at Pike's Opera House.

They first visited a photographer to sit for the ambrotype. George promised he would carry the picture for the duration of the war. The likeness would sustain him when he had no will to continue. They went next to the opera house to hear Phillips, the famous abolitionist. His graceful appearance, his resonate voice, and his flair for dramatic metaphor captivated her.

"I remember the news story." The reverend's voice pulled her back to the present. "A melee ensued, and Phillips almost didn't get out."

At least two thousand people had been in attendance. Twenty minutes into his speech, the hissing and cheering began. He said the war was inevitable, a result of the futile attempts by the framers to reconcile freedom and slavery. An hour into the talk, some people in the audience started hurling eggs and stones at the stage. A fight erupted. George stepped into the circle of danger with no consideration for his own safety and helped to lead Mr. Phillips out of the opera house.

"The Union Army considered George one of its rising young leaders," Rebecca said, a distinction she would gladly trade for George, the ambitious, industrious young farmer. "His commendations for bravery made his father proud."

The next day they'd returned to Red Oak, and the following day he left to rejoin his unit. That was the last time she had touched him, the last time they'd kissed. How could she go on, never holding him again?

She rose and searched for the right spot to lay the ambrotype. The hutch that covered the hidden door in the stairway would do. As the shock subsided, she leaned into the fullness of her loss. The floodgates unleashed another stream of anguish. The pastor moved close to her, and she fell into his arms.

When she'd stepped out of his soft embrace, the reverend thumbed through his Bible and placed his finger on a passage. "Forgive my inadequacy in offering the right words to assuage your grief. Will you allow me to share God's comfort?"

She nodded as tears dribbled.

"From the Book of Isaiah: Fear thou not; for I am with thee: be not dismayed; for I am thy God: I will strengthen thee; yea, I will help thee; yea, I will uphold thee with the right hand of my righteousness."

Both of them rested for several moments in the power of those words. "Thank you, Reverend." She reached for George's Bible and held it close to her chest. "I will need this."

Had her back not been leaning against the door when he left, she might have collapsed. Rebecca Johnston, self-reliant feminist and abolitionist, sobbed uncontrollably. She dropped to the ground. The swirling room—*was it swirling?*—made it difficult to breathe. When tears came no more, she sat for an hour, staring into space, emptied of all emotion and devoid of any connection to the world around her.

Yankee moved from his spot across the room to his master's side and nuzzled her shoulder as if he understood her sorrow and mourned the loss with her. How could she tell George's parents that his body lay with untold others? She didn't know if they even buried all those who fell on the battlefield. Would weather and wild animals scatter his remains before they could be properly laid to rest?

Still on the floor, her finger brushed against the letter in the Bible. She eased it free and unfolded the paper. The words blurred together on the page until she forced her tired eyes to focus.

June 10, 1862

Dear Mrs. Johnston,

I writing at 5:30 a.m. to personally convey to you my deepest sorrow at the passing of your husband George on the battlefield at Port Republic. He fought with great valor in this terrible struggle, but passed to glory defending his comrades against attack. George made his mark as a dedicated leader, and all who served with him and had the privilege to call him their friend shall miss him. Having witnessed his passing, I can tell you that your name was the last word to leave his lips, and your face was undoubtedly the last vision in his eyes. The Lord provided me the opportunity to carry his haversack off the field, and so I am returning these personal items to you.

With the utmost admiration and sympathy,

Private Hollace W. McDaniels

A life she once treasured had passed away with George. An uncertain future remained. She would have to face it alone.

"There was also very active a certain group of men who made a living by capturing the runaway slaves and returning them to their masters. These men were on watch day and night along the riverbank the year round. While they captured quite a few it was remarkable how many slaves we got through the line successfully. The feeling grew so tense Rev. John Rankin and his followers left the Presbyterian Church forming a new congregation who were given over to the antislavery movement."

- John P. Parker, Conductor, Underground Railroad in Ripley, Ohio (1885)

Fifteen

Sharpsburg Erupts

Woodard's Farm
Sept. 14, 1862

The intermittent cannon fire confirmed that two titan armies were amassing across the Potomac, somewhere around Sharpsburg. Woody sat on the porch with his parents as the sun began its descent into the western horizon, he and his father enjoying a smoke while his mother knitted. A big fight was brewing and the proximity to Shepherdstown occupied his attention.

Over the last few days Woody had monitored Boteler's Ford, the shallow crossing point from Virginia into Maryland, a mile from their farm. As he hid in the nearby woods, he'd watched General Lee's Army of Northern Virginia wade over to the Maryland side. Then Lee split his forces, sending some of them back south. Woody could not fathom why the general did so, but he prayed that Lucas had marched away with these men.

The uncertain events of the last few days left the citizens of Shepherdstown hysterical, anticipating the worst. A present-day Armageddon threatened to turn their peaceful town into a bloodbath. If Lee and McClellan threw the weight of their enormous armies at each other near Antietam Creek, Shepherdstown would experience a nightmare of death and destruction not soon to be forgotten. And with the Woodard spread so close to the field, his parents might also become entangled in the web of war.

Woody glanced at the letter sitting on his father's lap.

"To the honorable Reuben Woodard—looks official. From the mayor?"

"A personal note to keep on our toes. Take all precautions to ensure our safety and such. But he doesn't think harm is headed our way like so many of the townsfolk do."

Daddy winked and nodded his head toward Mama. Woody understood—no cause to heighten the concern that his mama had already expressed at dinner. She'd worried that Woody might change his mind about the short trip to Cincinnati he intended to take and trot into battle instead. The idea had occurred to him more than once.

The harvest had been completed with the help of some young boys who agreed to work if Woody would regale them with tales of heroism in the Stonewall Brigade. While his father recovered from a bad break below his left knee, Woody spent the next month doing chores and upkeep around the farm. To his surprise and delight, Woody made progress on his search for the unnamed girl, thanks to Daddy's inquiries through the mail about Private Henry Prescott, the Confederate soldier who might have yielded possession of the girl's likeness at Port Republic.

Mr. Prescott had joined the brigade's 5th Infantry at the beginning of the conflict. The private hailed from Staunton and died an unmarried man. Soon to be hitched, but definitely single at the time of his unfortunate demise. Thus, the unnamed girl was likely not Prescott's child, and it would be rare to carry such a valuable memento from a sister or other distant relation. Which meant the ambrotype most likely had belonged to the Union soldier from Ohio.

Woody had planned to launch his search there soon. Mama even packed his bag. He would rejoin the brigade after making some headway on finding the girl. He would have been gone already if the war hadn't made its way up to his doorstep. Now he faced a difficult decision.

Should he begin the journey to find the girl or jump into the fray? To whom did he owe the greater duty? The girl or General Thomas Jackson? In his heart, the answer was clear.

He must fight alongside his comrades.

* * *

Boteler's Ford
Sept. 17

A blanket of early-morning fog shrouded the ford and the bluffs on both banks of the Potomac, offering Woody cover as he waded across the three-foot-deep riverbed. A couple hundred yards separated each shore. He'd made the crossing many times before. But this time, as he passed the wooden dam upstream, he trembled. Nerves? The cold water?

He emerged on the Maryland side, alert for stragglers. The savage sounds of musketry and artillery blared with the ferocity of a thousand thunderbolts. Making his way slowly up the narrow road leading to the hamlet of Sharpsburg, he realized the importance of this emerging struggle.

General Lee had invaded the north to press the advantage after his recent victory at the Second Battle of Manassas. If successful and able to occupy this ground over the long term, the focus would shift from the war-ravaged Shenandoah to the northeast outskirts of Washington, D.C. Maybe the general could then sue for peace, and the business of war would be concluded. Woody and his daddy had expected such an attempt.

Before emerging onto the southernmost end of the battlefield, he opened his sack and hid himself amongst the trees. Everything remained dry. He pulled out the Bible his mama had given him when he turned seven. He flipped through the pages to his favorite passage and prayed for his and Lucas's safety, wherever he might be, and that his mama might forgive him for walking into a nest of vipers without saying goodbye. He'd thought to spare her the stress, but now he counted this a mistake.

If he survived, he would return to the farm, secure his

baggage, and leave for Ohio with all due haste.

* * *

Sharpsburg

As Woody moved northward, he recognized the steeple of the Dunker Church poking above the dissipating mist.

At the eastern outskirts of the West Woods, troops around this house of worship and the surrounding cornfields withstood a pummeling from artillery the likes of which Woody had never witnessed. He made a quick decision to skirt the east side of Sharpsburg, cross the road that led to Boonesboro, and sneak over the Hagerstown Pike. He searched for a fortified field position that had not yet been engaged.

When he peered toward Henry Piper's cornfield, the line appeared. Confederate troops had placed fence rails along the sunken road embankment that faced the Union lines to the northeast. The old lane, worn down by years of traffic and rain, had been fortified and was filled with hundreds of waiting soldiers. An ideal rifle pit: about five feet below ground level and a few hundred yards long. He hunkered down at the midpoint.

Woody turned to the man at his right side. "Do you know where the 2nd Virginia settled in?" he asked.

"Some of Stonewall's boys are up by God's house and the woods nearby. Been takin' a beating since early this morning. The 2nd marched outta here days ago for Harpers Ferry. General Jackson went with 'em to route out the bluecoats down there."

A second man said, "Guess they succeeded. I seen most'a them boys come back couple a days ago."

Disappointing news. Lucas might be somewhere on this field. Woody lifted his eyes to the rising sun. Mid-morning had yet to prompt an attack at the heart of his position. Then, as if the dark realm could read his thoughts, hell unleashed its fury.

Federals charged across the open ground. Woody and his comrades stood and let loose a withering fusillade, dropping almost all the soldiers in the front rank. Up the ridges of the sunken road came the next assault, bluecoats firing point-blank into a sea of gray and brown.

Woody loaded and fired three rounds per minute into waves of enemy soldiers—thousands of determined men set on breaking the line. Missiles of death flew down from their weapons, thick as waves of locusts.

A punishing volley sent countless Yankees into the ditch, dead and dying. Exhausted from the fight and the now-blaring sun, Woody reached his limit just as the middle of the road broke open. Federals streamed past him in pursuit of the retreating line. The wave pummeled Woody to the ground, where he lay helpless while a wild-eyed Yankee leveled a pistol at him and fired.

Intense pain set fire to his left side and his right thigh. Shot twice? He touched his side. Blood covered his hand. A pile of bodies surrounded him, some quiet, others groaning. He felt his vision closing down but forced himself to focus when he noticed something an arm's length from him.

The ambrotype. Somehow ripped from his haversack, like it had been loosened from its original owner at Port Republic. He stretched out his arm as far as his injuries would allow.

As his fingertip touched the case, the blackness wrestled him away.

* * *

Woody opened his eyes, expecting to see the glory of heaven. Instead, a woman gazed down upon him. Pulling his blanket down, the woman checked his bandaged stomach. Not an angel...or was she?

Her black hair was parted down the middle, and the sides had been braided and pulled to the back where they were joined in a neat bun.

How long had he lain in the road, and how had he survived?

He moved his hands across the cot, but the haversack was gone.

"Might these be the items you're searching for?" The woman reached to the floor beside him and then placed the gold case and his pocket Bible at his side. She also laid someone else's used haversack next to him. "Your sack is no longer usable, but here's another for your consideration."

"But how...?"

The woman, perhaps his nurse, explained that hours after the Confederates left the field, Union soldiers and local farmers collected the dead and injured. Every open space, church, town building, farm, and barn now served as a hospital where doctors and nurses worked feverishly to save brave young men from both armies. The farmer who'd found Woody discovered the gold case at his fingertips.

"He thought well to collect the item for you, along with your Holy Book."

"Thank you." He clutched the ambrotype to his chest. "Where am I?"

"You are in farmer Samuel Poffenberger's cellar. You will recover here for a while, but I'm afraid you will become a prisoner of the United States government in the end."

She turned away.

"What's your name?"

"Clara Barton. I'll drop in later and see how you're doing."

With that, his personal angel walked through the door.

* * *

That night, Woody awoke with a fright, reliving the events on the battlefield as if they'd just occurred.

As the clouds faded from his brain, he touched his side. This was no dream. He'd suffered a debilitating wound. He should be dead.

Picking up the case, he found an indentation in the top right corner. A blunt force had smashed into the cover but veered off without shattering the image. Then Woody lifted the Bible and ran a finger through a hole in the cover until it reach something hard.

As he chuckled, Lucas's voice tickled his ear. Many times his friend had reminded Woody how the Lord works in mysterious ways. Woody opened the book to where his lucky, now crumpled silver dollar marked the page. He read the verse he'd circled before the war. Joshua 1:9 sang out to him. "Have not I commanded thee? Be strong and of a good courage; be not afraid, neither be thou dismayed: for the Lord thy God is with thee whithersoever thou goest."

A favorite passage, one he would now rely on more than ever.

Sixteen

Two Camps

Camp Chase
Columbus, Ohio
February 1863

The Feds would have delivered Woody to one of two places in Ohio—Camp Chase in Columbus, or Johnson's Island in the Sandusky Bay of Lake Erie. The compound surrounded by water housed officers, for the most part, so they sent him to the Columbus facility.

Woody found himself in the middle of an outbreak of small pox that ravaged Camp Chase, providing the prisoners an unintended escape route in a pine box.

He tried to comfort Phillip Nesbitt, an inmate in Number Two, the sixteen by twenty-foot shanty where Woody, Nesbitt, and eleven others were held. The man lay in his bunk as the sickness progressed. Woody had recited Psalm 23 many times at his bedside. Private Douglas Simmons, another resident in that infested hut, accused Woody of harboring a death wish.

"Are you crazy? The pox is blowing through this hole like an Alabama tornado. Stay close to him and you'll be swallowed up."

Another storm dropped its own toll on the shanty. A driving

rain slammed against the outside walls. The roof had no shingles and water leaked on the beds. For the last month, Woody had suffered from a nasty chest cough that seemed to worsen each day. He worried that the wet weather might turn the cough into something worse, like bronchitis, or even pneumonia.

He had been a walking dead man in the battlefield, and while nighttime shadows still harassed him, he no longer feared the spirits arrayed in his dreams. Spared for some unknown reason, he would flirt with his own demise to provide peace to the lost and needy. Peace came to him through prayer and the silent encouragements of a little girl, a stranger who'd become a close friend. On the doorstep of the afterlife, Nesbitt had no one else to comfort him.

"What shall we do?" Woody asked. "Turn our backs on each other in our time of greatest need?"

He refrained from any physical contact, for Nesbitt's rash had turned into pus-filled sores all over his face and body within twenty-four hours. He suffered with uncontrollable shakes and a raging fever. A putrid smell filled the space where he lay, waiting for a blessed mercy to arrive and whisk his soul from this desolation. Shoddy blankets failed to ward off the insistent drafts that seeped through open cracks in the wooden planks. Woody put his own threadbare blanket over the dying man, who opened his eyes.

"An angel from hea…ven. Thank you."

Seconds later, Woody drew near as the man slipped into eternity. Many men had passed into the hereafter since the Confederates fired upon Sumter, most of them from one scourge or another. Closing his eyes, Woody lifted a prayer to follow Nesbitt. The other men, cadaverous and burdened with multiple maladies, stared at him through empty sockets.

The next day, with a soiled blanket around his thinning body, Woody strolled along the circumference of the camp. Samuel Barkley from Campbell County, Virginia, walked with him. Without warning, Woody stopped and let loose several deep coughs that caused him to double over. Samuel placed his hand on Woody's back. "Good Lord…you okay?"

"Fine. Just give me a few moments." He wheezed and coughed several more times before the spell subsided. "Had this for weeks now. Can't seem to shake it."

They continued walking. All around them cold and hungry prisoners sought time and space away from their vermin-infested sheds. In the yard, open excavations that served as latrines left a stench that permeated the camp.

"Horrible, nauseating, and disgusting," Samuel said as they passed by. They took it slow since Samuel had sustained a leg injury in battle that caused a permanent limp. In the short time since his incarceration, Woody and Samuel had become fast friends. The image of the unnamed girl had fascinated Samuel, and he relished their frequent conversations about Woody's plans to find her.

One soldier ahead stood in a pool of water and mud left by the storm. His eyes danced as he held a conversation with an imaginary companion. Like a band of thieves in the night, the horror of battle robbed some men of their sanity. Woody understood this all too well.

Filled with compassion, Woody stopped in front of the man. "Fine day for some sunshine, soldier. Bask in it while you can. Soon we'll have little or none."

The confused prisoner spoke with a stutter. "S-stopped 'em at Shiloh that first day. K-ilt me thirty-five or more of them bluecoats. A-course, m-my sister helped." A broad smile revealed a gummy mouth with three blackened, rotted teeth still planted. By God's grace, Woody had escaped a one-way ticket into the fractured world where such troubled souls resided. As a visitor, he always managed to claw his way back to the edges of reason.

"Good job, soldier. General Lee still needs men like you in the field." He and Samuel walked on. "How can charity be reduced to this? Hard to fathom."

Samuel added his list of wrongs to the conversation. "Not enough wood to cook the vile, rotting pork. No heat to protect against the blustering winter winds. This war has turned into an ideal stained with the blood of innocents."

As they strolled to the front of Woody's hovel, a prisoner approached them. "S'cuse me, gents. Got any tobacco you can share?"

"Not on me," Woody said. "But if you come inside here, I'll

share what little I have."

"Mighty kind. Name's Orville Mott…from Cincinnati."

Samuel's brow rose. "A Confederate from Ohio?"

"Yep. There's plenty of us from up there."

Woody perked up. That's where he was set to travel before his capture.

"I'm Jonathan Woodard, and this here's Sam Barkley." The men shook hands. "I know it's unlikely, but do you know a man with the last name of Braun? He's also from Cincinnati. Joined the Union side."

Orville thought a moment and shook his head. "No. Can't say I do. But with that name, chances are he came from our German immigrant neighborhood. A place called Over-the-Rhine." Orville's smile revealed a mouthful of large teeth, which appeared odd given his small face. "Had me some fun times on that side of the canal before this damned war."

Woody suppressed his euphoria. Locked up in this decrepit prison, good fortune had somehow delivered a second important clue about the girl right to his doorstep. The Confederate, Henry Prescott, was not the girl's father. Now, thanks to Orville, he had a place in Cincinnati to start his search. For the first time since his arrival, Woody thought about the possibility of escaping from the prison.

He nodded his head toward the shack. "Come inside, Orville, and I'll get you some tobacco."

The same day, a note from Lucas arrived. Woody also received mail from his mother, a response to the communication he'd sent after his capture to inform her of his whereabouts and encourage her not to worry. The words from family and friends acted as a salve that eased his loneliness. In a return letter to his mother, he asked about his brother Robert's welfare, and whether his father's leg had completely healed.

A few weeks later, they moved Woody from his shelter. None of the others could fathom where.

Woody took his persistent cough with him.

* * *

Shackled and wearing worn out federal clothes, Woody was

transferred to the Union prison on Johnson's Island. The train he boarded at the Columbus depot, which carried several Rebel officers on board, headed north toward Lake Erie. The word was that captives on Johnson's Island endured better conditions than those in the other camps. Fortune had smiled upon him, but he couldn't figure out why a mere private would be transferred to this detention center.

The small steamboat called the Little Eastern carried him, the commanders, and their guards from Sandusky City across the water. The commandant met them at the dock, along with his acting provost marshal and guard unit. They escorted the group a short distance to the prison.

The officer addressed the group after each man was processed. "My name is Major Pierson," he said. "This center has ten rules. The first nine you should not take issue with." Those commandments covered when and where one could venture outside the blocks, when lights would be extinguished, bedtime, and obeying orders from the sentinels. "Number nine reads as such: Nobody will be allowed to loiter between the buildings, and the north and west fences, and they will be permitted north of the buildings only when passing to and from the sinks. Nor will they approach the fences anywhere else nearer than thirty feet, as the line is marked out by stakes."

The highest-ranking Confederate officer spoke on behalf of the others. "Those rules are acceptable. What is the tenth order?"

Major Pierson walked over to the inquiring lieutenant, his face stern, his eyes as penetrating as a rattler bearing its fangs. "Number ten is simple. Anyone who fails to obey all the other rules will be fired upon."

Woody concentrated on his surroundings while being walked to his block, one of four structures dedicated to the enlisted men, political prisoners, and spies. A total of twelve two-story blocks would serve as their housing. The thirteenth building was the hospital. Seventy-five prisoners lived on a patch of land designed to accommodate hundreds.

"These numbers may change, now that there's hardly any prisoner exchanges," the guard said. "Grant doesn't want you Rebs back out on the field to fight another day. And Jeff Davis won't release Negro soldiers and their white commanders. More graybacks will soon be living in our little sanctuary. But for now, you all will be enjoying better conditions."

Woody noticed plenty of level ground that could be used for exercise. He wondered if the men played the new game called baseball here. His body and spirit needed such a team sport.

First, he would take stock of his overall condition. By his reckoning, the business of war—the endless marching, brutal fights, and overall lack of nutrition—had stolen twenty pounds that he needed back. The squalid conditions and disease at Camp Chase had contributed to his decline. His chronic cough lingered for months. He worried about pneumonia and knew how many had perished of that disease since the beginning of the war. But once the cough and illness was behind him, exercise would be just the thing.

"Behind each building is a temporary structure with two entrances," the guard said. "Sinkholes. When they're filled, the holes are capped and you boys dig new pits. Some of you may be lucky enough to work this detail."

The attempt at off-handed humor fell flat. As they approached Block Three, the guard checked his list. "Jonathan Woodard?"

"Here, sir." He stepped forward.

"Ah, we have one that speaks."

Friendly banter? The guard seemed an amiable fellow. War had introduced Woody to the best and worst in men. Like him, most just wanted to survive and return home to their families, so he made it a rule not to paint his comrades or his enemies with the same brush. By the same token, Lucas had taught him to be wise as a serpent and harmless as a dove. Discern the hearts of men, Lucas would say.

"Yes, sir," Woody said. "Paying attention to rule number…" He'd forgotten the number. "The one about following orders from the lookouts."

The highest-ranking Rebel prisoner among them lifted an eyebrow. Woody took note: If he sought favor from the enemy, the suspicions of others on his side might be raised.

"This is your new home for the foreseeable future." The Yankee officer moved ahead with the rest of the newcomers, but then stopped and came back to where Woody still stood. "My name is Sergeant Horatio Hicks, Company A of the Hoffman Battalion, the sentries keeping this place safe. Keep your nose clean, and you'll do fine."

Woody almost extended his hand out of habit, but he held back. "Thank you, sir, for the advice."

"Right. Carry on." An awkward silence filled the space. "We'll talk again."

Hopefully not from one of the lookout paths with Hicks's musket trained upon him.

Woody stared at the twelve-foot catwalks that provided a line of sight inside the camp, and then counted the sentry boxes lining the walks, which offered protection for the guards against the brutal cold and numbing winds that whirled about from Lake Erie. The temperatures had reportedly reached sub-zero levels in past seasons. Had any prisoners scaled the high walls and escaped to freedom?

Woody pointed his face upward to the sun. The bright rays signaled a late-March thaw.

With his haversack and a few possessions tucked inside, Woody entered his temporary shelter. Like the other new arrivals, he had been issued two used, second-rate blankets that were nearly devoid of wool. He wondered how much heat the small, antiquated wood-burning stove could circulate, and whether the camp would supply enough fuel for the typically cold Ohio winters.

He nodded to his new barrack mates. "Place looks to be survivable," he said.

"The wheat straw bedding in these bunks would hardly feed a cow," one man said as he walked over to the wall. "The cold drafts squeeze between these wood planks and turn our little paradise into an icy hellhole."

Another man lying on a bed nearby chuckled. "Welcome to the bullpen."

"Come again?" Woody said.

"Prison talk. I'm Peyton Bragg, French's Virginia Battery, Company C."

"Like—"

"Yep, like General Bragg. No relation." The man sported a

bushy beard and hair that fell in curls to the nape of his neck. Still, Woody noticed that his right ear was mangled and his eyelid on that side drooped. A friendly sort, Bragg seemed happy to welcome a new bunkmate into the otherwise empty building. He pointed to the reclining soldier. "And that there's A. J. Frazer, 5th Kentucky, Company E."

"The bullpen's our name for these box houses," Frazer said with a deep yawn.

Woody picked a bunk. "I see."

An older man with graying brown hair and a heavy stubble on his deeply lined face, Frazer reminded Woody that the Confederacy faced an increasing lack of younger men in the field as the war continued. The man showed little spark, and Woody assumed he'd been a prisoner for a long while.

"Not my old Kentucky farm, but I guess it's home," Frazer said. "For now, anyhow."

"And I'm Jonathan Woodard, 2nd Virginia, Company G—the Stonewall Brigade. My friends call me Woody."

Frazer's eyes widened. Both men scurried to Woody's side.

"One of Jack's boys," Bragg said excitedly. "We heard how y'all whupped ol' Sideburns at Fredericksburg."

Woody mentioned that he'd sat that battle out at Camp Chase, but that didn't diminish their enthusiasm.

"Heard how you butternuts gave McClellan the Shenandoah run-around back in '62," Frazer said. "Grab a bunk and we'll swap some camp canards."

Woody settled in, and they told each other stories about their exploits, the difficulties of army life, and the friends who'd been taken. They spoke of disillusionment and the fleeting honor in the conflict that lasted far beyond what they'd ever imagined.

Woody told them about his farm near Shepherdstown and how he and his best friend Lucas had joined Botts Greys back in Jefferson County in '61. He spoke about the battle of Port Republic and how he'd found the ambrotype between the two men and planned one day after the war to find the girl's family and return the photograph. He left out the part about the frightful dreams plaguing his sleep. They would learn about those soon enough. He suspected he wasn't the only one to suffer nightmares.

Woody's stomach growled. It had been two days since his last meal of stale bread, some strange meat, and a scoop of rice. "How are the fixings here? Needin' to put some meat on these bones."

"Prefer my momma's cooking," Bragg said. "The portions ain't what I'd like. But everyone gets the same share. Most of life is bearable here."

* * *

Over the course of several weeks, Woody's health worsened. A high fever accompanied the hacking and blood appeared in his mucus. The camp authorities transferred him to the prison hospital, where the medical care was much better than at Camp Chase. The doctors treated him with opium and quinine and eventually brought his cough under control. But they warned that the condition would likely return over time.

As Woody left the facility, he wondered if he would ever have the opportunity to search for the unnamed girl.

Seventeen

Luke's Crucible

Early July 1863

Lucas marched through Greencastle and Chambersburg to Carlisle, the farthest north the Stonewall Brigade had ventured since the war began.

Private Mark Randolph, who joined the 2nd Virginia as they broke winter camp, walked in formation beside him. The generosity of the citizens along the way surprised the conscript.

"The barns are full, and the livestock's plenty fat," Mark said. "These Pennsylvania folk aren't starving like some in the Shenandoah. And they sure ain't been stingy with all the food. The blankets will come in handy."

At seventeen and the youngest soldier in the unit, Mark missed the obvious. Face to face with a behemoth, the citizenry did well to cooperate. Lucas liked the young man, but found him callow about war. Much like he'd been in the beginning. Impulsive, bound to make a wrongheaded decision in the heat of battle, desperate to prove his manhood. He would keep the lad close.

Along the dusty road, he started teasing Mark as an older brother might, calling him by the wrong last name. From the top of South Mountain on the Chambersburg Pike, the familiar sounds of battle rumbled in the distance. The Army of Northern Virginia marched toward its destiny, and Lucas had tangled with fate on one too many occasions. He had long fought on borrowed time, and poking fun at Mark helped to ease his anxiety.

"Hear that, Randall?" Lucas said.

"Yeah. But my name's not—"

"The pounding of hellfire," and they were hoofing right toward the flames. This time, they didn't have their brilliant general, Stonewall Jackson, giving the orders. "Best we commence to asking the Lord to help us and General Lee."

"Like I said before…the name's Randolph. Not Randall."

"Right."

The men all up and down the long line choked on the clouds of trail dust kicked up by thousands of soldiers on foot, hundreds of horse-drawn wagons and other supply vehicles, and countless other horses and mules. Mark coughed out a question. "Where we all headed again?

"Seems we got a date with the Army of the Potomac at some Podunk up ahead. A place called Gettysburg."

"What's in...in…?" Mark sucked in a swirl of dirt that sent him into an uncontrollable dry cough. The hacking lasted a full minute, causing his eyes to water like a spring-swollen creek. He pulled a swig from his canteen. "My lungs are burning."

"You okay, Randall? Might wanna reduce your tobacco use, or stop altogether."

"The name is—"

"Randolph. Yeah, yeah."

"And I don't need to cut down on my smoking," Mark said. "Why we hoofing to Gettysburg?"

"Shoes…according to rumor." Someone in the ranks had started the story about a shoe factory in this Pennsylvania town. The lack of boots had sidelined many soldiers in Lee's army. That much was true. While Lucas didn't buy that as the reason for the march, he toyed with his friend. "Aren't you needing another pair?"

"My brogans are plum worn out. Take a look." He elevated his right foot to show the tattered sides, hopping as he marched.

"Not much leather left. Better off than some of our boys marching barefoot."

"Truth is," Lucas said, "I don't expect we're here for provisions, although we need boots something fierce. I figure we're taking the brawl to the Yankees where they live. Try to get Abraham to pull Mr. Grant away from Vicksburg. Bring him up and over yonder to protect Washington."

As they continued down from the summit of South Mountain, Lucas spotted other Confederate regiments resting on the side of the road. "Can't be much happening on the field, right?" Mark said.

"Don't believe it." Lucas called out, "Where you boys from?"

One man hollered back. "Anderson's division, Hill's Corp. You?"

"Stonewall Brigade, 2nd Virginia," Lucas said. Proud of his regiment, Lucas always added the unit's original name. "Men of Botts Greys. The few who are still left."

"Awful shame about Ol' Stonewall." The general had been accidentally shot by his own troops. Doctors had amputated his arm and he died of pneumonia several days later.

Lucas and Mark moved beyond the soldiers.

"Hey," Mark said, "they're just sitting around. Must not be much going on. This may not be such a hard tussle. Those boys are in good spirits."

"Maybe."

He would not burst Mark's bubble, but in his view they were walking toward an epic battle long in the making. The incursion into federal territory was meant to turn the advantage toward the Confederates. The bluecoats or Bobby Lee might pick another field or another day, but at some point, his beloved general meant to strike a crippling blow, one that would end the bloody conflict for good. Woody was confined somewhere far from this ground, and for the first time, Lucas was glad.

Moving forward on the Chambersburg Pike, they followed the rest of Johnson's Division and swung left to approach Gettysburg from the north. Spent from the arduous march, they made their way along the York and Gettysburg Railroad for two miles and filed to the right where they formed into a line. A second new recruit to Lucas's right asked him a question, the fear of death stamped all over his face.

"Think we'll engage the Yanks head-on tonight?"

The soldier next to that one whispered the Lord's Prayer. Another man recited a Hail Mary as he clutched his rosary beads. Lucas silently asked for heaven's protection—for him, Woody, Mark, and the rest of these boys who would sacrifice so much.

Another soldier answered the question. "If General Jackson was here, he'd engage. Try to catch the enemy off-guard."

The order to rest came as no surprise to Lucas. "Old Jack's not in charge anymore. He's dead—shot by our own boys, remember? On this spot we'll wait for what the morrow brings."

Lucas and the others rested on the southeast side of Gettysburg, at the extreme left of the brigade's line. A handful of skirmishers had been sent to assume different positions, and the rest of the men settled in for the night.

Through the long winter months and into the spring, Lucas had kept a diary. He wrote sparingly, for Woody's sake more than anything. If they both survived, Woody locked up and him still in the fight, someday they would be reunited. Woody would want a record of what transpired in his absence. An ominous shadow had draped over Lucas in recent days, a nagging sense that this time his luck would peter out. He pulled the diary out of his haversack to add an entry.

But the words wouldn't come. He gazed upward, the sky alive with blinking lights and the occasional streak to the horizon. Woody always marveled at creation and gained solace from its grandeur. Such notions might afford Lucas a similar peace on this night—a calm before the menacing storm.

So his thoughts tumbled to the brighter times of his youth. Most days brought backbreaking work. He would plant and harvest, each in their season, and tackle the endless chores that kept a farm active and productive. Sprinkled between were days when he and Woody would swim, fish, and play pranks on their fellow students and church friends—fun times unspoiled by the horrors of war. When the invasion had threatened their homes, they responded. Out of duty and honor to Virginia and the South. The life they traded seemed a distant memory.

Now Woody languished in prison. He longed to spend one more day with his childhood pal, or God willing, to join Woody's quest to find the girl's family. Maybe that would bring closure to everyone, including Lucas.

I wonder if you're looking at the same moon as me?

The universe appeared enormous. Had he never taken the time to contemplate its mysteries? Earth in all its vastness shrank by comparison, and yet what they fought for emerged paramount in the direction of his life. His heart wanted to embrace faith, to experience the closeness of God warming his spirit. Redemption must emerge from the ashes of man's inhumanity toward his brothers. Otherwise the killing would be in vain. But he had watched Woody ask for heaven's relief, and the Lord had remained silent. How could Lucas trust God to remove his own doubts?

Jesus promised to carry our burdens, but maybe Lucas and Woody and every other soldier toted too heavy a load.

Lucas tried to review his last journal entry in the dark. That time the words had come. About being stir-crazy in winter camp, and excited when the officers confirmed the tittle-tattle throughout the camp that the army would move out in two days. Winter had traded the freeze for a thaw, a weather change the men thought might never happen. And young Mark Randolph had become a friend.

Many yesterdays had passed, and now he faced tomorrow's crucible. So he wrote. At the end, he jotted a special entry for God.

> July 1 (evening)—Massive armies filled with men having no gripe with one another, who will pour out lead and canister on each other. May Almighty God save us from ourselves, and save Gettys'berg…

* * *

Sleep eluded him. He had rested in place before other fights, but this ground haunted him. After about an hour, his eyelids drooped and he slept.

"Say Luke, you awake?"

If I ignore him...

"Want to talk...?"

"Randall..."

"Randolph."

"I would be asleep, but for you asking whether or not I am." The young man lay in the line of formation to Lucas's left. Lucas sat up.

"Sorry. Can't sleep," Mark said. "Case of the jitters, I reckon."

This boy should be home tackling the daily chores around the farm or preparing for the fall harvest. "What led you to muster in at your age?" Lucas asked.

Mark thought for a few moments. "Love for my state. Anyway, I'm not so young that I can't kill me some bluebellies. Turned seventeen a month ago."

"Yeah, I suppose so," Lucas said. "I can see you're a scrapper. Kinda remind me of me."

"Had my nose busted twice."

"Hard to miss. Listen, war ain't like any fistfight back home. I want you to stay by my side when the fighting starts, in my line of sight. Understand?"

"Now you're starting to sound like my brother." His misty eyes bore witness to a deep loss. The subject was tender, but Lucas decided to probe anyway.

"Tell me about him."

"William, three years my elder, and my best friend. Good-for-nothing bluebellies killed him at Fort Donelson in '62. Pa passed from scarlet fever when we was young'uns. Left three boys and one girl. William taught me how to shoot, ride, work the farm. Almost everything I know."

It seemed Mark had signed on to preserve Southern liberty, but perhaps even more to avenge his brother's death. "Sorry about your brother. Don't allow the hurt to dampen your common sense in the battle that's coming. Keep a level head."

The young soldier shook his head. "I declare, you do remind me of William. First thing I thought of the day I met you."

A heartfelt compliment. All the more reason he would be vigilant in protecting the lad.

* * *

At dawn the Union vanguard and the Stonewall Brigade exchanged brisk fire for most of the day. At six o'clock, the Confederates advanced to the side of Hanover Road. Well-placed sharpshooters harassed them, so Brigadier-General Walker ordered Colonel Nadenbush and the 2nd to clear the wheat field and woods from where they fired.

"Here we go, Mark." He reminded the lad to stay by his side.

The young private asked Lucas if nerves ever got the best of him before combat. His experience made him mostly self-assured and unafraid, but not so in the beginning. The first time he'd witnessed a Minié ball shatter a man's cranium changed him forever. Slaughter on a mass scale left him numb to taking life on the battlefield, turning him into a death machine, focused on the survival of two men—Woody and him. And now Mark.

"A frightful feeling don't mean one's a coward, right?" Mark asked.

"Been through a mess of battles. Seen more trouble than you. No shame in a case of nerves."

Nadenbush gave his command. "Advance men, and do your duty."

As the regiment rose and dashed toward the enemy, they sounded the familiar high-pitched Rebel yell and drove the Yanks into the grove. Lucas and Mark ran three feet apart. After advancing some distance into the trees with the rest of the men, two artillery guns opened up and drove the Rebels back toward the open ground.

One shell found its mark nearby and knocked both men off their feet. Moaning and semi-conscious, Lucas tried to focus his eyes on Mark, who removed his belt and crawled over to him.

The circumstances confused him. "Hey, what're...where ya goin'…?" The men around him moved in slow motion, and the sounds of war were muted. Try as he might, Lucas could not regain his bearings. He raised his head and an excruciating pain almost overcame him. To his left, Mark reached over to Lucas's arm. Everything turned blurry, and Mark had doubled in his vision. The smoke from the explosion burned in his nose, and his mouth was gritty. He coughed and tried to spit out the dirt he'd swallowed.

A second sharp pain came from his arm. With a steady stream of blood flowing from a neck wound, Mark wrapped his belt around Lucas's arm below his elbow.

Why? The answer struck him like a charging bull. "Aahhh!" he screamed. "My arm…my arm."

Another cannonball exploded yards from them, throwing Mark on top of Lucas, and knocking the little bit of air from his lungs. Mark lay still over Lucas's body. He thought he might suffocate, but then Mark stirred and rolled off him.

"Oh God, I'm hurt bad," Lucas said. "My arm. I can't see straight."

Part of his limb hung by bits of skin and tissue. Incoherent, his mind sent signals to his fingers to move, but they ignored the commands. Mark's belt helped to stop the blood from squirting out of the stump. The Confederate troops at the edge of the woods provided cover, as Mark lifted Lucas to his feet and steadied him. He almost blacked out from the throbbing in his head, but his need to hold the dangling arm with his other hand kept him conscious.

"Come on now, Luke," Mark said. "Just a few steps to go."

Someone yelled, "Stay down. Snipers!"

Mark failed to heed the warning. The brave soldier half-carried Lucas, but within a few feet of the line, they both fell. Lucas blacked out, but then regained consciousness and crawled over to Mark's body. His head had been blown open. *No, Mark. Wake up!* Lucas managed to stand, and the landscape swirled in circles. He thought Mark would be fine once they got him to a field hospital.

A stabbing pain in his leg made him falter. Had he been shot? As Lucas stooped to pick up his fallen friend, another soldier pulled him back into the Rebel line.

Eighteen

Christmas

Christmas of 1863 brought with it a profound sorrow that stomped on Woody's Yuletide joy. The return of his cough earlier in the month had depressed him. He ignored it, hoping this was just another cold and that nature would take its course. He longed for the loving presence of his mother and another sunset chat with his father and brother as they watched fields of grain and contemplated the grand issues of life, like torn loyalties. The United States was their country, but Virginia would always be their North Star.

Steady, reassuring. Their first love.

Marylander Henry Kyd Douglas, an old acquaintance from the 2nd Virginia, Woody's regiment, had been captured at Gettysburg and transferred to Johnson's Island. When they talked, Woody learned the War Department had granted the brigade's request to be formally called the Stonewall Brigade. Douglas shared how Lucas had lost part of his arm at Gettysburg and returned home to recover. Woody mourned his friend's injury but rejoiced that he no longer faced the perils of war.

The unnamed girl and his plans to find her family sustained him. The quest for survival led Woody to direct his attention to the murmurings of escape. He'd been fishing for details from Private Nathan Harp of the 25th Tennessee, who'd arrived in July. The two men found an immediate kinship with each other. Nathan had an inside source of information about a possible escape.

An elaborate group of generals had organized into five planning units to develop different escape scenarios. Brigadier General Isaac Trimble, with whom Woody had fought in the Seven Days Battles, led them. The highest officer in the camp, Trimble had lost his leg at Gettysburg during Pickett's charge, which led to his imprisonment. Nathan had learned from a friend in one of the planning units that nothing concrete had been decided except for one detail. An escape would wait for a thick blanket of ice to descend on the island and surrounding waters.

The chilliest months elevated the misery index on the island but also offered the best chance of disappearing without being detected. With the waters of Lake Erie frozen, someone could walk across the harbor to Sandusky or Marblehead, or head the other direction toward Canada. The warship Michigan, otherwise anchored in the bay with its guns trained toward the prisoner barracks, moved to another location during these icy conditions.

Over the past year, desperate men had tried other means of escape, like tunneling under the wall. The elements and the guards proved too great a match though, and these men were captured.

Woody and Nathan had a lot in common—similar families, similar stories. Nathan's closest friend had died in combat six months before Nathan's capture, and he still reeled from the loss.

The prisoners braved the rain and plummeting temperatures in the yard to receive a carload of Christmas food boxes from their families. They enjoyed some merriment in guessing the contents of the packages. "Hey, Woody, what's in yours?" Nathan asked as he opened his own package. "Look here. A fruitcake."

Woody opened his box and let Nathan peek. A note from his mama was tucked to the side. He'd read that later. For now, he wanted to talk about a different subject. First he unwrapped a chocolate from his box and waited for Nathan to finish a mouthful of cake. A biting wind gusted over the prison walls and blasted through Woody, rattling his insides. The blast set off a series of coughs. Nathan's nose and ears turned a light shade of blue.

"Say, Woody…you don't look so good," Nathan said. "You feverish?"

Woody scanned the immediate area. "Any news?" he asked, careful to keep his voice down so others couldn't hear. He figured only a select few would be allowed to mount an escape, and he'd have to quietly position himself to be counted among them.

"Word is," Nathan said, "Major Winston's on the lookout for the perfect chance to walk out of here. Been collecting clothes and making a ladder. Gonna hop the wall and walk to Sandusky, but they're waiting for this storm to turn more harsh."

"Hmm…that's about what I figured." Woody shuffled his feet to coax blood into his toes. "How many will throw in?" With small numbers, he might convince Winston to include him.

"A faction. The major is the boss dog."

Maybe he would be invited into the inner circle if one of his friends were involved. "Which commanders?"

Nathan insisted they walk the grounds, away from inquisitive ears.

Woody was eager to comply.

"Now you must keep this to yourself. Tell anyone and—" Three men came toward them so Nathan stopped. One dragged a limp foot behind him. The others walked at a slow pace so the disabled soldier could participate in the conversation. Nathan addressed them as they passed. "A happy Christmas to you, gentlemen."

After the men moved on, Woody said, "You can trust me." He would never share the information with anyone else. That would endanger the plan.

"Appears that Captain Waller Boyd's the ringleader."

Both being Virginians, Woody and the captain had connected on a personal level. He was a pious man of stern integrity. If Captain Boyd decided to climb the prison walls, Woody would follow right behind him.

* * *

The weather cooled on New Year's Eve day. The snow started falling, big, wet flakes perfect for a classic snowball fight. General Trimble and his grand army of snow launchers assembled to do battle with Brigadier General Jeff Thompson's proud fighters. Thompson was renown as "the Swamp Fox of the Confederacy" for his battalion's exploits in the swamps of Missouri.

Woody approached Captain Boyd as he loosed a volley of ice against the other side. The fight became a matter of regimental pride. "Fill your grip and do your duty," Boyd called. As ordered, Woody tossed some well-placed shots, one striking General Trimble in the forehead. A pause in the bombardments gave Woody the chance to talk to Boyd.

"A word, sir." Boyd nodded. "If you ever devise a plan to leave this island, I wish to be included."

Abrupt…and awkward. Boyd's eyes narrowed. "Can you be trusted to keep the secret, let alone tow the mark?"

Woody's reputation in the prison ranks would speak for his discretion. "My word is my bond." He examined the captain's face, small clouds of cold air streaming from his nose and flecks of snow falling on his brows. Boyd shook his head to release the snowy remnants from his beard.

"Escape is near impossible. Dangerous. If we do bust out, the likelihood of being filled with lead is far greater than that of crossing the bay successfully. Those who do reach land are likely to rest in a frozen tomb until the Second Coming. Best to ride out the war here on this rock."

The captain's dire warning gave Woody pause. This kind of death scared him. Freezing would be slow and agonizing. He weighed the alternative of remaining in the prison, unable to taste the freedom of the outside world. The inmate population on the island had swollen to more than two thousand men. Other conditions were tolerable, but even if it meant he must rejoin the fight, Woody would leave if given the chance.

"All due respect, I'm not afraid of Minié balls or the cold." He launched a few snowballs, and then leaned in close. "Are you planning anything, sir?"

Boyd motioned for Woody to step away from the snowball fight and spoke in muted tones, his eyes darting back and forth between Woody and the others walking the grounds.

"A small group of officers are on standby alert, waiting for the right opportunity. So far the weather's been mild for these parts, but we intend to jump the fence and cross the lake once the freeze begins."

"Would you be willing to include me?" Without responding, Boyd walked back into the danger zone, only to be blasted in the lower half of his body.

"Bad form!" Boyd called out.

Packing some snow into a tight ball, Boyd launched the frozen weapon and hit his attacker in the head. Woody followed suit, but his intended target dodged the snowball and it whizzed past his face.

Numbness worked its way into his fingers. He examined his hands, which were almost as white as the snow he tossed.

Boyd followed his gaze. "Take the biting, mind-numbing sting in your hands and multiply that by five or ten, and you're getting close to the frigid conditions you'll face if you tag along. Are you sure you want to come?"

"I can't go another winter cooped up in here."

The officer thought for several moments. "No promises, but I'll try to send word to you, if and when we decide to break out. Stay alert. Gather every bit of clothing you can, and keep your blankets at hand."

"Much obliged, sir."

The snow war in the courtyard went on for another three hours until the weather ended the contest. Like so many real battles these men fought, no clear winner emerged. No one landed a knockout blow, but everyone left the field wet and bone-weary cold.

Woody's head throbbed as he dragged himself back to the barracks.

* * *

That night, a frigid, shrieking wind descended upon the

island's inhabitants.

The temperature plummeted. A bitter freeze crept into the unheated barracks. The weather and lack of firewood turned Woody's stove cold.

The rapid change in conditions left the prisoners and guards in shock. Woody donned every stitch of clothing he owned and draped himself with blankets. With fewer sentries posted, this was the night the escape planners had waited for. A prisoner from another block entered Woody's structure. "Who's Woodard?" he asked.

"That's me." The man handed him a note and left.

Come to Block Ten when the drum calls for lights out at nine o'clock. Captain Boyd had fulfilled his promise.

Woody kept his timepiece handy in case the howling wind drowned out the drumbeat. At nine, he stepped into the night. A rush of bitter cold blasted him with a sobering truth: He needed heavier clothing. There was no turning back now. A frozen death while attempting to break free surpassed the option of staying another day.

He ducked into the officer barracks undetected as Captain Boyd stepped into below-zero temperatures at the entrance. "You got this far at least," Boyd said. "Are you sure you want to give this a try?"

"Without a doubt, sir."

"Bully for you."

Woody lowered his head and coughed.

"Sounds bad, Woody. Are you sure about this?"

"Yes, sir. I'm ready to go."

Boyd nodded, bade good luck to Woody and the other officers committed to the plan, and trudged toward the snow-tipped wall. When he reached the section where the men had hidden their makeshift ladder earlier, he changed directions and moved out of sight. What had happened? The onlookers remained at the door, but Captain Boyd seemed to have disappeared into the howling wind. Five minutes went by. Nothing.

Through the swirling snow, Woody caught the silhouette of a man with his hands raised in the air. "Over there," Woody said.

Then a second shadow appeared. Boyd walked ahead of a sentry's rifle aimed at his back. The men scurried away from the door and took casual positions on the bunks and near the furnace. After the sentry released Boyd and trudged back into the storm, the men planning to follow Boyd to freedom surrounded him, clambering for an explanation.

"Is an escape possible in this Arctic hell?" Major John Winston asked.

"What happened to you?" Captain C.C. Robinson said.

The captain's skin had turned blue from the whipping winds. White frost encased his eyebrows. Several minutes passed before his body stopped quivering. He told the men that surviving the cold would be possible, but only with the right clothes and a strong will to be free. Woody qualified on one count. Just as Boyd had reached the ladder, a sentinel turned the corner to assume his duty on the wall. The captain had nowhere to hide. On the walk back to his quarters, the guard told Boyd the temperature had fallen to twenty-seven degrees below zero, the lowest level ever recorded. The frightening number sank in.

The men eyed one another warily to gauge any fear or doubt in continuing their mission. They remained undeterred. Woody looked over at Thomas Davis and John Stakes, both Virginians, and to N.W. McConnell from Kentucky. They all nodded.

"Understood, Captain Boyd," Woody said. "If the guards don't catch us, the weather most likely will."

The captain reiterated the extreme danger involved but also gave the men the renewed hope they needed. "The other side thinks fleeing is impossible under such conditions, so they are lax in their duty. Like us, they're just trying to stay alive. The howling wind has rendered their reflector lamps useless. They can't see much beyond a shadow. With no extra personnel posted, it's clear they don't expect any further attempts."

"This is reassuring," Winston said. "Mother Nature provided an opportunity in this miserable storm. The gift may never be presented again."

"I'm prepared to light out," Woody said. He suppressed a cough.

"As am I," Winston said. The other four men pledged their involvement as well.

The violent tempest continued. Winston and Davis checked the sentry walkways. The guards remained hunkered down, paralyzed by the gale and freezing temperature every bit as much as the prisoners. "My turn," Winston said as he lumbered out to the fence, retrieved the ladder, and began his climb. Again, the men who'd joined the group of escapees watched at the door of the barracks.

As the attempt unfolded, Woody expected Minié balls to fly at any moment, but none came. With his eyes shut, he uttered a quiet petition to heaven, and the men around him unexpectedly pronounced a group amen. He gave each man a steady, intense glance, and realized separation of rank meant nothing at this moment. They were courageous men, tired and cold, and in need of hope.

Major Winston had climbed most of the ladder when the sentry who'd caught Captain Boyd before emerged from his box to assess the conditions. The major stopped and remained still until the man returned to his refuge. By the thinnest thread of luck, Winston crossed the catwalk and went over the fence. The men inside the barrack exhaled in unison. The next three prisoners ran to the ladder as fast as their thick layers of clothes and the heavy snowfall would allow. The three made their way over. As Stakes climbed up and over and dropped to the ground, the sentry shouted.

Woody barely heard the sentry's command, standing at the doorway to take his turn.

"Halt!"

He watched the confrontation unfold, heartsick at the prospect of being denied the chance to leave. He could barely see the guard looking down from the catwalk to the ground outside the prison wall. Was he speaking to Stakes? By some miracle, the sentry just turned and retreated to the protection of his box, probably to keep from freezing himself. It appeared that Stakes was allowed to continue walking outside the prison walls.

Woody rushed toward the ladder, expecting his freedom vault over the wall to be cut short by gunfire. No shots. Might his luck hold out? He started to climb, but the same guard, who now appeared to be working solo, stepped into the blizzard again and held a bead on him with his rifle. It was Horatio

Hicks, the sergeant he met his first day on the island, and with whom he'd exchanged warm greetings throughout the following months.

He peered deeply into Woody's eyes, an expression of disapproval frozen on his face. For the longest fifteen seconds of his life, Woody waited for the shot. Instead, Hicks lowered his rifle and scrambled back into the box.

Woody climbed faster than he thought possible and leaped over the catwalk, marveling at his luck. He stepped down the fencepost the others had used, and lowered his feet to the tree trunk serving as their landing pad. All but one waited for him in the woods beyond. What happened to the fifth man…Stakes?

Woody walked through the snowdrifts, resigned to the fact that he'd probably die from the cold even though he'd escaped the bullet. The frigid conditions they had waited for became extreme, and Woody suffered a number of maladies. He didn't possess the proper clothing to shield him from the elements. His hands and feet turned numb after a few minutes, as did his nose and ears.

Despite the three pairs of socks he wore, the bitter cold broke through his tattered shoes and traveled up his body. He shook with the chills.

Nineteen

Reawakening

Red Oak, Ohio
Jan. 1, 1864

Eighteen months had passed since Rebecca received the news of George's death. She tried to wear a cheerful face around friends when shopping in Ripley, pretending that life had returned to normal. But inside, the loss sapped her joy for living with each passing month.

She cried herself to sleep most nights, praying that George would appear in her dreams every morning to ward off her desperate loneliness. Sometimes she stayed in her room for days. Her church attendance became spotty, and she rebuffed the community's efforts to reach out. Her father saw through the facade.

James Wallace had moved his young family from Scotland to America to find opportunity and a better life for his children. He had pledged his fidelity to this land and taught Rebecca and her five brothers to honor their new flag. The war compelled his two oldest boys to fight for the Union, and Rebecca served in her own way by helping slaves escape their bondage. When George died, James carved out one day a week to help around his daughter's farm. But the spread fell into disrepair.

On this Wednesday morning, she forced herself out of bed, lit her bedroom lamp, and dressed for a day of work. Her father would arrive before sunup to pitch in, and she intended to prepare a hearty breakfast for him. His presence always lifted her spirits. Yankee lay at her side, content as she brushed her hair, until something prompted him to rise and bare his teeth.

"What's wrong, boy?"

The staircase squeaked. It was only four-thirty, still dark outside. An intruder, someone or something, had entered the house and was climbing. She froze in fear. What to do?

Yankee leaped out the door and toward the staircase. A few seconds later, she heard a scuffle, Yankee barking and growling and a man yelling, "Shoot the dog!"

It sounded like someone was tumbling down the stairs. She grabbed her lamp and rushed to the top, where she saw the faint outline of the dog at the bottom, standing on a man who attempted to fend off the dog's vicious attack.

She saw a second man and the glint of a gun.

Then a boom.

Yankee yelped and rolled off the man. The dog lay still, bleeding from his haunch.

Fury and fear mixed. Fury won as Rebecca hurried down the stairs. "You killed my friend."

The first man stood and smiled. He picked up his blue kepi and placed it on his head. *A Union deserter?* His knotted hair fell to his shoulders. His companion, still holding a smoking Derringer pistol in his hand, pulled up a chair at the kitchen table.

Her father wouldn't arrive for another hour, so she was on her own. Her heart beat wildly. She knew these men would have their way with her if she didn't assess the situation and act. The single-shot Derringer had been discharged, and the man failed to reload. The intruders seemingly carried no other weapons. These were Union drifters who wandered and took, with no regard for the people they harassed.

Was Yankee still alive? Rebecca edged past the reclining intruder and snatched a towel from the stove. She stooped down, set the lamp on the floor and petted Yankee's head. With eyes closed, his chest rose and fell. Her four-legged hero wasn't dead. As she applied pressure to his wound, she lashed out at the men. "Take what you want and leave. You've done enough damage for one day. Get out!"

"Sure…sure."

The man stepped closer, wiping blood from the dog bites. A foul stench followed him. As his face came within inches of hers, she prepared to put up a fight. He stroked her hair once, and then unexpectedly picked up the lamp and wandered about the house, pawing at her things instead. The need in his lustful eyes told her that an attack had only been delayed.

The man at the table rose and looked about the kitchen. "I'm 'bout half starved to death."

The comment gave her an idea. *Delay.* If she could hold them off until her daddy arrived, then…then what? That would only put him in harm's way, but she had no choice. She would fry some eggs. "If I make some breakfast for you boys, will you take your leave? The trouble must stop now."

The hungry man looked to his sidekick who said, "Maybe we'll skip the food and first get to know each other."

"No!" the hungry man barked. "We eat—now."

She fired up her wood stove and cracked some eggs into a pan. Both men took a place at the table. She glanced over at Yankee, who lay in the same spot and appeared to be breathing normally. But he might bleed out if she didn't get him to Doctor Hooper's house soon.

"Coffee'd be good with them eggs, lady." The shooter held the derringer but still had not reloaded. They didn't expect that she'd be having company, and that would give her daddy an advantage when he arrived. Rebecca served everything up and stood by the stove rather than go near the men. "About time," he said, setting the gun on the table.

When they'd finished eating, the man who'd wrestled with Yankee kicked his chair away and approached Rebecca, while his partner sat and smiled. Again, he stroked her hair, which she wore down at night. Emboldened by her seething anger over the shooting, and determined to make things difficult for him, she brushed his hand away. He brought it back and petted her cheeks, the skin on his fingers cracked and dirty. As he yanked her hair back, a strong snarling jaw sank its teeth into the calf of her restrainer, forcing him to release his grip.

"Ahh...!" Yankee had waited for the right time to strike. He mauled the man, who kept screaming, "Get him off me!"

The man at the table reached for his gun, dipped his hand into a pocket, and loaded a bullet into the chamber. As he stood to fire again at Yankee, Rebecca's father arrived and jumped into the fray. A large, muscular man, James broke the shooter's nose with a strong blow to the face, stunning him. James then turned to pull Yankee off the man on the ground, and as he did, the intruder pulled a knife from a holster at his ankle. He lunged at James when his back was turned, the knife lifted high to strike a deadly blow.

"Daddy!" Rebecca screamed.

Yankee tore into the man's arm, knocking the knife from his hand. Rebecca commanded Yankee to heel, and the second man, bleeding from his arms and legs, followed his partner in crime out the door.

Yankee whimpered and laid down.

"Oh, Daddy." Rebecca fell into his embrace, sobbing.

"It's over now, honey. They won't be back anytime soon." He petted her hair, but this stroke was familiar and loving. "Deserters. Like rodents scavenging for morsels."

He held her until she remembered. "Yankee..." Turning back to her rescuer, she got on all fours and rubbed her face into his. He moaned, but his short tail wagged.

"You're the second bravest soldier I've ever known." She scratched his nose and the top of his head.

"Best we load our friend here into the wagon and hightail it over to Doc Hooper's place," her daddy said. "He'll need to pull the ball, clean the wound, and bandage Yankee up. He sure saved the day."

* * *

Red Oak Presbyterian Church
Two weeks later

She'd hitched her buggy on Sunday morning, dressed in her

finest outfit and anxious to attend worship. A light rain had soaked the ground over the last two days, but on this morning Rebecca watched the sun rise over the fields. This sunrise felt like a renewal. If not for her faithful dog and her courageous father, she might not have lived to see another day begin or attend another church service.

As she approached the front entrance, young Willie Williamson called out, "Morning, Mrs. Johnston. So nice to see you again."

"And you, Willie."

He directed her to pull up next to the wooden planks leading to the door, placed there so congregants would not have to step into the mud. She climbed down and walked into the sanctuary as Willie parked the buggy at the side of the building. She'd attended church only a handful of times since George's death, and she felt anxious about how the congregation would receive her.

Reverend Matthews met her near the door. "Welcome, dear Rebecca. We've missed you. Are you well?"

"Hello, Rebecca," said Constance Warren, as she and her husband Simon scooted into the last bench. She acknowledged the greeting with a smile and then turned to Matthews.

"Yes, Reverend. Now I am."

Rebecca explained that after many months of mourning George, she'd finally become aware that she had been nearly as dead as him. In the last couple of weeks she felt more alive than she had in a long time. She wouldn't allow herself to slip backwards. From this day on, if she started to mope in bed, she would rise and work. She would find joy in her farm, in her friends, in her faith again.

"Life is for the living," she said, "and I'm not going to spend another minute of it wallowing in sadness."

She slid into the row next to the Warrens.

Another fact became clear. These were dangerous times for a woman living alone on a farm. She needed farmhands, but she couldn't afford to pay. Or a husband, but she didn't envision a wedding anytime soon. Nor did she wish for one.

For now, she would continue to face the danger on her own. She decided to keep the squeak in the stairs.

Twenty

Escape

Johnson's Island

They waited a long time for Stakes, the escapee who'd exchanged words with the sentry after he dropped to the ground. The soldier must have told a convincing story about his identity and how he came to be outside the compound. Their chances for a successful escape diminished with each passing minute. Major Winston was in charge so he made the final call.

"He was probably arrested. We should head out." After they slipped past the guard barracks and the prison cemetery, Winston suggested they make their way to Marblehead, a mile and a half over the frozen Lake Erie.

"Calmer waters in that direction," he said. "That means stronger surfaces. Less chance of taking a cold bath that we'd not survive."

Thomas Davis said, "But sir, Sandusky City is the more direct route to the South. Don't you think we're better to head toward Sandusky?"

"Sure, if we want to crawl through territory swarming with Federals. Bulletins about our escape are being prepared as we speak."

John Winston spoke with the assurance of an educated man.

On a few occasions, Woody had spent time walking the prison yard with Winston, and learned he'd graduated from Trinity College with a Master of Arts degree. He'd delayed his plans to practice law when war broke out, and soon after he joined the Confederate Army. The major, a single man at twenty-four, practiced the Christian faith with ardor. Unlike many in prison, Winston took pride in his appearance. His hair always neatly combined back and the beard stretching across his lower jaw kept trim. He struck a solemn pose, his forehead broad and cheekbones high. Like Woody, Winston breathed the idea of escape, and that had increased Woody's admiration for him.

The others on this dangerous journey were just casual acquaintances, men that Woody might have greeted with a friendly nod on the yard. He already worried about Davis's pushback against Winston's authority.

"The major's right," Captain C.C. Robinson said. "Patrols will be searching for us by land, and detectives will be covering the railways. Our chances increase northward into Canada, where fewer Union troops are stationed."

"We watch our backs, avoid the citizenry, and we might pass undetected," Winston said.

Davis shrugged, "If the cold don't kill us first."

While the way forward made sense, Woody wasn't sure he'd make it. The congestion plaguing him over the last several months racked his chest with pain, and he could barely feel his feet. If the deep freeze killed anyone, he would be the first. Each man committed to support the others, whatever may come. How long would their commitment to each other hold once Woody became an albatross around their necks?

They slipped their way across the bay to Marblehead and headed west, careful to walk beyond the farmhouses beckoning them with warmth and food. Woody's agony increased with every step, and he could barely contain his cough. The icy wind whistled and whirled with a vengeance, but he didn't complain. The men walked through the tempest, and when Woody was about to give up and submit to nature's violent outburst, the major called for a rest.

The leader faced him to get a closer look. "Woody, you're ragged. Can you resume?"

He nodded, unwilling to quit the fight. A minute later, Winston motioned for the group to move ahead. Anxiety-ridden, exhausted and bone-weary cold, Woody trudged forward. After a short distance, a troublesome coughing spell erupted from deep in his chest. The group stopped again. "I…I'm fine. Continue..." In addition to everything else, Woody now became racked with guilt that he'd not disclosed to Winston how sick he'd become in the last week. His selfish desire to escape had put the others in danger.

Winston pulled the cloths wrapped around Woody's neck and ears and removed his own makeshift glove. He put his hand against Woody's forehead and quickly rewrapped the material around his face. The major's grim expression spoke volumes.

He turned to the others. "May the Lord help him, he's hot as a brush fire. He needs shelter and rest and nourishment."

"Keep going," Woody said.

Each labored breath made him weaker, depleting what little energy remained in his reservoir. Traces of blood colored the discharge from his lungs, a sign of pneumonia or some other lung ailment. If they figured out how sick he was, his comrades would drop him somewhere and he wouldn't blame them. The condition of his feet also worried him. Numb from the ankle down into his left foot, he couldn't feel his toes. The same symptoms appeared in his right leg, but not as bad.

In spite of his weakness, Woody put one foot in front of the other. Three hours later, the major put his hand up and the group stopped. All eyes were on Woody. He tried to make them understand why he'd insisted on continuing.

"Must find her," he said, shifting his focus from man to man. "So...tell them about her father...let them know...about the battle...and he died. Never met him. So sorry, but your daddy's dead."

Davis spoke out. "Good God, Major Winston. The man's delirious. He cannot continue."

"He's right," Captain Robinson said.

"What would you have me do? Leave him here in the bleakness of winter?"

Neither man answered, so they continued through open stretches of land and through forests. Woody lumbered for some time toward a remote place he'd never visited, but where the girl marked time. His eyesight played tricks. A farm jutted through the snowy wind and trees ahead. Or was it a house in a major city? The girl called for him, eager for news about her father and how much he missed her. Lucas walked by his side, clad in a single shirt, untroubled by the driving cold.

Woody said, "Put on your jacket and cover yourself with a blanket, Luke."

Major Winston stopped the others. "A confusion has overtaken him." He woke Woody from the strange trance.

"Major? Where are we?" Bewildered, Woody turned a full circle. Somehow, someone had whisked him to this place in an instant. "How am I here?"

"Gonna find someone who can help you," Winston said. "Hang on."

* * *

The next day, the group pressed across northwestern Ohio, on their way toward Toledo. The storm had lessened in intensity, but the sun was still nowhere to be found. Woody's will to survive astounded the other men and gave them added courage to finish the journey. Dark clouds released a soft snowfall that added to the white landscape that stretched as far as the eye could see.

Finally, with many miles between them and Johnson's Island, and the worst of the storm behind them, Winston gave the order to build a makeshift camp in the midst of a forest. They settled Woody and spread about to find firewood, which they dumped into an icy pit and managed to set ablaze with matches. The warmth of the fire, and the limited rations they'd been able to carry over the prison wall, revived Woody but did little to relieve his burning fever and the lack of feeling in his ankle and foot.

The men pulled blankets over their bodies and slept on the icy ground, and that brought sweet relief. When Woody awoke, he pulled the girl's photograph from his sack and gazed for several minutes. When he looked up, he saw the others had been staring at him. Dropping the photograph, he coughed into his cupped hands and left a bloody residue that he wiped against the snow.

Winston gave the order to break camp and continue on. Along the way, they stole two horses from a barn, one of which Woody rode until an hour later when they spotted a farm down the road. Winston rapped on the door and asked for refuge. The owner invited them inside and led the party to the fireplace. Once they'd warmed up, he fed them. Woody refused to leave his place at the fire, so the owner brought the stew to him there. His chills continued despite the heat, and he could barely eat a morsel.

The only sounds coming from the table were of the men slurping and moaning with delight. The farmer broke the silence.

"Your friend here is in dire need of a doctor," the farmer said. "Bad cough, high fever. What brings you boys out into this nastiness? This man should be in bed."

Listening from the fireplace, Woody felt grateful at first. To crawl into a warm bed would be heaven. But the man's curiosity also made Woody uneasy. Too many questions might turn into suspicion and involve the local authorities. By now, word would be circulating about the men who'd escaped from Johnson's Island prison.

"Sir, you've been most kind," Winston said. "We learned a powerful lesson in this storm. Surveying is best done under the warmth of a shining sun."

"So you're surveyors." Woody heard a tinge of disbelief in the farmer's voice. No one else appeared to reside in the small farmhouse, but the two doors that led to other rooms remained shut. Was he alone?

Winston seemed concerned too. "Yes, sir, we'll be moving on, but we're thankful for your hospitality."

"Best for your friend if you stay the night."

"Why, thank you kindly," Winston said. "We might just take your offer."

An hour after the farmer retired to his room, Winston rallied the men. A clandestine departure put some distance between them and their host. With Woody still on horseback, they kept off the roads as they passed Port Clinton, crossed the Portage River, and continued south of Oak Harbor, where they stopped at an inn. The proprietor inquired as to their status.

"Surveyors. Army. Investigating lands suitable for future development," the major said. "Got stuck in the havoc of this storm."

"No rooms available tonight, but you can huddle by that fire long as you like."

"Much obliged."

The quick answer satisfied the man. Woody and McConnell, tormented by the cold and on the cusp of being unable to finish the journey, huddled closest to the fire. Later that night, some Federals entered and talked about the Rebs at Johnson's Island who must have been near frozen on a night like this. None of the escapees uttered a word. Woody held his breath, hoping the innkeeper would not query the men about their work in front of the bluebellies.

As they left at dawn on the third of January, McConnell announced he would not proceed. He would stop at the next farmhouse in hopes of finding benevolence, some rest and food. "With any luck, I'll be right behind you and we can meet again in Canada," McConnell said.

Winston glanced at Woody. "How about you?"

"I have a mission to find an unnamed girl."

The major nodded. "Okay, Woody."

Throughout the night, Woody's sleep was disturbed by intermittent outbursts and nightmares. With each startled awakening, he caught Major Winston staring at him. At one point, the major tried to talk some sense into him. "Listen, Woody…your face is pale, your eyes sunken, and you're burning up. At first light, we'll find someone who will help you."

Most men would have given up, but Woody still possessed enough grit to ignore the ravages of cold on his legs and the horrible cough. Rising to walk that morning, he grimaced with pain and started to crumble. The major supported him as Woody forced his unsteady legs to move, one step at a time. The mental deterioration—his clouded mind—now matched the physical state. His body twitched like a horse shaking away flies. When he looked around, all eyes were upon him.

He stood as straight as his body would allow. "I won't slow us down." The promise sounded implausible even to Woody.

McConnell bid his friends goodbye at the first house they passed, hopeful that the occupants would show him mercy. The rest of them walked on until they came to a simple two-story house near Toledo, where Woody collapsed. Darkness threatened to close in, and Woody welcomed the relief that would come. But he remained conscious.

They carried him up to the door and knocked. A man and his wife, and too many children to count, greeted them from across the threshold. The man sized up the situation and moved quickly. "Bring him in here, by the fire."

Major Winston thanked him as he and Davis carried Woody to an empty bed, where they lowered him and positioned his head on the pillow. The man's wife removed the thick layers of clothes. His coat was frozen solid, and his underclothes were soaked from the sweat generated by Woody's fever. His haversack hung from his neck and shoulder, and when the woman tried to remove the bag, he grabbed her arm.

"No." As Woody lay on the threshold of existence, he still held the sack tightly. Cobwebs stretched across his mind as he struggled to explain. "Must not...the girl can't..."

"The sack will stay right next to you on the bed."

Woody opened his eyes long enough to glance at the kind lady and allow her to remove the strap from around his neck and torso. As promised, she laid the haversack by his side and put some dry clothes on him. That's when they examined his legs and feet. The woman pointed to the bluish-gray color around most of his foot. "This boy has severe frostbite. I seen it many times before."

"Maybe gangrene." Winston touched the tissue from Woody's ankle down to his toes. "The limb is hard."

Woody moaned. Even in his delirium, he understood every word whispered around the bedside. His body shook from the chills. A gob of ruby phlegm followed his cough.

"Never did any doctoring, but this man suffers a pneumonia," the man of the house said. "I'd bet on it."

Startled, Woody opened his eyes and doubled his efforts to clear his murky mind. The man was balding and wore a long mustache that stretched across to both cheeks. He examined Woody's leg and then came close to look into his eyes. The man's gaze reached deep inside and filled Woody with an unexplainable sense that he would pull through this ordeal. He must be the patriarch here. The man's wife stood by his side until she noticed that their children cowered in the corner. She scurried over to comfort them. They stayed silent as their mother hugged the young ones and ushered them all into another room and closed the door.

The father spoke with an air of urgency. "This man needs a sawbones. No time to lose."

Winston asked, "Where is the nearest doctor?"

Through the fog, Woody predicted his friends would leave him behind in the care of these people. He smiled wearily, welcoming such an outcome. The major would provide fake identities and an explanation of why they'd traveled on such a troublesome night. The need to fetch a doctor might work well into his story. Woody closed his eyes but fought the need for sleep. What if his eyes never opened again?

The woman asked her husband, "What about John Wesley Bond?"

"Bond...hmm. The new doctor over on Glenwood Avenue, right?"

The couple conferred for a few minutes, and came back to Winston and the other men. The man reviewed the plan. "One of you will call on the doctor and request his services at our home. The trip won't take much time. Saddle up our two horses; they're hearty animals."

"How can we thank you?" Winston asked. "At least our friend has a chance, thanks to your kindness."

Woody opened his heavy eyes again as Major Winston shared some story about them being woodcutters surprised by the storm's fury. The man's brow furrowed, his eyes unblinking, as he chose his next words.

"We don't know you or where you're from or what you do. Might be desperate soldiers, for all I know. We align with neither side, and don't approve of the bloodbath that's stealing our young men. Nor do we abide in slavery. But do not take us for fools, sir."

Winston was sobered. "Rest assured. We do not."

"Charity is what keeps us from turning you back out into

Satan's vengeance," the man said. "As Lutherans, our faith and compassion tell us to help your friend."

"Understood, sir. By the Spirit, we're at your doorstep for the same reason."

Woody believed this to be true. His vision began to blur, and for a moment, the girl stood at the end of the bed. Just as quickly, she smiled and vanished like dew on a June morning. His tired eyes followed as Winston extended his hand to the man of the house.

"What name shall I give the doctor?" Winston asked.

The man returned the handshake. "Name is Herschel Myers, and my wife is Adele. An American flag will fly at my door. Old Glory and a general description of our place should be enough for the doctor to find us. Tell him we suspect pneumonia. Better tell him to bring his cutting kit and waste no time."

The major set out. The nightmare would soon be over.

Would Woody's life on earth also fade away?

He pressed hard to understand. What would the doctor be cutting?

Twenty-One

The Procedure

The Myers Farm
Near Toledo, Ohio

Words floated through the air in random patterns, many dissolving, unattached to a sentence. Apprehension muddled Woody's thinking. Some kind of threat loomed ahead, but he couldn't get his mind around what it was.

Then, a comforting touch. The slight lifting of his head. The water he requested, but in short sips. He thirsted for more. As he opened his eyes, an angel of mercy, the unnamed girl, held the cup to his lips and whispered words of comfort. At last they could talk about how her father died a hero, and how much Daddy loved his little girl. About how, after months of being comforted by her innocence, Woody had plodded through the storm to find her.

"Been looking...everywhere...on the field your daddy..."

"Here, now. The doctor will help you."

Not the girl's voice. Startled, Woody tried to focus his eyes. The girl still stood at the side of his bed, dressed in a hooped dress, her hair flowing down to her shoulders. Her cheeks were painted a pink hue, radiating warmth from her face. But a woman's voice came from her mouth.

"Doctor, he burns with fever," the woman said.

The young girl shattered into pieces like a vase dropped to the floor.

"A temperature of a hundred and four. The cough indicates a bad case of pneumonia."

The others talked, though Woody didn't understand much of it. One word rose above the rest. Procedure.

What procedure?

The roundness of the doctor's voice matched the rotundity that bulged from his clothes. He had a bewhiskered face. Intelligent eyes. What were his intentions? The instinct to flee dissolved when Woody commanded his legs to move but they disobeyed. Or never received the message. He would proceed cautiously. Lucas would sort these confusing matters out when he…where was Lucas? He promised always to watch his…? Woody racked his brain. To always watch his…what? He couldn't remember.

The doctor examined Woody's other leg, and covered him back up. "This foot also is frostbitten, as are his ears and fingers. But these extremities are not as far-gone. A couple of toes may need to be removed, but I can treat everything else."

"What about his left foot, Dr. Bond? Can you save it?" Herschel asked. "The boy's young to go through life a cripple."

"Sorry to say, but I cannot. An immediate amputation is the only remedy. Otherwise, he dies."

As the doctor opened his cutting kit, Woody lurched forward in bed. He stared straight ahead and pleaded. "No, take your hands off her."

Someone eased him down to the pillows.

* * *

Woody watched the doctor methodically set out his instruments, naming each one—surgical saws, pliers, and a curved probe. He placed them in the order of use, along with his lamps, a retractor and brush, and trepanning implements.

"Do you understand what I'm doing?" the doctor asked him.

The doctor moved ahead with his preparations, not waiting

for an answer.

Turning to Adele, he rattled off a list of necessary items. "Plenty of warm water in a basin, and as many towels or rags as you can spare. And something we can use to restrain him."

Restrain me...for what reason? The doctor put a couple of blankets under the bad leg, causing Woody to groan.

Woody tried again to focus. Death did not concern him. The sojourn would be over, and he would awaken in heaven. The doctor leaned down and whispered in his ear.

"I must take your left foot so I can save your life, son. The drug we're about to administer will put you to sleep. Afterwards, I will inject some morphine into your hip. That will ease the pain as you wake up. I will use all my skills to provide you a rounded end to accommodate a prosthetic device. Once you've healed, this will allow you to farm and do most things you did before."

Medicine. Darkness. Blessed slumber.

The last thing he remembered was the sparkling eyes and broad smile lighting the face of the cherub who held his hand. The unnamed girl's devotion allowed him to find the elusive peace he so long had pursued.

Twenty-Two

Recovery

February 1864

"Turn to your left, Luke!"

Woody stepped between Lucas and the bluecoat who was about to thrust a bayonet into Lucas's back while he remained locked in a fierce hand-to-hand fight with another soldier. A couple of volleys whizzed past Woody's head, musketry missing its mark. Explosive shells and case shot canister from multiple howitzers rained fire and death around him, but not on him. Providence cast a protective hedge around him, denying entry to the missiles that sought to tear and maim.

Woody used his Springfield to parry the soldier's deadly force. Both rifles tumbled to the ground beside Lucas, who continued in the struggle to best his opponent. Now Woody and his enemy also relied on brute strength, as they punched and wrestled in the thick mud to gain an upper hand. The man landed a blow to Woody's face, stunning him. The next thing he knew, a long blade moved toward him.

"No-o-o..." He lurched up from his pillow, wild-eyed and drenched in sweat. For a moment longer, he thought the Yank had found him in the safety of his family's farmhouse. Sarah

Woodard charged into his room.

"Do not be fearful, son. You're safe." The sound of her voice covered him like a woolen blanket, shielding him from the cold he'd endured for so long.

She pulled back the curtains covering his window, and his room brightened in the morning sun. He looked at the familiar space. The timepiece on his dresser and the mirror on the wall. The washbasin and personal items—his shaving tin and razor, and a bone-handle toothbrush. All appeared in their proper places. Even the chair, a treasured family antique, sat in its usual spot opposite his bed. The heirloom was his connection to the present.

One item had been taken off the wall. The cross. Odd—it had always hung there.

His gaze settled on his mother's concerned face as the frenetic pounding in his chest gave way to a normal rhythm.

Suddenly, a Union soldier exploded through the door to his room. The bluecoat leveled his Springfield and fired at his mother. The projectile left a hole in her forehead, a ghastly exit wound he could see through as she lay sprawled on top of him. Blood flowed onto the blankets…onto him. Lifeless eyes stared into his face.

"No, Ma!" Blood-curdling screams reverberated through the house. In the midst of this horrifying scene, he noticed the coward had no face.

* * *

The Myers Farm
Near Toledo, Ohio

Woody emerged from a deep sleep to that familiar place where one is half awake and half asleep.

"Dear Woody, wake up."

With her hands clasping his shoulders, Adele Myers shook him over and over until the tremors ebbed and the deep fear subsided. The strange double nightmare left his dead mother in some shadowy world.

He stared up at Adele and perused the room where she'd

nursed him day and night since the surgery four weeks before. She wiped his face with a cold compress. The woman's touch had vanquished his persistent fevers. The pneumonia had subsided, and Dr. Bond reported his stump had healed with no secondary infections. Between the doctor and the Myers family, Woody had received excellent care.

Without warning, Adele left the room and returned with a bowl in her hands. She lifted the spoon to his mouth. "No offense intended, but you're cadaverous," she said.

He didn't have the energy to chuckle, but he managed a smile. "None taken."

"All right, young man. I know you don't feel much like eating, but I'm not going to permit you to rest until this soup is gone. Eat while it's hot."

"Not hungry, Mrs. Myers."

She set the food to the side and propped up his pillows. "Nevertheless, it's time for some nourishment. When I count to three, you can ease yourself backward." He decided it best to obey his new commanding officer. "Good. Now I can feed you without spilling."

"Just for you." After he ate a few bites, he asked a question that had been burning in his mind for weeks. "Why did you rescue me? You know I'm a Confederate soldier. Most folks would have turned me in."

"I'm not them." The small, sturdy woman wearing the plain dress of a farmer's wife dipped the spoon into the bowl, brought it to his mouth, and allowed him to sip the contents. Several sips later, he raised his hand to indicate he could take no more. One more mouthful was lifted to his lips, but he refused.

"Please, no more for now." He readjusted himself lower in the bed. "Your house is filled with young children and a husband, yet you save a stranger's life—a traitor some would say—and you work around the clock to nurse him back to health. Why?"

This time she breathed deep and exhaled, long and slow.

"Herschel's younger brother, Max, lost his first son at Shiloh." She stopped a quick tear before it could roll beyond her eye. "Little Maxie was wounded on the sixth of April in '62. According to the letter his commanding officer sent to the parents, Little Maxie suffered and bled on the ground until the end of the second day. Time just ran out for Little Maxie."

So much woe. Could the two sides ever settle their differences and learn to live together again?

"I'm so sorry."

"Who knows? If someone had tended to his injuries in time, Little Maxie might still be with us. You reminded us of him."

Twenty-Three

A Crossroads

The Myers Farm
Near Toledo
Late June 1864

The night stretched on. Woody tossed and turned, causing the iron bed frame to squeak like his old church shoes back home. Somehow the family slept through the racket, or they lay in their own beds with open eyes like him.

He'd been sleeping on the same bed where Herschel and Adele placed him that January day. A torturous day when creation's fury led him to believe the sun had been blotted from the sky forever and that he would be removed from the earth. Instead, Woody hovered between life and the hereafter on this wool-stuffed single mattress. Adele had nursed him day and night until Dr. Bond proclaimed her patient free of pneumonia.

He carefully swung his legs over the side of the bed. The black of night robbed him of all visibility. As he fumbled around the nightstand for matches, he knocked over a water cup. The clang when it hit the floor made him cringe, certain the noise could raise the dead. He listened. Nothing. Just the quick bursts of the katydids outside, in crisp and harsh tones that usually lulled him to sleep.

This time he found the matches and lit the small kerosene lamp. He strapped on his prosthetic and gathered his clothes for the day. The rhythmical throbbing in his leg ran from his hip to his foot, but the appendage wasn't there, only leather, wood and iron. Would he ever get used to this strange sensation? His limp had lessened over time as he relearned to walk, but an uneven gait still revealed his disability.

He could not fathom how a woman would ever look upon him as a whole man again. What would his father say when they were reunited later that morning? The anticipation of seeing him again had robbed Woody of his rest.

In the kitchen, he lit a second larger lamp and started a fire in the cast-iron stove. He took the coffee grinder from the top of the wooden icebox and crushed some beans, hoping again not to awaken the sleepers. Then he sat on the rocker by the small kitchen table as the water in the coffee pot began its slow boil.

The rectangular table came alive once more, if only in his mind. The family of nine managed to fit around this space for their meals. Franz, the oldest child at fifteen, would hold Margareta, the three-year-old on his lap. Luther, the next oldest, did likewise with a younger sibling. It was a tidy country kitchen, filled with pots and bowls on shelves lining the walls. Buckets sat on a wooden floor decorated with soft carpets. More than anything, this space brimmed with the love Herschel and Adele stirred within it.

The sound of water boiling in the coffee pot gently roused him. Soon he would share a last meal here with these friends. He sighed and mixed his coffee. Lamp in one hand, coffee in the other, Woody walked to his favorite chair on the porch where he waited for the sunrise.

As he regained his strength, Woody had hatched plans to find the unnamed girl. In a letter mailed weeks before, he informed his parents about his long recovery at the Myers farmhouse all these many months. He told the story of his harrowing prison escape, and how he'd survived pneumonia but lost his ankle and foot. A prosthetic supplied by the doctor who performed the amputation allowed him to move about, so he did small chores while his stump healed.

The letter beseeched his father to come to the Myers's farm, and to bring some clothes and money so he might journey to Cincinnati to find the girl. Woody lamented asking his father to undergo such a long train ride, but he needed more than a suitcase and some cash. Some of his daddy's quiet confidence would help prepare him for the task. Finding the girl would be like grasping the gusts of wind that ruffled his hair on this cold pre-dawn morning. Alone and filled with doubt, Woody hoped seeing his daddy would help him to focus.

The wartime nightmares had faded. And his need to view the photograph diminished with the dreams. Why then put his life on hold to accomplish the near impossible?

"Didn't get much sleep, did you?" Herschel stood at the doorway dressed for the morning chores, the vapor from his coffee cup winding upward. Woody shook his head. "Me neither. Adele didn't do much better."

"Sorry about all the noise."

"Oh, that didn't bother us. Mind if I join you?"

"Please."

"Still a bit early to start pulling on them cows."

Woody smiled at the morning routine he'd witnessed so many times before. Herschel's short five-foot-six frame stooped over a stool, his still jet-black hair and angular face buried beneath the cow's udder. As he pulled each teat, Herschel would sing out a pleasant song in German. This was the only place he'd heard Herschel sing.

Straightforward in manner, Herschel spoke sparingly and never wasted his words. The crooked smile under his long mustache showed up occasionally, but only when he let his guard down. Like when he reminisced about meeting Adele in Cincinnati, and how they sang folk songs together in the city's German Sängerfests. His bushy brows danced when he told Woody about those community festivals.

When Woody told Herschel he'd be searching for a family named Braun in that city, the proud German mentioned his old neighborhood, Over-the-Rhine. He'd said, "Start there." This was the second time Woody had received this advice.

Herschel was like a surrogate father to him. They sat in silence for a while until Herschel turned to him, tears rolling around his mustache to his chin and said, "We're gonna miss you. You're like family now."

The unusual display of emotion shocked Woody.

The patriarch patted his coat pocket and then reached into his pants. "Drats."

Woody handed him a kerchief to dab his eyes. Moved by compassion, Herschel and Adele selflessly ignored the danger to themselves and their family that stormy night and chose to save a stranger's life. A Confederate soldier, no less. "How can I ever repay you and Adele?"

The mooing of Herschel's cows interrupted the tender moment.

Herschel straightened his shoulders and stood. "Sounds like them cows are ready for me."

"Let me help. I'll pitch some hay while you do the milking."

"Deal." As they entered the barn, Herschel grasped Woody's arm and pulled him to a stop. "First I want to ask. Are you prepared for this mission of yours?"

"Funny. I was trying to remember why. I mean, after all this time, why am I still driven to accomplish this goal?"

"Son, you told us the first night you struggled through our door. You're doing it for the little girl."

* * *

At midday, after Woody and Herschel repaired a broken fence on the property, Herschel hitched his buggy and headed for the Toledo train station.

As he waited on the porch, Woody sipped a glass of Adele's lemonade and reread a recent letter from Lucas. He wrote about being in prison right there on the Halverston farm and that he needed a good adventure. The transition from soldiering to sowing and planting had been difficult. Many tasks required two hands. He wrote, "And don't try to talk me into I wearin' a fake hand for broken down soldiers. I'll pin my sleeve back and parade my stump arm around like a badge of honor."

Both men suffered the physical ravages of war, but it sounded like Lucas had made peace with his injury. Not so with Woody.

The wait on the porch unnerved Woody, so he walked a portion of the sixty-acre wheat field, ripe for harvest. The warm summer sun on his face and the bright blue skies made him think again of the three days from hell that brought him to this place. Thankfully, those days passed and new beginnings emerged. What would this fresh start bring?

The buggy pulled up to the front of the farmhouse. Woody

peered across the field as an imposing figure stepped down and met his gaze. A tingling passed down Woody's spine as he walked toward his father. Reuben Woodard stopped a few yards away from him. "Hello, son. I've come like you asked."

"Look at me, Daddy. I'm half the man I once was." He fought to keep his composure.

"No, Jonathan. You're so much more than that man."

They walked the last few feet and fell into each other's arms.

* * *

Two days later, Woody drove his daddy to the train station.

"Remember, son. You're posing as a discharged Union veteran in town seeking business opportunities," Reuben said. "Be careful who you talk to. Steer clear of the men in blue."

"Will do."

At the depot, Reuben bought his ticket and they walked to the platform where the train awaited. The conductor called out, "All aboard."

"Well, son. Time for me to board." Their eyes met. Nothing more needed to be said. Woody nodded, and his father turned and climbed the steps.

* * *

The following day, Woody stepped aboard a similar train as the entire Myers family bid him farewell. The locomotive rolled forward, drowning them in a cloud of steam. He craned his head out the window to catch one more glimpse, but the train banked to the left.

They were gone. The search had begun.

The rail car would carry him from the northernmost tip of Ohio to its southwest border with Kentucky. He was headed to Cincinnati, shipping point and connector city between the east and west. As the train raced ahead, he prayed. *Be my lamp, Lord.*

Through much of the ride, Woody gazed out the window at the landscapes that rushed past as if the land bounded backwards toward the Toledo train station. After several hours, the smoky basin of Cincinnati lay below on the banks of the Ohio, signaling the train's imminent arrival at the new Baymiller Station.

They passed through the hilly suburbs, dotted with expensive estates and painted green with trees and vegetation. A vibrant city jumped through the train windows. A living organism filled with belching smokestacks, commerce, and a riverfront where flatboats and steamers of all shapes and sizes entered and left the docks like clockwork. Woody exited the train in silence, aware that his presence in this place was no accident.

He summoned the courage to begin the adventure. On the street, blue cloth defined the moving wall of people.

Yankees everywhere.

Twenty-Four

Cincinnati

June 30, 1864

The streets of Cincinnati pulsed as people and carriages and wagons and buses dodged each other. Urgency filled the air. Woody picked a well-dressed passerby and stopped him with a slight bow.

"Pardon me, sir. Can you recommend a top-rail place to stay in your city?"

"Why, yes," the stranger said. "Check out the Burnet on the corner of Vine and Third. Quite famous around these parts."

"How so?"

"The president spent one night there after his election, the same day the Rebs opened fire on Fort Sumter. And Generals Grant and Sherman huddled there a few months back to plot an end to the war."

"How do I locate this fine property?" Woody asked.

The man directed his attention to the horse-drawn street coaches with iron wheels revolving on rails, conveying people to various points in the city.

"Hop onto one of those." He sidestepped Woody and continued on his way.

Minutes later, another boxy tramcar pulled by two horses rolled to the boarding point. Woody climbed the narrow steps through the rear door, paid the five-cent charge, and sat on the wooden bench seats along with the other passengers. The interior was varnished, and the outside painted with elegant stripes and letters. The operator, who wore a full jacket and hat, stood on the platform in front, reins in hand. After some distance, he rang a bell and applied the brake, signals the horses responded to. The car rolled to a stop. Some passengers disembarked, others came aboard.

Woody rose from his seat and edged past the riders and found a spot to stand next to the conductor, hoping to engage in some cordial repartee.

"Seems like this is one of your busiest times," Woody said, glancing to the street.

"Yep. T'is."

Woody tried again, commenting about the efficiency of the city's transportations systems, but the man had little interest in small talk. The car quickly pulled to its next stop. The new travelers paid their tolls and took their seats. Woody stood the rest of the way in silence until he realized he'd better ask one more important question. "Where do I jump off for the Burnet? Hate to miss my stop."

The man pointed forward. "The building up ahead with the large dome. That's the Burnet."

With a quick pull on his bowler, Woody thanked him and stepped to the street at the next stop. The magnificence of the building left him awestruck. He had no business staying in such a high-class hotel. His father had stayed there once and insisted Woody register for at least one night. The elegance of the interior matched the grandeur of the outside structure. He decided to stay this first night and then switch to more modest accommodations if the search became prolonged.

At the front desk, he registered as Andrew Alexander. The clerk welcomed Woody like he was the Prince of Wales. He reviewed all the available amenities and passed Woody his room key.

"The second floor, sir," the clerk said. "Please tell us if we can assist you during your stay, and we will be pleased to accommodate. May we help you with your bags?"

Woody tipped his hat, feeling quite the dandy in the suit his father brought from home—a jacket, waistcoat, and trousers. Old clothes, but not worn often enough to become tattered. He had notched his belt tighter than usual to account for the ten pounds he'd yet to replace. "A gracious offer. Not much to carry." He lifted his one bag. "Thank you, though."

He climbed the staircase to the second floor and walked the long carpeted hallway to his room. As he turned the key, a sharp pain traveled the length of his bad leg. He groaned, and then checked in both directions hoping no one had heard him. Upon entering, he sat on the soft double bed, removed the prosthetic, and rubbed his stump until he gained some relief. He lay down. The furnishings—the dark walnut headboard that reached almost to the ceiling, the matching baseboard and six-drawer dresser, the shiny blonde wood flooring and spotless white walls—were exquisite. He felt guilty.

Too extravagant a room for a country bumpkin like him, he remembered thinking before he fell into a deep sleep.

* * *

The next morning, Woody filled his stomach with an oversized omelet of kidney beans, ham, and bacon. He topped that off with one of the Burnet Hotel's famous waffles and plenty of real coffee. With one final swig, he rose from his seat and left the cavernous dining room still buzzing with breakfast-goers. The time had come to visit Over-the-Rhine and find the Braun family.

He stepped again into another world where big-city streets came alive, eclectic in their sights, sounds, and smells. The roadway spoke with the click-clack of horses drawing different vehicles and single riders. The thoroughfares reeked of urine and manure, conditions that sanitary workers in horse-drawn street sweepers tried unsuccessfully to keep clean. In the distance, smoke billowed from factories and contaminated an otherwise pristine sky. Another unpleasant but acceptable cost of advancement.

This major hub had emerged as a landing spot for

newcomers seeking the American promise of a better life. Shoppers ducked in and out of stores and restaurants, businessmen bustled from door to door, children laughed and danced all around them. Like a living organism, the city had a heartbeat. A short visit might be tolerable, but Woody would choose a farm on the Shenandoah River any day. He hailed an open-air carriage.

"Where to?" the driver asked.

"Your German community."

"Ah, yes. Over-the-Rhine."

As the vehicle rolled through the streets, Woody noticed evidence of strong municipal development. There were paved sidewalks and thoroughfares, and they passed workers installing new sewer lines and gaslights. The North apparently prospered and modernized during the course of the war. Meanwhile, the South continued to incur a heavy cost.

The driver, who spoke with a German accent, defined the locality called Over-the-Rhine for his passenger. It lay north and east of the Miami and Erie Canal. The locals and new arrivals dubbed the area as such because they likened the canal to Germany's Rhine River. Across the canal, the driver pointed to Sängerfest Hall, where the singer and song festivals were held. He explained how German immigrants had influenced the structure and culture of Cincinnati. Woody pictured a younger Herschel Myers, who long ago sang with his beloved in this place.

They passed the breweries, furniture showrooms, markets, and shops springing up. Many societies had formed through the years—literary, musical, and political—and entertainment houses like theaters catering to fun-seekers did a healthy business. Institutions like Saint Mary's Church and the Turnverein also established the cultural character of this part of town.

He stopped the carriage. "That's the Turnverein across the street."

"What's the Turn...?"

"Turnverein. The home of the Turners, German immigrants active in physical education and social and political groups."

When war came, the Turners established the 1st Ohio Regiment, later to become the 9th Ohio, made up of men of

German and Dutch descent. The driver shared his recollections of the two days at Turner Hall, when a thousand patriotic men—many unable to speak English—answered the president's call for volunteers.

Woody said, "Since you are familiar with this neighborhood, might you be acquainted with a Mr. Braun? Perhaps one of the hundreds who enlisted in the German unit."

The driver thought for a moment. "I used to live here. Never met him personally, but I do recall a Braun family. Check across the street at Turner Hall. They keep strict records. Or perhaps at Dennison or Harrison, the military camps in these parts."

"I wonder if..."

The driver checked his pocket watch, glanced at Woody, and sighed. "Sure, I'll wait. Got nothing pressing at the moment." A marked contrast to the tramcar driver the day before.

"Mighty kind. Thank you."

* * *

The Turner clerk told him Gustave Braun had enlisted and went missing after the Port Republic engagement in Virginia.

"The 9th fought bravely, made us all proud," the woman said. "We lost some fine men."

Woody forgot to breathe. "May I ask your name?"

"Not many people outside of Over-the-Rhine bother to ask an old white-haired lady her name. I'm Frieda Grober."

Based on the wrinkles in her face, Frieda had to be one of Cincinnati's oldest German citizens. "I imagine your history here is long and distinguished," Woody said.

She told him she had four children and twelve grandchildren. Two of her kids had moved on to glory, as had her husband of fifty-five years. Frieda's deep-set eyes shined like the blue glitter of the sea, but those numbers did not tell the whole story. She boasted about her twenty great-grandchildren, and several others on their way. Three of them had died in the war.

"God has granted me peace in my losses, and thankfulness for my blessings."

Woody suppressed his excitement over being so near to the girl. All he needed was an address. "Will you point me to the Braun residence, if he still lives in this fine city?"

She started to answer, then stopped. "What is your business with the Brauns?"

"I served with the 7th Ohio at Port Republic. Mustered in around the same time as Mr. Braun but in the Cleveland area."

This part—the lies—Woody hated.

"Why do you seek the family now?" Frieda asked.

"Found this near his body." His hands trembled at the thought that perhaps he'd found the unnamed girl. He reached into the Union haversack his nurse had given him after Sharpsburg and pulled out the ambrotype. "Maybe the likeness is his little girl. Assuming Gustave Braun is the man who gave his life for our nation on the Port Republic battlefield. This might give the family some closure."

He opened the golden case. Frieda's eyes widened as she studied the photo.

"She looks familiar?" Woody asked. "The daughter of Mr. Braun. Am I correct?"

"Oh, no. I mean...I don't know. Never met this sweet one. But I will give you the location. Your intentions are kind."

He noticed Frieda's tears and handed her a kerchief. "With no connection to the family, why do you cry?"

"A good cry needs no justification. It's a grace."

She handed the case to him, along with the address written on a slip of paper.

The unnamed girl lived practically around the corner.

Twenty-Five

The Appearance

Red Oak, Ohio
June 30, 1864

The bonnet was old, but Rebecca felt new on this Thursday morning.

George had purchased the hat on their first anniversary. Made of dark straw and topped with a green ribbon ornately bunched at the top, the gift lay tucked away in her closet for three years, waiting for the right opportunity to be worn again. Today's marriage of two older friends, both of whom lost their spouses to illness in recent years, qualified.

She glanced one last time in the mirror, adjusted the brim, and tied the strips below her chin. As she smoothed her dress down, she smiled at the memory of her vivid dream the night before. Her daddy would say sometimes heaven sends us messages when we're asleep. Desperate for such a childlike faith again, she decided to share the vision with Reverend Matthews at the reception.

The buggy horse needed little direction, for they'd traveled this route together many times before. In addition to Sunday services, Rebecca attended many prayer nights and spearheaded bake sales at the church. She'd formed sewing and quilting groups that met in the sanctuary on weekdays as the pastor toiled away on his next sermon in a back room. And before the winter holidays, she would organize fundraisers to support the Underground Railroad. The theme—"Buy for the Sake of the Slave"—set the tone for these events. The women would turn their efforts into acts of moral commitment.

This place of worship, built in 1816 after the previous log structure burned down, was home to more than twenty-five pro-abolitionist families, a close-knit congregation. Rebecca thrived in this community. Since the end of her self-imposed exile in January, she'd reintegrated and longtime friends welcomed her back.

The buggy passed the stacked-stone wall that enclosed the nearby cemetery. She parked and took a seat inside the old building as the procession started.

Ophelia Teague, the bride, walked forward and joined her betrothed, Lionel Rix, at the altar. She wore roses in her hair and carried a matching nosegay. Having buried their own mates, they'd rallied around Rebecca when George died. But she had shut them out like everyone else as she drowned in self-pity. Her heart soared when she learned the news about their engagement.

Reverend Matthews began with the familiar words, "Dearest friends, we are gathered here in the sight of God." Rebecca was swept back to a similar ceremony held years ago in this place. Her father walked her down this aisle as George stood in front, a crescent smile on his face. When she stood before him, his moist eyes glistened, the way they did when George first said he loved her. The way they did the day he proposed.

In her wildest dreams, she never imagined marrying such a handsome man with an equally beautiful heart, yet she stood by his side below the cross. George's blondish-red curls fell beneath the new bowler hat he bought for the occasion. He'd shaved off his bushy beard at her request. Afterwards, he complained about his freckled face and said he looked like a pubescent boy. "No," she'd told him. "You, George Johnston, are all man."

George echoed the words spoken by Reverend Matthews as he slipped the simple band on her ring finger. When he promised to love and cherish her, to care for her in sickness and in health, she trusted him. George lived his life with the highest regard for honor and moral character. On that special day in front of family and friends, she had expected they would grow old together, surrounded by their own Scottish clan.

Lionel placed the ring on Ophelia's finger, snapping Rebecca back to their ceremony. At the reverend's invitation, Lionel pulled Ophelia's small veil back and kissed his new wife. After the ceremony, the couple walked toward the front door, followed by the guests. As the last person left the building, Rebecca removed her band and read the inscription: George and Rebecca, June 10, 1860. No matter what happened in the future, she would never forget that date.

A celebratory breakfast meal was offered at Lionel's home in Ripley, where the couple would reside. In a buoyant mood, Rebecca greeted several friends, stepped into her buggy, and headed for town. The warm rays of the mid-morning sun filtered through the trees like a painting come to life.

George's appearance the night before could not have been an accident.

* * *

Rebecca pulled her vehicle alongside the others.

The small house couldn't accommodate all the people, so the party was moved to the front yard under the scorching June sun. The women swiped their hand-held fans back and forth as they engaged in conversation. Most of the men huddled together smoking pipes and cigars under what little shade existed on the property.

Rebecca stopped for a brief chat with a Ripley storeowner who always stocked her sorghum sweeteners. Then she walked into the house to address the couple, the only ones seated in the parlor. Their adult children and grandchildren stood behind them. Rebecca was careful not to congratulate Ophelia, as that would have implied she was lucky to have received a proposal. The custom made little sense to Rebecca.

Lionel and Ophelia beamed when Rebecca called them Mr. and Mrs. Rix. "Things have a way of working out for the good," Lionel said as he winked. "Don't give up on second chances."

"And what's next for you, Rebecca?" Ophelia asked.

She thought for a moment, uncertain how to answer. "We'll have to see where God leads."

As Rebecca moved out of line, the person she most wanted to speak with approached her. Reverend Matthews had delivered the devastating news of George's death. As a man of the cloth, he was qualified to answer her questions.

"A wonderful service," she said.

"Thank you. This is a joyous day."

"Can we find a place outside to talk?" He nodded and they strolled to the backyard where fewer people mingled. "Last night I had a visit and I'm not sure what to make of it."

"Tell me about it, Rebecca."

She described the vision in full detail because she remembered each feeling and spoken word. The hour was two-thirty when a strange sensation woke her. At least, she thought she'd awoken. She sat up, lit the lamp at her bedside, and checked the clock on her nightstand. When she gazed over to the end of the bed, she saw the faint outline of a man, half-seated on the mattress, watching over her, a bowler on his head. The room was dark, so she couldn't identify the man, but she didn't fear him.

He spoke to her, but she didn't recognize his voice. "Rebecca, it's okay. I release you." The words warmed her in a familiar way. At the same time, she realized a stranger in her room should be cause for alarm. The conflicting sensations had confused her.

She asked the man, "Release me from what? Who are you?" He repeated the same words, so she asked again. This time he didn't respond. She lifted the lamp and slowly walked to the end of the bed. Now side by side, she raised the light higher, and when he shifted his bowler upward, she recognized him. "George! My George," she had called out, weeping with joy.

"I want you to move on." When she tried to hug him, George vanished into the darkness.

"That's when I woke up...I think," Rebecca said.

He nodded and smiled. "A good dream. The kind we wish would last all night."

She hesitated to ask, but might this have been a visitation

from above? Did the Almighty send her beloved to deliver the message that something more waited for her?

"I guess I wanted to know..."

"If George actually came to you from beyond?"

"Or was it just my yearning to gaze upon his face again. The conjuring of my mind to allow it?"

"Hard to know." Matthews pulled out his pocket Bible and thumbed through many pages until he found the verse he wanted. "This book says our Lord can come to us in such a way as this. Remember this passage in Matthew's gospel? The angel appeared to Joseph in a dream and said, 'Joseph son of David, do not be afraid to take Mary home as your wife, because what is conceived in her is from the Holy Spirit.' The Holy Word is filled with stories like this."

She'd read many of these references but never paid much attention. But this reunion was personal, meant for her. This much she believed.

The people lined up to pelt the couple with rice as they left for their honeymoon. As the gathering wound to a close, Rebecca collected her boxed-up piece of fruitcake at the front door. She bid farewell to many friends and strolled over to her horse. He nudged her and nickered. She rubbed his snout and climbed up to the seat.

"Whad'ya say, boy? Let's go home."

Rebecca pondered the dream's meaning again on the ride home. The idea of another man taking George's place seemed inconceivable, and yet many years of life stretched ahead of her. Must she live them alone, without companionship?

As she turned toward her farmhouse, Yankee barked and ran out to greet her.

This had been a good day.

Twenty-Six

Mrs. Braun

The driver had waited, true to his promise. Woody shared the story of the unnamed girl and then showed him the ambrotype.

"I know it's too much to ask, but—"

"Come on, then," the driver said. "Can't leave you now."

"What's your name?"

"Ernst Weber."

Woody stuck out his hand. "Thank you, Ernst. I'm Jonathan Woodard, but you can call me Woody." He handed Ernst the address.

"We're close," Ernst said. "Shall we go?" Woody took his seat, and Ernst wove his way into the oncoming traffic. He stopped in front of the row house in a neighborhood of mostly brick apartment buildings.

The ambrotype in his hands did little to calm Woody's nerves. He inhaled deeply and hopped down to the street. At the doorway, he froze. He had lived this moment in his head countless times and now the hour had arrived. How would the gesture be received? No answer on the first and second knocks. On the third, the door swung open. The woman who answered appeared to be in her fifties.

"Afternoon, ma'am. Does Mrs. Braun live here?"

"I am she."

Gustave's aunt or older sister? This silver-haired Mrs. Braun was much too old. "Do you know a Mr. Gustave Braun?"

"I'm his mother. Wait here, please." She closed the door.

Woody looked over at Ernst and shrugged.

After two minutes, the door opened again to reveal an attractive woman with thick brown hair, no older than thirty. Her coiffure was intricately plaited and rolled, adorned with flowers and beads. Her skirt was stylish, flat and narrow in front and more gathered in back. "May I help you?" she said.

Woody glanced behind her in hopes of spotting a ten-year-old girl whose round face he would easily recognize. He shifted his gaze back to the woman, who waited for his reply.

"Please excuse my hesitation," Woody said. "I'm a bit nervous. My name is Drew, short for Andrew. Last name is Alexander."

"Afternoon, Mr. Alexander." She extended her hand to Woody. "Why would you be so anxious, Mr. Alexander?"

"The business that brings me here is delicate…and important," Woody said. "I want to do this right."

He'd long assumed his message would help close an unresolved mourning period for the family of Gustave Braun. For Woody, finding the girl would further his own release from the scars of war. Now at the doorstep of his mission, he questioned if his motives weren't self-serving. What if telling this unsuspecting widow the truth about her husband didn't bring closure, but instead reopened a heart wound that might never close? And what if the resolution he'd envisioned for himself never came to pass?

The woman's wide smile turned hesitant. She stepped backwards. Her brows wilted like rose petals, as her eyes darted between Woody and the vehicle that waited on the street. Mere words fell short, deficient in the task of conveying so many of Woody's jumbled emotions that cried out for explanations.

"Ma'am…" He cleared his throat. "I fought with your husband at Port Republic, and came a long distance to tell you..."

"Yes?"

"Um…" Woody's mind went blank.

Seconds seemed like minutes. His mouth turned dry.

"There is no easy way to say this, so I'll come straight out with it. It sorrows me to inform you that…that…Gustave fell in battle, mortally injured."

Before Woody uttered another word, her feet buckled. He guided her into the living room, and the older woman directed them to the sofa. She dashed into the kitchen and came back with a cold compress that she applied to her daughter-in-law's forehead.

"Meine Tochter," she said repeatedly.

As she regained her composure, the younger Mrs. Braun sat up, a gentle stream flowing down her rosy cheeks. He allowed the widow time to come to grips with her loss. Mrs. Braun the elder broke down as well as she gave her daughter-in-law a handkerchief.

As Woody expected, shock and sorrow held this family firmly in its grip. He fidgeted in his chair until Gustave's wife finally spoke.

"You say you served with Gustave?"

Woody's gaze dropped to the floor. He nodded, hesitant to voice the lie again. "Gustave performed his duty with courage and did his community and people proud."

"That's just like my husband," she said.

"A respected soldier, and a fine man."

She rose from the couch and walked to a likeness of Private Braun displayed on a bookshelf. Woody focused on the picture but the man's face did not register. He'd viewed Gustave in death for a brief moment two years before.

Mrs. Braun traced her finger down the photo. "He served his new country proudly." She turned back to the stranger in her home and tried to smile through her sadness. "I can see you also sacrificed for your nation, and I thank you. Why did you come all this way to tell me? Were you friends with my husband?"

Where should he begin?

"Just in the way soldiers serving on the same battlefield become comrades."

Woody wanted her to grasp his motivation, the solace her daughter gave him through all the months of torturous marches and brutal fights. To understand the soldier's attachments to home while in the field. To share his desire—the same conviction Gustave must have had—that he not be laid in an unmarked mass grave, his family burdened with a lifetime of unanswered questions about his fate.

With her husband listed as missing in action, perhaps knowing how he fell would grant her peace and allow her to move on with her life. He told her the whole story and more, but left the part about finding a treasure for last.

"Most kind," she said. "Yes, this is helpful to me, and will help me now to grieve with closure."

"It pleases me most to return this, madam." Woody pulled the golden treasure from his bag. "From what I gleaned on the battlefield, this gave your husband an extra measure of solace. The frame lay exposed near his body."

Woody handed her the image, which she opened and stared at for some time before looking up. "I'm afraid I don't understand."

He plucked the likeness from her, unsure of how to respond. "Is this not your little girl?" Woody asked.

The blood drained from her face.

"We are—were—unable conceive. I am not acquainted with the child."

* * *

Before Woody left, the elder Mrs. Braun gave him directions to the Cincinnati *Daily Gazette*, where he might find lists of men killed, wounded, or taken captive from the 5th and 7th Ohio regiments. Both fought at Port Republic.

Ernst must have read the disappointment on his face. "That didn't go as you expected, it seems."

"No, my friend. One final stop, I promise, and then back to the Burnet. The *Daily Gazette* on the northeast corner of Fourth and Vine streets."

"I know the building," Ernst said, as he guided his horse into a slow trot.

On the way, Woody reviewed the hitch in his plans. The setback discouraged him. He'd been so close to success, only to have his one solid lead drop through his fingers like grains of sand. At times like these, Lucas always showed him a bright side, helped him to recognize the possibilities around the next corner. The *Gazette* building occupied that corner, where he hoped to get back on track.

Maybe the prisoner on the battlefield that day had mistaken the dead soldier's name for something that sounded similar to Braun, like Brown. If Woody failed to make any progress at the newspaper, he would give up the search and head to Shepherdstown. He missed home.

Inside, reporters scribbled away on their notepads. An older woman, a clerk or manager and the only female in the office, sat at the desk closest to the entry. Three sets of files lay stacked below her nose. A cigarette, smoked halfway with a trail of ashes attached, hung from her mouth. The ashes dropped to her desk as she poured through a document. She swished the residue away.

When she'd finished her task, she looked up, a scowl etched on her face. "Can I help you?"

Not the genteel manner of a Virginia lady. Caught by surprise, Woody didn't answer. He managed only to clear his throat.

"People in Cincinnati like their newspapers on time, and our competitors are anxious to get a head start. So...?"

Woody found his words. "Yes, ma'am. I'm new in these parts, handicapped in defense of our proud nation. Name's Drew Alexander."

This time the woman clammed up. Her eyes squinted through the cigarette smoke as she sized him up. Proper social graces required a response. Hers was brusque.

"McPherson. Miss Tildee McPherson."

"A pleasure." He lied.

He chose his next words carefully. "I'm on a mission of mercy, Miss McPherson. Looking to find the family of a fallen comrade and return his personal effects. Perhaps you can help me."

McPherson consulted her timepiece and perused the newsroom floor. When had he learned to lie so easily? The untruths stacked up like McPherson's files and smothered him with the foulness of deceit.

"Suppose I can spare a few minutes. Who is it you're looking for?"

* * *

McPherson led Woody to another room where all the paper's master files were stored. As she rustled through several containers, he asked about the kinds of articles the *Gazette* published on a regular basis.

"Usual stuff. The latest news from the war fronts, casualties, and other such reports."

When he asked if she was a correspondent, McPherson pressed her lips together into a thin line. A sore subject? He couldn't imagine how she'd found work in this capacity, let alone as a reporter. The world of newspapers was dominated by men.

She lit another cigarette, blew a cloud of smoke to the ceiling, and continued the search. "Here we are. The casualty lists for our local boys. What battle are you inquiring about?"

"Port Republic, in the Shenandoah Valley Campaign," Woody said. "The fight happened on the ninth of June in '62. Look for the name Brown, or something like that."

Her suspicions were raised. "Wait a minute. I thought you said this was a fellow Union soldier. A fallen comrade. Wouldn't you have known his name?"

He had to think fast.

"So it might seem, Miss McPherson. I—"

"You've been nervous since you walked in here." She took a long puff on her cigarette and peered into Woody's eyes. "The Pinkertons have offices in town. The city is crawling with Union soldiers. Your stay here will be troubled if you are found to be a spy."

He pulled up his pant leg. "Miss McPherson, please rest assured. I sustained this wound protecting our flag." The lie seemed to calm her.

McPherson shared a story of treason from the previous year, implicating people in Cincinnati and Columbus and a couple of smaller towns. The perpetrators plotted to free more than three thousand Confederate prisoners at Camp Chase, take possession of the facility, and embark on a military crusade to capture the state. In the end, they failed to overthrow the local government. Since then, she'd been wary of strangers.

"Yes, I can understand the need to be on high alert," Woody said. "As to the dead soldier's name, almost four thousand of our boys took the field that day. I'd spoken to this man only once before he fell. He showed me this and shared its meaning."

Woody opened the gold cover and handed the image to McPherson. Her quick glance betrayed no emotion. She stubbed out the end of her cigarette and lit another.

He took the cover from her. Would she continue? The stillness in the small room stood in marked contrast to the scuttling about and boisterous chatter of newspaper reporters working under deadline. He suddenly became clammy and pulled his kerchief to blot a bead of sweat from his forehead.

"The girl's photograph, his daughter most likely, lay on the ground next to Mr. Brown's body," Woody said. "Perhaps his last vision before passing into the next life."

Without warning, she turned back to the files and shuffled through several folders until she found something.

"Ah, here we are." She combed through the record for Port Republic, noting almost two hundred fifty losses from the 5th Ohio Volunteer Infantry alone. "Here's a William Brown from the 7th Ohio. Joined up in Cleveland. Went missing at Port Republic. Might this be your man?"

An interesting but disappointing lead. Cleveland was a considerable distance away. He hoped to find the girl's family in the southern end of Ohio and head home to rebuild his life. A journey to Cleveland would require some planning. He'd need to purchase train tickets and find a decent place to stay in Cleveland. He had experienced his fair share of campfires, so sleeping in the wilderness would suit him as a last resort.

Woody took a note with the man's location. "Much obliged for your time, Miss McPherson."

As he turned to walk out, she called back to him. "Wait a minute. Just found a second Mr. Brown."

Woody returned to her side. "Yes?"

"The list shows a Clancy Brown, 5th Ohio Infantry. Also unaccounted for."

"Where might this Mr. Brown be from?" Woody asked.

The question made Tildee smile. "Brown County, of all places."

She scribbled another reference on a small piece of paper. "It's two counties over from Hamilton. No city is listed. The family might live in the countryside. Start at a river town called Ripley about forty-five miles east of here."

"Again, thank you for all your help," Woody said.

"A woman lives north of there, about five miles. Her acquaintances in those parts are widespread. Wrote her name for you. Enlist her assistance if you choose."

As they walked through the newsroom, Woody assured her that he would pursue the lead.

She sat down at her desk. "Public's always thirsty for news," she said, as she buried her nose in another file. She lit a cigarette and inhaled.

Woody stuffed the note into his coat.

* * *

"Back to the Burnet, Ernst."

Woody wasn't excited like he'd been at the Braun residence. Just thankful he had one more card to play.

"Well…?" The driver's expression pleaded for a report on the visit.

"Let's get going and I'll tell you on the way."

When they pulled up to the hotel, Woody paid the driver handsomely for his services. The sun had almost completed its arc across a cloudless sky, ready to end the day and birth a new evening. The hotel lobby reverberated with the sounds of some patrons checking in and others settling their bills. Some stood in small circles dressed in their formal evening wear, perhaps deciding where to dine or waiting for another party member to descend the stairs. Woody took in the reverie for a few minutes, but loneliness stole his hopeful mood so he decided to turn in.

He settled the bill and informed the front desk clerk that he would leave early in the morning. He asked about the easiest passage to Ripley and learned a steamer could take him to the town. He would catch the boat, secure a room, and rent another buckboard at the local livery.

As he climbed the stairs, Woody pulled the scrap of paper from his pocket. Scribbled in Tildee McPherson's illegible penmanship was a name he could barely read. His best guess was Reba Johnston.

Woody pictured another silver-haired old lady with a wrinkled smile, a stalwart member of the community. A fixture on the porch of a house she'd owned long before he'd made his entrance into the world.

Johnston…for some reason the name awakened an impression. An elusive echo that he couldn't quite place.

Twenty-Seven

Independence Day

Red Oak, Ohio
July 4, 1864

Rebecca brought her coffee over to the kitchen table. The steam swirled upward from the full cup, delivering the familiar aroma that granted permission for her day to begin. As she scanned the front page of the *Ripley Bee*, she took her first sip and burned her tongue. "Aghh," she blurted out, angry with herself. She let the coffee cool.

She'd risen before the sun to clean the barn, feed the animals, milk the cows, and collect the eggs and water. Then she sat on her porch and greeted a sunrise that burst onto the horizon in swirling yellows and oranges. As the dawn swept down the hillsides, she'd strolled with her lantern amidst the ripening sorghum canes in the field. This morning transpired like most others, but today differed in one respect. The Fourth of July gave this day special meaning and should be giving all citizens a cause to celebrate. But Rebecca expected some of Ripley's townspeople would not feel the same pride of country as her.

A new writer for the *Ripley Bee*, J.D. Buckner, said it best in his column: "It is like the anniversary of a divorced couple's wedding." Rebecca knew people on both sides of the argument. She hoped the traditional Ripley Fourth of July Parade and Picnic in the afternoon would not be marred by any squabbles.

Buckner's articles impressed her. The two talked one Sunday after church at the community meal. He sat alone at a small table so she'd asked to join him. A well-manicured and handsome man, he barely responded when she asked about his family background. She thought this strange for a man who made words his business.

They ate in silence until she brought up the subject of abolition, which Buckner so eloquently wrote about in the paper. That opened a floodgate of talk about slavery, the end of the war, and the kind of country that would be left.

Rebecca enjoyed the topic, but on the ride home she realized he'd volunteered little about himself, other than feeling old at thirty. And a strange distance separated them, something in his eyes that she couldn't identify.

Yankee rose from his spot and laid his head on her thigh. "Come, boy, let's go to the porch and write Israel another letter."

He followed her to the writing table where she collected a pen and paper and her old stained recipe for sorghum cake. The sweet memory of his eyes lighting up when he took his first bite of that cake so long ago flooded back. He'd raved about the taste so much she showed him the list of ingredients, but then quickly pulled the page away, assuming he couldn't read. But he could. An old learned slave on the Wills plantation had taught him several years before. When caught in the act, the overseer brutally flogged both men, the old man to within an inch of his life.

When Israel and Fannie first settled, he wrote to Rebecca to let her know their location and that they and little Parker were fine. She'd postmarked a return letter, and two more after that, but never received a response. Perhaps the family moved on and the letters were never forwarded to a new address.

Never one to give up easily, she tried again and included the recipe for sorghum cake.

July 4, 1864

Dear Israel,

On this day of celebration, I am reminded of how happy I was the day you and Fannie and Parker left my farm on your journey to freedom. While parting was difficult, Independence Day held you in its palm. So I am thinking of you on this day. But I'm also worried for your wellbeing. I have sent two letters in recent months but never heard back from you. Write immediately if you receive my correspondence so I shan't worry any longer. If this is the first letter to find its way to you, let me share both the sad and joyful goings on in my life. Not long after you left me, I received word that George had died in battle. I became so despondent..."

After writing her final words, she tucked the recipe inside the message and sealed the envelope. The Ripley Post Office would be closed for the holiday but she would return to town tomorrow and mail the letter.

"Well, Yankee, it's done." The adoring dog wagged his short tail and followed her upstairs. She chose a suitable outfit for the occasion and said her goodbyes in the kitchen. "This party might make you too excitable, boy. Best if you stay home this time."

He walked behind her to the front door. She heard his whimper as she left.

* * *

Rebecca loved a good parade.

The procession featured the traditional marching bands and cavalcade of officials representing both local government and the town's most popular charities. Union soldiers wounded and discharged from the service marched to loud hurrahs as they passed. A sea of Stars and Stripes colored Main Street, dwarfing the few Confederate flags being waved.

Rebecca stood with her family and cheered the participants. At the end of the procession, everyone gathered at City Hall for the traditional reading of the Declaration of Independence.

Mayor Clark stepped forward. Document in hand, he read the familiar opening passage. "When, in the course of human events, it becomes necessary for one people to dissolve the political bands which have connected them with another—"

A man's voice rang out, "Long live the South," followed by three loud bursts. Rebecca ducked. She assumed this was gunfire and expected an attack had been launched. Her father huddled the family together, and then advanced toward the sound along with several other brave men. Moments later, amid all the confusion, the mayor announced the bangs came from firecrackers set off by a prankster who'd fled the scene. People stood and spoke in hushed tones about the scare.

"All right now folks," Clark said. "No cause for alarm. Allow me to continue."

Clark finished his recitation with no further interruptions, after which a subdued crowd made its way to the picnic grounds. Rebecca's family sat together and enjoyed a feast of fried chicken, potato salad, bread, and watermelon. After eating, she rose to greet John and Jean Rankin. From the corner of her eye, she spotted J.D. Buckner headed her way on the arm of an older woman. They stopped in front of her.

"Thank you, Mrs. Fordham. Give me a few moments, please." The woman stepped away. "Hello, Mrs. Johnston. Wonderful parade, don't you think? The little prank excepted."

"Yes, Mr. Buckner. A rousing celebration."

An uncomfortable silence followed.

"Well...I just…that is, I mean…" His words stumbled out, disconnected. She charged to his rescue.

"I read your piece on our holiday and how Southerners are mixed in their acknowledgment of the day's meaning. Quite interesting."

"Thank you, Mrs. Johnston."

"Please do call me Rebecca."

"Yes...Rebecca it is," he said with a smile. Another pause.

"Well, I better continue on," she said, quietly stepping away.

Glancing over her shoulder, she noticed his gaze hadn't shifted. He mumbled something as if she still stood in front of him, but she couldn't understand a word. Suddenly, the obvious occurred to her for the first time. She saw him, but he couldn't see her. A.J. Buckner was blind. She stepped back to where she stood before.

"So, anyway, I'd like to do this properly," Buckner continued on. "I mean, you being married once, I wasn't sure if I needed to get permission from your father."

"For what?"

"Mrs. Johnston...? For what I've been saying. May I call on you?"

How could she have been so unaware?

* * *

As Woody returned to the buggy he'd rented from the Ripley Livery, he allowed the parade and festivities to wash over him. Independence Day had always been a celebration of his country's founding. But in recent years it represented the hope held by Southerners that their fledgling nation would also achieve freedom from tyranny. Woody was caught between both ideals, and this small-town celebration left him conflicted.

He'd found Ripley right where Tildee McPherson had described. After renting the buggy and checking into a hotel, he'd retired to his room, exhausted and in need of sleep. That morning, the clerk told him about the days events, and he'd ventured out after breakfast.

After patting down the horse, he backed into someone behind him. "Oh, so sorry," he said as he turned. The woman who stood before him took his breath away. Hair as red as a ripened strawberry, netted just above her neck. Skin the color of ivory. Bright blue eyes that twinkled like moonbeams against the Ohio River.

Who was she? He had to know.

"No damage done," she said as she took her seat.

The introduction he wanted to make got stuck in his throat as she hurriedly pulled away. Like a mirage, she disappeared. Perhaps forever.

Twenty-Eight

The Widow Johnston

Red Oak, Ohio
July 5, 1864

Woody emerged from his room in the quaint Baird House Inn, a block from the shore of the Ohio River. He'd rested well, except for the faint singing he thought he'd heard twice during the night. Strangely, when he inquired about the songstress, the proprietor quickly changed the subject. He directed Woody to the Johnston farm, due north in Red Oak, when Woody asked about its location.

"The woman's name is Rebecca, not Reba," the man said with a smirk.

As he turned to leave the lobby, Woody overheard two men talking about the storied Baird House ghost, thought to be the former owner of the inn. Not one to normally believe such balderdash, his past nightmarish visitations had left him uncertain.

The pristine day invited Woody to walk, but the five miles would play havoc on his leg. He decided to drive the rented buggy.

A dog announced his arrival. In a display of neighborliness, or maybe complete confidence in her safety with a watchdog by her side, a woman opened the door without making any inquiries from within. Woody walked toward the porch as a tall, muscular dog rushed out to inspect him. The dog's short tail wagged uncontrollably as he sniffed all around Woody's legs and boots.

She stepped from the dark into the daylight. "Oh!" Her hand covered her mouth. "Aren't you the man who—"

"Rather clumsily bumped into you at the—"

"Fourth of July picnic?"

"Uh-huh," Woody said, astonished. What were the odds? "Are you…?"

"Rebecca Johnston. And you are?"

His stomach jumped to his throat. A tense moment passed before he answered, "Alexander…Drew." He avoided direct eye contact.

"Well, Mr. Drew. Pleasure to meet you."

He smiled. "Last name's Alexander. But please call me Drew."

"And you must call me Rebecca. Come in. You seem to have passed Yankee's smell test." The dog came to her side and sat. "Good boy, Yankee."

"An excellent watchdog." He stepped up to the porch to greet her properly with a tip of his hat. "Pleasure, ma'am."

She surprised him by extending her hand to a stranger. Not the gesture he was used to in Virginia, at least not between strangers of the opposite sex. He raised his hand and shook. He noticed the band on her ring finger. His sailing heart sank.

"The best," she said, beaming.

"Ma'am…?"

"Yankee, here. You wouldn't want to provoke him. He's fiercely loyal to his family. Can sniff out bad intentions before they can be acted upon."

She smote him again, like at their accidental meeting. Not a day over twenty-five, and not the gray-haired lady he'd imagined. Those blue eyes, twinkling like stars, magnets that reeled him in like a fish on a hook. He tried to avert her gaze, but he couldn't unlock eyes from her.

She'd been baking. The sweet smell of a confection wafted

through the door, inviting Woody to remember carefree days gone by. Some of the raw ingredients covered the patterned pinner apron she wore over a plain white morning dress. His sniff turned into an inadvertent snort. The woman stepped back, laughed.

"Stand in the heat all day, or you can come inside for some milk and cakes," Rebecca said. "Your choice, but I'll be getting on with things either way."

"I...thought...uh..." Embarrassed, Woody couldn't string together a complete sentence. She broke into a full smile, revealing a small dimple that enchanted him even further. He removed his hat. "That is to say, yes. That would be wonderful."

Upon entering the house, Yankee conducted a further probe, sniffing Woody's shoes, pant legs, and open hands. He lifted his front legs to rest on Woody's chest. A thick tongue slobbered the dog's approval across Woody's mouth. The canine affection reminded him of winter nights at home by the fire, his own hound, Gracie, curled up beside him. The days of hunting with Gracie were long passed now. He scratched the bridge of Yankee's nose.

Rebecca invited Woody into the kitchen, where he stood and watched. With a thick glove protecting her hand, she pulled open the oven door and withdrew the first batch of golden brown cakes. She placed a second sheet filled with small dough-balls into the oven and turned to face him. Yankee stood in the space between Woody and the woman. He admired the dog's instinct to protect his master.

"A warm cake for you, sir." She handed him the confection. "Milk or water?"

"Most kind of you, Mrs. Johnston," Woody said. "Water would be welcomed. I'm a bit parched. I obtained your name from Mrs. McPherson."

"Ah, yes. Tildee's an old friend of my parents, and a mentor of sorts to me." Rebecca dipped a cup into a bucket of drinking water and carried it to the table. "Lived in these parts before moving to the big city years ago. Quite the character, don't you think?"

Character was the perfect word. Rebecca explained how Tildee had influenced her views about the need to advance equality for women, to vote and work in careers if they chose. The abolitionist movement, the war's conclusion, and a compassionate reconstruction also moved both women to activism. Woody may have differed on some of Rebecca's views, but debate did not interest him at the moment. She did.

"This banged-up soldier has certainly seen enough of war."

Woody took a bite of the dessert. She glanced at his leg. Did she view him as a pathetic a cripple? Deep within, the sin of deception took another bite of his conscience.

"Listen to my jabber song…I apologize," Rebecca said. "For me, God and family come before anything."

Guilt clouded his thoughts, so Woody sought to change the subject. He savored the sweet taste of the cake. Where did she find the sugar? Soon after the war began, sugar became scarce as hen's teeth. Brown sweetener and molasses had doubled in price. Domestic production had all but ceased, and imports into southern ports dwindled to almost nothing due to the blockades. Before his brief stay at the Burnet, Woody almost forgot what sugar tasted like.

"Where'd you get the sugar for these cakes?" he asked.

She pulled a jar filled with a thick substance from her cupboard and handed him the container.

"This is syrup made from sorghum canes, grown here last year on a half-acre," she said. "Go ahead—open the top and dip your finger."

He dipped and tasted. Impressive.

"Well now, Drew. I'm sure you have a purpose for your visit. What can I do for you?"

"Yes, ma'am. Perhaps we can sit…?" He gestured toward the couch and chair.

"Of course."

She led the way into the living room and invited him to sit on the couch. As he did, Woody glanced at the photograph resting on the hutch against the stairway. Rebecca and Mr. Johnston, no doubt, dressed in a Yankee uniform. Woody remained fixed on the couple's image.

"My husband, George." She'd caught him staring. He quickly turned his gaze toward her, embarrassed. "We believe the sorghum industry is ready to take off. We'd planned to expand our crop to yield commercial quantities. The war came, and well…so many plans were put on hold."

He'd seen her ring, but the picture of them together filled him with selfish disappointment. "May I ask…under whom is your husband serving?"

She walked over and picked up the image. "George passed into the presence of God some time ago." Her lower lip quivered for a moment as she stared intently at the photograph, and then returned it to the hutch.

Had Tildee mentioned that Rebecca was a widow? "Please forgive me, Mrs. Johnston."

"For what? I've made peace with my loss." Her brows narrowed. "Now, sir, I insist you call me Rebecca."

Ashamed, he fought against his wrongheaded relief that she no longer had a husband. But who could blame him? She was beautiful in skin and spirit, and a good baker.

He thought of the husband's name again. Familiar, but why? George Johnston. Did he ever run across a man with this name? The gap in his memory troubled him.

As he had approached the Johnston farm, Woody noticed the spread suffered from disrepair. She needed help. There was a hole in the barn roof and he'd bet his family's West Virginia farm that he would find wood rot if he were to look. A coat of whitewash would give the farmhouse a new face. In its current state, the coop couldn't hold much of anything, let alone chickens. A plan took shape.

"Rebecca…" She nodded and smiled. "Before, you asked if you might do something for me. I'm hoping we can do something for each other."

He talked about finding the gold case, and his long-standing desire to return the likeness to the family of the dead soldier; to tell them about their loved one's sacrifice. At least that part was true. He showed her the ambrotype, and told her the name of the soldier who owned it. Or the name he now assumed was correct. According to Tildee McPherson, the family of Clancy Brown lived somewhere in this county, and he needed help to find them.

She studied the image, then placed the case close to her heart. Did she recognize the unnamed girl? After several moments of silence she leaned toward him and grasped his hands. "I can tell you are an honorable man." That comment stung. The charade would be harder to maintain this time. Each time the lying chipped away a little more of his integrity.

He swallowed his misgivings one more time.

"I think this Clancy Brown is the right man, but his family could reside anywhere in the region. They may have moved after he went missing. This county must be home to thousands of people on farmlands."

"Yes."

He issued a heartfelt appeal. "Miss McPhearson said you possess a vast network of friends in this vicinity. This is a lot for a stranger to ask, but might you be able to point me in the right direction? Perhaps in return, I could do some work around your farm."

An awkward hush followed, and she rose from the table and began cleaning the oven. The silence spoke volumes to him as she tidied the kitchen. He'd overstepped his bounds.

* * *

The proposal sounded intriguing to Rebecca. Heaven knew that she needed the daily help around the farm.

She set a plate of desserts on the table and sat. "Help yourself to another." How might this work? She bit into a cake, lost in thought as she chewed.

She could lead the hunt for Mr. Brown's family in exchange for help with some long overdue repairs. The barn roof was beyond patching, the hayloft crumbling. Fences needed mending. There were broken windows. The sorghum and potato crops would soon need harvesting. If Drew would help her bring the farm into proper working order, she would not rest until they found the family. Assuming the right Brown family lived in this county.

But would people talk? A stranger spending time on her property would be perceived as inappropriate without the proper safeguards. Where would he stay?

This good man had served their country in her time of greatest need, driven by nobility and selflessness. Still, she mustn't be too trusting. The trauma of her past experience with Union soldiers who drifted colored her judgment. Perhaps her daddy would allow Drew to bunk in his barn, and each morning loan him a mule to ride to Rebecca's place about two miles away. Daddy would certainly welcome an additional set of working hands around her farm. He could accomplish only so much on the one day a week he pitched in.

Rebecca dabbed the sweat on her forehead with a kerchief, and moved her hand fan across her face in a futile attempt to cool down. Drew now appeared anxious to leave. As he stood, she said, "I'm giving some thought to the idea and might see a way forward."

The whites of Drew's eyes flashed. He quickly sat, this time on the edge of the couch. Drew attracted her attention. Handsome enough in looks, he carried an awkward boyishness she found appealing. Perhaps in time, he would feel comfortable enough to share how he'd sustained his injury and where he called home.

"Drew, what you said in the kitchen is accurate. The county is indeed large—hundreds of miles, thousands of people," Rebecca said. "But perhaps we can serve each other's needs."

"Where do we start?" he asked.

An inquiry with the Browns in Ripley would yield no results. The elderly Mrs. Brown and her long deceased husband never bore children. Nobody with this name resided in Red Oak. A search must be conducted in other townships.

"We'll start at Daddy's farm. He will want to approve the arrangements."

"Of course."

"Then we'll head to town and return that buggy. No sense in wasting the rental fee. Might also buy supplies to start repairing the mess in my own barn."

Before they left, Woody assessed the damage to the barn roof and the loft, and started a list of materials needed to execute repairs. He shared concerns about the size of the list and how she would pay the costs.

"The storeowner in Ripley will extend full credit for what we need," she said.

"How will you retire the debt?"

"I'll swap him for sorghum syrup and sugar to sell in his store."

* * *

Woody's mood soared after meeting Rebecca's father. He'd agreed to the plan and would set up a cot and other essentials for Woody to stay in his barn. Afterwards, she followed him to the Ripley livery to return the rented unit. Next they traveled a short distance to the general store. When Woody finished loading supplies into her buckboard, they stepped up and took their seats.

She turned to him. "If you're of a mind to join me, we'll attend Sunday services at Red Oak Presbyterian Church on Sunday. Afterwards, the McAllisters are preparing a feast with lots of dancing. Hope you'll choose to come."

A dance with her would be exhilarating, and worrisome. Could he dance without stepping all over her feet? Would she even want to be seen among her friends dancing with a cripple? Woody didn't mind delaying his efforts to find the unnamed girl. The schoolboy in him had been caught staring at the pretty girl in the seat across from his. Would this joyful moment last or would it die, like most everything around him had over the last two years? Shouldn't he maintain a healthy distance between them, for the sake of the mission?

So many questions.

"I'd be pleased to accompany you," Woody said, hoping he would not regret the decision later.

Twenty-Nine

Seeds of Love

July 10, 1864

"Jesus loves me, this I know," the congregation sang, "for the Bible tells me so."

The words spoke to Woody of certainties he once believed in a childlike way. His faith had been shaken to its breaking point. The simplicity of this new song gave him a stepping-stone toward a rebirth. As he sang with his fellow believers, the worship turned the small Red Oak church into a great cathedral.

Simple blessings, like his friendship with Lucas and the outpouring of love from his parents, made him profoundly thankful. And now this: a picture of normal life. His attention turned to the beautiful woman who sat at his side. His heart raced as he contemplated what might become of their arrangement. Was there someone special in her life, or was it too soon after her husband's death? Was the girl in the photograph the daughter of Private Brown, and would they find the family? Or was the search a fool's errand?

"Jesus loves me, loves me still. Though I'm very weak and ill."

The song lyrics tugged at his spirit, almost like a whisper from God. He'd longed to hear from his maker, who had remained silent for three long years. How he'd thirsted for the living water.

He'd almost forgotten how to pray. Now, in the middle of a community of believers, that familiar stirring he'd longed for whisked him into God's presence. He realized that God had never left, but had carried him across the sandy desolation of a seemingly endless desert of heartache.

The flock turned their hymnals to the John Wesley standard—*Jesus, Lover of My Soul.* He had sung this hymn at the Presbyterian Church in Shepherdstown. This time the words moved Woody more powerfully.

When they finished, the pastor opened the oversized Bible and turned the pages.

Woody glanced at Rebecca as she leaned forward in anticipation, a picture of loveliness. Her hair was parted down the center and drawn back, with soft loops on each side of her face. A vertical gold broach adorned her neckline, the only color against an all-white dress. She waved a small fan in front of her face, but the effort did little to offset the stifling summer heat inside the building. A closed parasol sat propped against the bench, her protection against the sun's rays on the ride to church.

She peeked at him.

Did she catch him gawking?

He focused on the pastor, but guilt stained his joy. The pretense of being a Union soldier with a different identity had become more burdensome over the last few days. He'd prefer a Colt Navy revolver aimed at his head to this dishonesty with her. He wanted to introduce her to the real Woody. The ruse had gotten him this far, though, and must remain in place for now. At the right time, he would unmask Drew Alexander and hope for her forgiveness.

The preacher began as Woody tired of his mental gymnastics. He tried to climb into the message, something about the meaning of life without God…living below or above the sun.

"When we take a good thing or deed, and try to make it the ultimate thing or deed, it is vanity…like chasing the wind," the preacher said. "Are your good intentions pure and true, or is there deceit? Are you chasing after wind? Are you connected to God, the only good life under the sun? For without him, all we do is vanity."

The words pierced him. He'd justified the lies he told to good people. Put his father and himself in harm's way. Spent his family's hard-earned money. And all for what? The message made him wonder whether his good intentions had indeed been a vain attempt to find his own peace.

Woody would wait on God to show him the way out of this quagmire. The decision quieted his restless spirit. For the second time since he'd found the girl's photograph, an assurance had been spoken over him: All wrongs would be righted in due time. He trusted the promise.

After the service, Rebecca introduced him to several neighbors. One tall, lanky gentleman, wearing a top hat and frock coat, walked toward them. An older woman had her arm locked in his and seemed to be guiding the man's steps.

"Here we are," the woman said softly. The man released his arm and bowed in front of Rebecca. His gaze was slightly off-center, his eyes unblinking. Woody had seen these kinds of uncertain movements by men injured on the battlefield. This man was blind. Woody guessed he'd been without sight for a short period of time.

"Rebecca, I hope you were blessed by the service," A.J. Buckner said.

"Very much so, A.J. May I introduce you and Miss Fordham to Mr. Alexander. He's a new member of our community, at least for a while."

Woody spoke first so the blind gentleman could place his location. "A pleasure, sir. And you as well, madam." He gave the woman a slight bow. "Mr. Buckner, I read your article on benevolent reconstruction in the local newspaper. Cogent writing."

A.J. turned slightly. "Thank you, Mr.—"

"Call me Drew. All my friends do." All his new friends did, anyway.

A.J. offered a handshake, which Woody accepted.

"Yes, well…" A.J. turned back to Rebecca. "Now remember, Rebecca, you promised me a stroll at the McAllister's hoedown tonight."

Rebecca's face turned pink.

* * *

Was there something between A.J. and Rebecca? As they spoke, Woody wandered over to another group of churchgoers and introduced himself. When they asked what had brought him to Red Oak, he pointed to Rebecca.

"More like who brought me here," Woody said. "Mrs. Johnston and I have a reciprocal business agreement. Work around her farm in exchange for helping me to find someone here in Brown County. Been staying with her father, James."

He listened to their chatter about the silliest of matters and about their small circle of life in Red Oak. They shared hopes and dreams for the future, even as the national conflict dragged on. He missed this kind of community; the sense of belonging to something larger than oneself that war had stolen. This time in the presence of other believers whetted his appetite for reconnection.

Later, the two of them sat on Rebecca's porch sipping lemonade, as Yankee stretched out at their feet. She walked into the kitchen to cut them each a piece of pie. Red Oak appealed to him, as did nearby Ripley, but Rebecca Johnston lighted his very being. Her giggle made him grin, but then her attempts to avoid full-throated laughter failed half the time and that made him chortle. Rebecca's sunny outlook infected him.

The name Johnston continued to tickle an old memory. Why? He once knew a drunkard named Shamus Johnston, but the old man died long before his body put him under the ground. That happened when he and Lucas were tadpoles. And it wasn't just Rebecca's name. It was the name of this place. The recollection wouldn't come to light, and he remained puzzled.

Woody surveyed the farm. The mill near the house and the tall stalks surrounding the structure would soon be the focus of his labors. He scanned the acres beyond, where other subsistence crops grew. Along with the canes, the potatoes should be lifted by September.

The chickens clucked, pecking at their food, and the roosters joined in the lively farmyard dance. The pigs would soon roam free if the pen remained in disrepair. He made a mental note to complete that task tomorrow. He'd slept well over the last several nights in James's barn. He bunked with horses, a mule, and three cows, none seeming to mind the intrusion.

After enjoying their Sabbath rest, they climbed into her buckboard, the mule that would carry Woody to James's farm after the dance tied to the back. As they approached the McAllister's farm, the music and merriment gave evidence of a raucous party in progress. The aroma of red meat and chicken being seared on a grill clung to the air.

They walked past the food and into the barn where the participants danced a jig and folks around a circle clapped to a familiar fiddle-driven breakdown. The ladies wore long dresses, some hooped, and the men danced in various coat and trouser ensembles. The band, comprised of a banjo, two guitars, fiddle, and washtub bass, alternated between jigs and reels and quadrilles. Woody led Rebecca to the outer circle, self-conscious that the pace of the music would be too difficult for him to manage on his prosthetic.

Two men sidled up to Rebecca at the same time. "Miss Rebecca, I'd sure like—"

The other man interrupted. "To have the next dance with you."

"Now, Amos. I believe Clinton asked first." The man bowed, she curtsied, and they entered the dance area just as the fiddler began another breakdown. Woody watched with a slight tinge of jealousy. After that, Amos hurried into the circle to claim his dance with Rebecca. When that dance ended, she walked over to Woody, out of breath, perspiration flowing from her forehead.

"Whew! It's rather warm out there."

Before he could answer, A.J. Buckner approached, Mrs. Fordham at his arm. Her graying hair, styled back and up, was covered by a blue patterned bonnet.

"Afternoon, Mr. Alexander. Miss Rebecca." He greeted them with a slight tip of his straw hat. "Rebecca, might I have that stroll now?"

She glanced at Woody.

"Do declare," Woody said. "My mouth's collecting more water than the great Ohio. I'm 'bout half-starved."

A lie on her behalf. He'd rather take her to the dance circle and hold her close while the band played a serenade.

Instead, he joined the food line as the band started up a rousing tune. A.J. offered one hand to Rebecca, and they too left the barn to join the people outside. The sun's late afternoon rays shined through the trees lining the McAllister farm. A breeze brought relief from the highs of the day, but the heat still wilted Woody in his Sunday suit. He loaded chicken and beef and an oversized potato onto his plate and found a shade tree.

The words of the next song floated out of the barn and tickled the ears of the people around him, who tapped their boots and shoes on the grass as they visited together.

I come from Alabama with
a banjo on my knee
I'se gwine to Lou'siana
my true lub for to see

Oh! Susanna, do not cry for me
I come to Alabama wid
my banjo on my knee...

When he'd finished eating, Woody re-entered the barn and sought Rebecca out. She stood alone so he joined her. After a brief huddle with the players, the fiddler called for everyone's attention. "Here's the *Prima Donna Waltz*."

Another man was about to ask Rebecca for the dance when Woody held his hand out and said, "I think this one is promised to me." She smiled and curtsied, and put her hand in his. The sensation of her skin on his sent him over a waterfall. Before he knew it, and much to his disappointment, the dance ended. The struggle he anticipated with dancing never happened. Their eyes met as the dancers clapped their approval to the band.

"You dance well," she told him.

His heart leapt to the moon.

The fiddler announced the next song. "This one's dedicated to those who are sweet on another. Sing it from where you are. Most of you know the words."

Beautiful dreamer, wake unto me
Starlight and dewdrops are waiting for thee…

Woody and Rebecca stood together and sang. He soaked in the sentimentality of the popular Stephen Foster composition, hard-pressed to remember the last time he'd enjoyed himself so much. For this day at least, he forgot about the photograph and the whereabouts of the unnamed girl. This time would be for him, and he would enjoy each moment.

* * *

Several weeks passed. Each morning, Woody rose before the first cock-a-doodle announced a new day. He saddled up James's donkey and rode to Rebecca's farm before first light.

Nights of peaceful sleep, uninterrupted by horrible scenes of human carnage, refreshed him and released boundless energy. He'd opened the ambrotype case only three times to view the likeness of the girl. While still determined to fulfill his mission, his fixation on the image waned. A bond between him and Rebecca had emerged, confusing and exciting him. When their eyes locked, neither of them looked away as hurriedly as they once had.

Did she feel the same way? What about the newspaperman, A.J. Buckner? He'd called on her several times, leaving Woody with covetous eyes as they rode away in his buggy.

The perfect opportunity to tell her the truth never came.

Thirty

The Foaling

Red Oak, Ohio
Late August

Rebecca greeted him with a cup of coffee. When his hand brushed across hers, he held it there for a moment. The sight of her grin made him want to join the song sparrows as they greeted the dawn. She released the cup.

"Morning, Rebecca."

"Marnin' to ya, Drew."

Her cheerfulness and the purposeful hint of her fine Scottish accent buoyed his mood. He described her as high-spirited in a letter to his folks, a positive soul in most circumstances. She made him want to become a better man. Fate had flung obstacles at her that would have buried the bravest women in their tracks. Like the death of a husband and the need to maintain a farm alone. She persisted, one day at a time, and he was grateful to be a part of these days in her life.

"If you'll collect the eggs and tend to the animals, I'll be starting our breakfast," Rebecca said.

In the barn, he pitchforked hay through the trap doors and into the mangers where Rebecca's cows, horses, and donkey fed.

Then he milked the two cows and led them and their calves into four acres of nearby pastures, careful to avoid the free-ranging bull. He carried the milk into a root cellar where Rebecca made and stored butter and cheese. Several jars of molasses, left over from last year's crop and stacked neatly in one corner, made him eager for the upcoming sorghum cane harvest.

As he passed the chicken coup, one of the first things he'd repaired, the hens screeched and cackled a pitiful song. Sure enough, when he unlocked their nesting area and let them roam around the enclosed pen, he saw the reason for their chorus. A dozen or more eggs lay unprotected in their nests. After collecting breakfast, he fed and watered the flock, and left them to enjoy the rest of their day without further human interruption.

"Here you go, Rebecca." He placed the full basket on the kitchen table. "The old gals have been busy."

The days on the farm settled into a nice rhythm, marred only by the betrayal of trust that continued longer than he'd ever intended. Rebecca had taken him through Union and Byrd townships in search of the girl. The effort yielded no results, but there was much more ground to cover. Meanwhile, he would begin harvesting the canes in the next week with help from Rebecca's father. First, he would chaperone her to Cincinnati for a few days while she nursed an old friend who'd taken ill. Afterwards the search for the girl would be extended to another two townships.

He made a decision. On the boat to Cincinnati, he would tell her the truth about who he was and where he'd come from and make an impassioned plea for forgiveness. He would profess his affections and hope she would respond to his vulnerability. Better judgment had advised him to rein in his emotions, to keep a healthy distance while they served each other's purposes, but love trumped wisdom.

Was this love? He could not imagine being apart from her.

* * *

With the morning chores completed, Rebecca set a hearty breakfast of eggs, bacon, and bread on the table. Over the last several weeks she'd succeeded in adding a few pounds to his skinny frame. As usual, Drew gazed deep into her eyes as they ate and talked. He seemed taken with her, and she'd developed romantic feelings for him, but she must be sure.

After they cleaned the kitchen, she invited him on a walk through the sorghum field and over to the small mill to review the process for converting canes to syrup and sugar. As they strolled through rows of ten-foot stalks, Drew asked about her husband for the first time.

The inquiry left her speechless. Memories of George had their place, but she didn't anticipate talking about him now—with this other man. Would this violate the sanctity of George's special place in her heart? She couldn't blame Drew for asking, and his inquiry was a sign of his interest. She recalled her visit from George a few weeks before. Had he not released her for such a moment as this?

Drew gently prodded her again. "Do you think of him when we're together?"

She stopped walking and looked down to the ground, desperate not to hurt him and at the same time to be honest. The tender touch of his finger under her chin lifted her head until they made eye contact.

"George and I were always meant to be. Our time together was effortless. Sometimes we thought each other's thoughts and expressed them at the same moment. I'm sure we had rough patches, like in any marriage, but I can't remember them now. When George passed, the light went dim in my world."

"Do you curse the men who did this to your husband?"

Why would he ask this question?

"My curses would only fester. The pestilence would kill me, sure as any plague. So...no."

"You are quick to forgive, Rebecca."

"I hate injustice, and so did George. He died to free the slaves. If liberty is extended to all in our land, his death will have meaning. I will always miss him, but I accept the sacrifice."

They continued walking, but Drew became distant. He told her he'd fought for the Union and its preservation. The question of slavery might be another matter, though, and she didn't know where he stood on the matter. While it was the primary issue to her and George, others who answered the nation's call to arms did so to keep it from fracturing forever. That was their priority, as it was for President Lincoln before he issued the Emancipation Proclamation. Rebecca harbored a deep affection for Drew, maybe even love, but she didn't know if the seeds of love could blossom for someone who felt neutral about slavery.

She tried to set the question aside. Being here with Drew in the midst of hundreds of tall canes would be enough, at least for now.

* * *

He feared she would never understand how, in a similar way, preserving Virginia's self-rule required his service to the Confederacy. His sense of duty had compelled him to take up arms against any invader seeking to rob Virginia of her independence. Hadn't the nation's founders responded the same way against England's aggression? The reasons for their choices differed, but the ideal remained the same. The principle of freedom had led George to leave Rebecca and join the Union Army. In the same way, the call of liberty had compelled Woody to leave his home and take up arms with the Stonewall Brigade.

The temperature settled at a tolerable level, as the sun popped in and out of sight behind the rolling clouds. He glanced at her as they walked, and she returned his attention with a full smile. The sensuous bow in her upper lip and the width of her mouth sent a tingle down his spine. She'd allowed her long, red hair to fall to the middle of her back, adding to a feminine mystique that threatened to overpower him. He wanted more than anything to kiss her.

She returned his question. "Do you detest the men who took your foot?"

He thought for a moment about his answer. "No, I don't hate anyone either. But I do despise the war—brothers killing brothers—families torn apart—children losing their fathers. The lines are blurred, and the devastation people experience is no greater or less than the other."

She nodded. "A national tragedy."

"I have to believe most Southern boys got no personal stake

in slavery and want to live in peace. In the same way, most Union soldiers are farmers or city folk. They want to get home to their families and communities."

Perhaps this truth would soften her reaction to his confession.

Forget waiting for the steamer to Cincinnati. He would tell her now, right in the middle of the sorghum field. He searched for words, tried to find the best way to share his bad news.

Lost in those worries, he was shocked when Rebecca pulled him close and planted an innocent kiss on his mouth. This kiss differed from any other he had experienced. The brush of her delicate mouth on his filled him with an assurance—they would be a masterpiece together.

Her cheeks burned red. Did he read too much into one kiss? The debacle with Becky made him question his own judgment about picking a mate. "Rebecca, I want you to—"

"I'm sorry. It seemed like a good idea in the moment."

"No. I mean...yes. I'm glad you did. But what about A.J. Buckner?" Her nose and forehead scrunched up, and one brow rose. "I've noticed the two of you together."

"Do I detect a bit of jealousy in your tone, Mr. Alexander?"

"Perhaps."

She smiled. "Mr. Buckner and I are only friends, Drew. We enjoy talking about deep subjects, but he's merely an intellectual sparing partner."

He paused, more determined than ever to unpack the deceit threatening to separate them. His mouth went dry, and the house in the distance turned blurry. "Rebecca, I need to tell you something right now. I—"

The voice of Rebecca's father drowned him out. "Come quick! The mare's water has broken. She's foaling."

It came from outside the barn. What was James doing here? Did he witness the kiss?

They ran to where the horse lay on a bed of fresh hay, spread each morning in anticipation for this moment to arrive. Woody quickly sized up the situation. Distressed and uneasy, the mare needed assistance.

"Oh, God. Rebecca, she—"

"Ssh. We'll upset her."

The white sack containing the foal was visible, but only one leg protruded from the birth canal. They waited with great anticipation for the other leg as the filly pushed and groaned but made no progress. Woody shifted to the horse's side and stroked her head.

"I have to open the sac," he said, turning toward Rebecca and James.

He slid his arm into the canal and followed the exposed leg until he found the foal's chest. The second leg had extended in the wrong direction, so he moved the limb in place while he spoke soft words of encouragement to the mare. With a tight grip, he tugged the foal through the canal.

"That'a girl," Woody said. "Easy now."

The other leg emerged, and the nose and head followed. With one more pull, the rest of the foal's body slid into its new world.

"Beat the Dutch," James said. "Will you look at that?"

Woody moved away with a slow deliberate movement so he wouldn't startle the mare, which lay side by side with her foal. After several minutes, she severed the umbilical cord and washed the new member of the family.

The foal tried its luck on all four legs. After wobbling, the young horse tumbled to the hay. Another attempt, and the foal fell again. Then, as with untold millions of newborn horses before, the foal remained upright on the next try and stumbled into its first steps. The new arrival practiced moving about, interested in its dam but also taking in the new setting.

Rebecca looked admiringly at Woody. "Nice handiwork." Then she turned to James. "Daddy, what a surprise to see you. Why are you here?"

"A hunch. When your mother and I visited last night, I forgot my hat. So I thought I'd pick it up and check on the horse at the same time. This is what I found."

Good thing. The mare might have died. As they walked back to the house, the miracle of new life dominated the conversation.

James recalled how George and he once rode to the edge of his fields to repair a fence when they came across a similar situation. One of James's heifers was calving but the cow couldn't deliver. George had turned the calf inside the birth canal so it could slide into the world.

"George Johnston was a top-notch gunner and a pretty good animal doctor," James said, as they stepped up to the porch.

In an instant, Woody's world caved in. George Johnston. Artillery gunner. Port Republic. These were the missing pieces, the gaps in his memory. A horrible possibility struck him like a dozen lead balls finding a single target.

George Johnston, from Red Oak, Ohio, had taken his final breath at Port Republic. If the Yank who invaded Woody's campfire was to be believed, he may have fired the fatal shot.

Had Woody been the Confederate soldier who killed Captain Johnston and stole the future from his wife...Rebecca?

Thirty-One

Betrayal

The next morning, Rebecca and Drew drove the buckboard through Ripley, while her daddy rode beside them on horseback. Soon she and Drew would be passengers on a steamer to Cincinnati.

The harvesting and stripping of sorghum canes would commence in earnest when they returned, and the pressing operation and packaging would follow. In addition to caring for her friend, she planned to call on storeowners in hopes of bringing her sweetener to market. Most of her sales would occur in Cincinnati and towns like Ripley and Georgetown in Brown County. If all went according to plan, there would still be stock for individual sales, personal use, and gifts. Before marketing her products, she and Drew would explore the surrounding townships in search of the unnamed girl.

Over the last few weeks, Drew had mentioned the girl much less than when he first arrived at the farm. But she needed to fulfill her end of the bargain. "If the Browns are in this county, we'll find them," she told Drew as they left the farm that morning.

The buckboard meandered south on Ripley's Main Street, past some of the shops she had visited since she was a little girl.

Proprietors like Elizabeth and Hugo Witherspoon, the owners of Ripley's grocery, had attended her wedding. When she and George moved into their farm, the Witherspoons were the first couple to grace their table. And when word came that George had died in battle, they cooked meals and helped with the funeral service.

The tombstone marked an empty grave. A similar emptiness lingered in her heart whenever she visited the site.

As they moved adjacent to the grocery store, she called out to Elizabeth who was sweeping the walkway in front. "How's Hugo?"

"His same old cantankerous self." Elizabeth's slight accent gave her away as a Brit. She continued sweeping and lamented, "Some things never change."

"Please say hello for me. Tell him I'll be visiting soon with some sugar and molasses."

The old woman nodded and waved again as they passed. The thoroughfare bustled with activity. Shoppers visited retail stores, children played, and horseback riders and horse-drawn carriages moved along the road. The early morning mist had dissipated, leaving behind a few wispy clouds and a brilliant late-summer sun. A delightful day in town, and the ideal hour to begin their journey to the big city.

As they came to the junction of Main and Front on the riverfront, a loud steam whistle blew from the sternwheeler about to carry them downstream. The signal informed the other barges and flatboats of the captain's intent to moor his vessel. Smoke and cinders snaked from the two tall stacks into an otherwise unspoiled sky. Twin double-acting pistons powered the paddle wheel at the stern, churning frothy water that resembled the foamy head on a glass of beer.

They all stepped down from their rides. Drew took the bags from the buckboard and her daddy tied the reins of his horse to the back. "Take care of my girl," James said to Drew.

"Will do, sir." They shook.

James turned to Rebecca. "Don't fret about the animals and such. I'll handle everything until you come home."

"Goodbye, Daddy. Should be gone no more than two weeks. I'll send word about our boat so you can pick us up. My love to Mama."

She hugged him.

As he pulled away, he said, "I'll try to get a head start on the sorghum harvest while you're gone. Shouldn't take long with just a few acres."

Another resounding whistle announced the ship's arrival as the captain pulled parallel to the wharf boat. The floating dock served as the entrance and exit for ticket holders, and the pathway to load and unload commercial goods. The assembled crowd began to board, so Rebecca and Drew crossed with them from the wharf to the steamboat. She had looked forward to this time. The kiss still stirred and surprised her.

She'd never been so forward with a man, even George. Now she was boarding a boat with Drew, without a chaperon, and they would be together in a big city for several days. He would take a room in a nearby inn while she stayed with her friend.

The next kiss would have to be his doing.

* * *

Along with several others, Woody and Rebecca discovered a comfortable place on the deck for day sojourners and those longer-distance travelers who purchased inexpensive tickets. For the next few hours, they would lounge on a bundle of straw covered by their blankets and dine on the home-cooked food she'd packed for the trip. The carriage trade would travel in private rooms, sleep on soft feather beds, and eat the ship's cuisine served on fine China.

They stowed their bags and strolled to the bow. An uncertain silence fell between them. This was the first time they'd been alone since the kiss. Woody wanted to hold her the way he did in his dreams.

She dominated his vision of a time yet to come, a life together of planning and building and being in a community. The thrill of her kiss awaited him. Now facing each other at the bow, his inner desires screamed...*kiss her!* A cold sweat poured from his forehead as he turned his head and blurted out the first harmless words that came to mind.

"Beautiful out here, don't you think?" Before she could

answer, the pilot again sounded the whistle. Traffic on the waterway increased with passenger and commercial shipping boats.

The interruption led to a prolonged silence between them. He welcomed the chance to cool his burning need to hold her. The difficult talk had to come first, and then he could gauge whether she would return his affections.

The bright sun continued its ascent, rays beaming down on the water, creating diamond sparkles that waltzed on the surface. The steamer's wheel interrupted the easy sway behind them. Soon the upper class, dressed in their finery, emerged from their quarters to enjoy the natural beauty of the Ohio River and the hills beyond.

"It truly is," she said.

The comment came out of the blue. "Sorry, Rebecca. Is what?"

"Beautiful. As you said. And I'm so happy you're with me."

He stumbled over the opportunity to come straight out with it. The right words still wouldn't come. Where was Lucas when he needed him? *Say something!*

"Rebecca, there is something important I must tell you."

"Let me go first," she said. "Since you arrived, I've realized how much we…I mean, how much I…need your assistance on the farm. And you need me to help find the girl's family. We..."

Even she slipped over her words. Did she have feelings for him too? Could he dare to believe it? He must protect her by revealing the truth before she professed her love.

She shifted her gaze to the shore, where the leaves on the trees were just starting to change. Soon nature would paint a kaleidoscope of hues over them.

"It's amazing how autumn turns the death of summer's foliage into a thing of visual magnificence," Rebecca said.

He paused, not wanting to miss the occasion to share a deeper connection, to be vulnerable with this woman who'd captivated him. But he couldn't concentrate on nature.

"Yes, I appreciate the colors. But…"

In the pause, she stared at him with a steady intent. This time, she waited for him to make the first move. His desire intensified, delaying his best intentions. His confession could wait a little longer.

The moment for transparency yielded as his lips explored the newness of linking with hers. This romantic kiss slayed his honest intentions to reveal his true identity and talk things out. He kissed her again, deeply; her shudder of pleasure increased his own.

Push away!

"Rebecca…" The situation grew more complicated with each moment. "You're the most amazing woman, but I'm not the man you—"

Before he finished, a voice rang out behind them.

"Jonathan...? Jonathan Woodard?"

He squeezed his eyes closed. The voice sounded familiar, but he couldn't match the lilt with a face. He didn't dare turn. If he ignored the call perhaps the impending disaster would disappear. To his dismay, a smartly dressed passenger approached. Woody glanced at Rebecca, who already seemed confused. As the man came closer, he became more animated by the encounter.

"As I thought," the man said, now facing both of them. "What a stroke of fortune, Jonathan, to bump into you after all these years."

Woody's heart jumped to his throat. The man, a friend of his parents, had been to the farm for dinner several times. They had not spoken since before the war. Desperate, Woody turned to her. "Please understand how badly I wanted to tell you."

Her eyes widened, then narrowed.

"Tell me what?" she asked.

The man also appeared surprised by Woody's lack of response.

"I'm not sure what's going on, but this here's Jonathan Woodard. I was down to see your folks in Shepherdstown only last month. The rich Virginia soil is bringing in a bountiful crop this year."

"Woodard?" she said. "No, I believe you're mistaken, sir. This is Drew Alexander." For several unpleasant moments, a hush fell between them. Rebecca's icy glare stabbed Woody with indignation.

The man blinked, bowed slightly. "Please forgive me."

She faced Woody, a pink flare widening across her cheeks.

"What *is* your name, sir? Seems I don't even know you."

The man now appeared more puzzled.

Was this what God intended when he said all would be settled in due time?

"This is Randall Young, a family friend from Baltimore." As he confessed, a joyful tomorrow slipped through his fingers. A wall of mistrust rose around him instead, hemming him in, brick by brick. "Rebecca, please..."

She turned to the stranger. "Please, sir. Give us some privacy."

Young backed away and disappeared inside.

Rebecca's eyes grew wild with fury. "You—Jonathan, or Drew, or whatever your name is—are a traitor and a liar. Heaven grant me to never lay eyes on you again."

She stormed off.

"Let me explain, Rebecca. Please."

He wanted to follow her, to demand she listen to his explanation, his apology, but as she disappeared inside, he realized his apology would evaporate into thin air. He'd lied to the woman he loved, and there was no way to undo the damage.

Thirty-Two

Forlorn

At the stern, Woody stared into the frothy water generated by the rhythmic rotations of the paddle wheel. The trail of disturbance, and the calm waters that settled well behind, made him wonder…when would lasting tranquility replace the incessant turmoil in his life?

A blast from the steamboat jarred him from his stupor. He would find her and appeal to reason. Love argued for reconciliation and would bridge the steep divide that separated them. But the final secret must also be revealed. The Minié ball that snuffed the life out of George Johnston that day near the Coaling might have been fired from Woody's Springfield. Could Rebecca forgive him for pulling the trigger?

There simply was no way to know whether he had released the deadly force that felled the man.

He turned and walked back to their spot—the place where he had envisioned a different dialogue between them. Here he'd planned to share the most intimate things, his deepest hurts and regrets.

When he reached their resting place, he walked to the side of the boat, clutched the rail, and stared at the trail in the water. Lost and alone, he stood like a statue. The banter and laughter of other passengers, their enjoyment of the riverboat experience, left him bereft. Life seemed perfect for everyone else. How could his be crumbling so?

When he walked to the port side he saw her, staring at the water. Doleful, he gazed at her for several moments, trying to collect himself. The course of his life hung in this moment. He would speak his heart, and if the door remained locked, he would do whatever necessary to find the key.

He heaved a sigh and approached. "Can you ever forgive me?"

She turned, wiping her eyes with a handkerchief. "The thing is…" She hesitated. "How strange to call you by another name—Jonathan. I've only known you as Drew."

"But Jonathan is who I am. The same man I was this morning. I am—"

An elderly couple ambled toward them, locked in their own world. Arm in arm, they came within a few feet of them, and stopped to engage a man walking the opposite direction. Impatient, Woody waited until the three strolled off together toward the dining room. To walk with her at his side, her arm folded inside of his, now seemed like an unachievable dream.

"I am Jonathan Woodard."

"Only in name. How you live is who you are, and you support an inhumane practice. One I will spend my life trying to stamp..." Voice quavering, she stopped. "No, I don't know who you are. And I'm not sure I can withstand the discovery."

"The same man who asked for help to locate a little girl. The child is real. The same fellow who can't get you out of his head." He paused to gauge her reaction. Cold as stone. Mortified at the prospect of losing her for good, he stepped forward. "What about forgiveness?"

She moved back two steps. "Love is an easy word to toss around. Intimacy is what I long for."

"Please trust me."

Puffy, wet eyes scanned his face.

"How, after such a violation? My heart is broken and I don't know if it will ever get better."

He clung ferociously to one hope. Providence had engineered their union, and would not be turned away empty-handed. He told her the reason for the lie, that it allowed him to seek information about the girl without rousing the suspicions of others. As he'd made his way to her farm, the story about him fighting for the Union, the name he'd been using all along…the lies were all perpetuated to meet his goal. The one thing he hadn't counted on was meeting her and falling in love.

Her eyes softened. "Perhaps..."

Perhaps what?

Lifting her chin with a renewed purpose, she told him how she would proceed. When the steamer docked in Cincinnati, she would travel on to her friend's residence without him. She expected him to be gone when she returned home. The constant people in her life—her family and community—would help her gather the crops, produce her sweeteners, and distribute the products to her customers.

"Rebecca, there's one more thing I must tell you." The hardest words he would ever speak came next. As he told his story about George Johnston, he choked back tears of regret. She tried to respond and stuttered.

"Oh, God. How…? I can't…"

"There's no way to know who actually caused George's death. I understand if you can't live with that uncertainty and still…"

What else could he say? He was powerless to remove the sting of this revelation. To forgive this much would take the deepest grace. The kind of forgiveness that God heaped upon his chosen.

As she turned and walked away, Woody prayed.

Don't let this be forever.

* * *

Two days later, Woody boarded a steamer back to Ripley. He'd rented a buggy and driven to Rebecca's farm, where he continued the harvest that James had begun.

He allowed the canes and the leaves to dry for three days as Rebecca had instructed. Woody's initial resolve to make things right waned with each passing day as he withdrew into his shell again. He toiled away in Rebecca's mill from dawn to dusk. The retreat into his sadness became more pronounced each time the old mule circled the floor. It plodded along, doing its part to advance the rollers that crushed out the juice from the canes. The sweet extract dribbled to the next station. The procedure became second nature after a while—extract, filter, and settle the juice, then boil it in the evaporator. Once boiled and skimmed, the syrup turned thicker and darker.

He would strain the contents again as the molasses ran into a metal receptacle. After an hour of cooling, Woody funneled the substance into multiple pint- and quart-size bottles that he stacked in Rebecca's root cellar, ready for sale or barter.

By the time he'd completed several days of production, Rebecca had many gallons of syrup and several hundred pounds of sweetener. Retail sugar prices had jumped from four cents a pound in 1861 to an average of twenty-five cents. Woody projected Rebecca's profit potential and felt glad he'd contributed to her success, even in the midst of their separation.

The time had come for him to return to Shepherdstown. He sat on the porch after a light breakfast, with Yankee curled up at his feet and Rebecca's father seated at his side. James had dropped in to say goodbye. He'd been disappointed to hear about Woody and Rebecca. Though he had expressed his own disappointment with Woody's deception and how he'd hurt Rebecca, he also encouraged Woody to hold out hope.

Both of them lit their pipes to enjoy one last smoke together.

James puffed his pipe to life, blue-gray smoke billowing from his mouth. "New life's been bubbling up in my girl," he said. "I've seen it, son. Rebecca's a forgiving sort. Give her time."

"Time may not heal these wounds."

Woody seized the branch he kept handy on the porch. An accomplished whittler, he steadied the wood with one hand. With the recently sharpened pocketknife his daddy gave him on his fourteenth birthday, Woody shaved the left side of the horizontal beam of a cross, removing the excess from his almost-finished memento. The icon would fit on the kitchen wall, or perhaps in the parlor if Rebecca chose to keep it. It was a rough-hewed apology for the duplicity.

He put the final touches on his woodwork and etched his

real name on the back along with the date. Lowering the blade to the porch floor, he stared at James. "Time's come to head off. My work here is done, and Rebecca will be returning any time now. I don't think she'll want to see me here."

"Right. I'll drive you to town so you can book passage on the next steamboat. Maybe reserve a hotel room until the ship arrives. I'll care for Yankee and the other animals until she gets home."

"Thank you, sir. Allow me get my things together and collect your mule."

They both rose, but as Woody turned toward the barn, James place his hand on Woody's shoulder. "One minute, son."

Woody gazed into the eyes of a man for whom he'd gained great respect. Next to his daddy and Lucas, James had become his most trusted male friend. The loss of Rebecca also meant he must say goodbye to a man he'd be proud to call his father-in-law.

"Sir…?"

"Write her a letter. Leave the words of your heart in her bedroom. Or in the kitchen. Be a shame to give up on her now."

After a moment of contemplation, Woody nodded. "I've already ruined the best thing in my life, so there's nothing left to lose. Give me a few minutes, and I'll wind up this business and go home."

With a new resolve, Woody returned to the house. Twenty minutes later, he emerged with the correspondence in his hand. James handed him the carving. "Might want to leave the note and your gift together on the kitchen table."

Woody nodded, and they both ambled to James's buggy for the ride into town. Not wanting to be left behind, Yankee followed them. Woody stooped down to pet the dog, and spoke to him for the last time.

"Go back home, boy."

After one last back scratch, he turned and left his canine friend in the road. The obedient dog first barked his displeasure, then trotted back to the house. There he lay, next to the rocker where so many hours had been shared. As the buggy rolled away, Woody looked over his shoulder one last time.

The porch disappeared.

Thirty-Three

Fannie Returns

Red Oak, Ohio
September 1864

When Rebecca walked through the door, Yankee could not contain himself. He had waited dutifully for his master's return. Now she belonged to him.

He barked and rolled and nudged, lavishing blind affection upon her with his thick, wet tongue. When he settled down, she sat on the floor for several minutes with his head nestled between her arm and lap. "Okay, boy…I need to get moving."

She scratched his snout one more time and stood. In the kitchen, she glanced at the table and saw a piece of paper, a letter dated two days before. She couldn't read it. She couldn't. Yankee followed her to the porch and sat beside her, a look of utter surrender. Could humans ever share this kind of blind devotion?

She petted his backside. "You're a good boy." He wagged his tail. Judgment be damned. She opened the folded page, inhaled deeply, and started to read.

Sept. 10

My dearest Rebecca,
When I was a boy, my daddy once whipped my backside because I stole some money from a friend. The beating hurt, but not as much as knowing how much I'd disappointed Daddy. Or having to stand before my friend and repay the money I owed him. I learned about integrity that day, how one falsehood can strip away the hard-earned trust of a loved one. Rebecca, I never intended to be disloyal to you, but I fell in love and became intoxicated by your charms. No matter how well intentioned my desire to find the girl, I owed you complete honesty when we met. Love requires nothing less. I believe you would have embraced me the same way you did because these are matters of the heart that you understand very well. If there's any way I can regain your trust, your love, I pray the God of heaven will show me.

I remain forever yours,
Woody

Woody…she'd not heard that name. Pouring through every word and phrase, she pictured Jonathan's gentle face, so tortured when they'd first met. Over time, he had become a man more at peace with his troubles. Her eyes moistened with might-have-beens. She clutched the note in one hand and the cross in the other, and made her way down to the root cellar. What she found shocked her.

A couple hundred gallons of syrup and several hundred pounds of sugar sat packaged and ready for distribution.

What had she done to this kind man?

* * *

Three weeks passed.

Rebecca had not written back to Jonathan, but in the last week, she'd received a second letter from him.

"I will never deceive you again, Rebecca," he wrote.

Those words softened her. Like before, she was desperate to believe him, but she chose not to answer. She busied herself with upkeep around the farm and delivered sugar and syrup to shops in Ripley, Cincinnati, and nearby townships.

The weather shifted. The days turned cloudier and the temperatures dropped as the month of October wore on.

She'd been baking bread in the kitchen when she turned to Yankee and started one of their frequent conversations.

"The winter will descend upon us soon."

Lying on the floor five feet from her, the obedient dog lifted his head, stretched it over his two front legs and cocked to the left. His tail wagged. She walked over to him and stroked the top of his head. Yankee's almond eyes oozed contentment.

"I'm chilled in my bones. What about you boy? We best plan on finishing all our firewood chopping before the first snows arrive."

Yankee's attention turned to the front door. He rose and sniffed at the threshold as though he expected a visitor. A few moments later, Rebecca opened the door. It was Josiah Kingsman, one of John Parker's foundry employees and an assistant conductor for the Underground Railroad. He appeared disheveled, his clothing rumpled and his hair tousled. This was not a social call.

"What's wrong, Josiah. Let me get you some water."

She turned to the kitchen, and he followed. "Sorry for how I'm lookin', Miss Rebecca. Had to leave in a rush. Drove the horse and buckboard a bit hard."

She poured the drink and grabbed three cakes, then set them on the table in front of him. "Tell me the reason for your hasty trip."

He took a bite. "Good cakes. It's Miss Fannie. She's back, but without Israel or little Parker." He washed the first cake down with a gulp of water. "Mr. John Parker sent me to fetch you and bring you back to Miss Jean's house. He told me to lose no time. Trouble has found its way to Israel's family."

"I'll gather some things and be right down."

She didn't ask about the nature of the problem. She would learn the details soon enough, but her suspicion centered on one plantation owner across the river. Two years had passed, but her fears about that cruel overseer never did. She would bet any high-stakes gambler that Israel had been taken, but why hadn't little Parker been left with his mama? Rebecca prayed her fears were unfounded. Within moments, she made her way downstairs and headed straight for the front door.

"Let's be off, Josiah."

The young man complied, but first he grabbed another cake. On her way out, she whistled for her four-legged friend. Yankee darted through the kitchen, his mouth dribbling with the water he'd lapped up from his bowl, and he jumped into the buckboard bed.

"That's a good boy, Yankee." She told Josiah, "Do as you did to get here, lad."

"Ma'am?"

"Make haste."

* * *

Josiah parked the rig in the barn, and they walked to the back door, followed by Yankee. Before she knocked, the door opened.

"Hello, John," Rebecca said. They gave each other a warm embrace. "Been a long time since our last visit."

The Reverend John Rankin placed both his hands on her shoulders and gently guided her one step backwards. His eyes scanned her face. "You seem a little tired, but it's wonderful to see you."

"And you. I'm well nigh tuckered out from delivering sugar and molasses. Been on the highways and byways, crisscrossing counties." She looked up and pointed to the house. "I notice you've made some changes. Has it been that long since I've been here?"

She always thought the Rankin house to be appropriate for a pastor—small and comfortable. The brood of Rankin children had grown and moved on to build their own nests, and the number of Underground Railroad passengers had lessened to a trickle as the war progressed, especially after President Lincoln's Emancipation Proclamation. Israel Rankin's family was the last she had conducted. She imagined the frenetic pace of life for John and Jean Rankin in years gone by.

"A small addition over here on the east side, and a little remodeling," he said.

They stepped inside and made their way to the front parlor,

where heat from a box stove kept the space comfortable. This room, always her favorite, remained the same. The grandfather clock still occupied the same spot against the wall. The two built-in cupboards flanking the fireplace lent an old-fashioned charm to the room. A writing table and piano indicated that creative people resided in this quaint house.

Visiting these friends was always like coming home, but this visit would be different. She locked eyes with Jean, who stood to greet her. They met in the middle of the room with an embrace.

"I've missed you," Jean said. "I wish we were together under different circumstances."

"Okay, it's my turn." John Parker rose from his seat to hug her. "How are you, Rebecca? You're always in my thoughts. Life on the farm must be hard without George."

She nodded, but said nothing. How could she tell him about Jonathan, and how he and George now occupied her thoughts?

"Can I help you with your harvest?" John asked.

"A hired hand and my daddy have been keeping things up."

She realized that under trying circumstances, she too could be less than honest with someone she cared deeply for. The hired hand had been long gone for some time. Jonathan's empathetic gaze poked through miles of separation to tell her…*I understand.* Rebecca sat on the couch. Familiar with the surroundings, Yankee curled up at her feet and fell asleep.

The room, a place of happiness and celebration, became a parlor of gloom.

She turned to Reverend Rankin, eager for details. "Where is she, John? What has happened? Where are Israel and little Parker?"

Before he could answer, the door connecting the parlor to his bedroom and study opened. Fannie stood at the threshold, her face lined with fear, her cheeks wet with distress.

Rebecca stood and embraced the woman, overcome by this somber, bittersweet reunion. She pulled Fannie close and held her tight. The former slave trembled until she broke down and sobbed. Rebecca had expected the worst, and this confirmed a terrible tragedy had taken place. She kept a kerchief in her hand to dab the heartache away from Fannie's face.

She turned to Reverend Rankin. "Where are they, John? Tell

me…are they alive?"

"Sit. Miss Fannie needs to sit."

"Of course." Rebecca led the woman to the sofa, and they sat close enough to hold hands.

The reverend explained. The family had left Rebecca's farm that night two years ago and traveled to the next railroad stops. When they made it to Columbus, en route to Canada, Israel decided they would run no farther. As a free American, he insisted on living in his own country. So they stayed, and Israel soon found work at one of the local blacksmith shops.

Fannie picked up the narrative. "Things went real well for us, Miss Rebecca. Israel made fair wages, and he looked into the sugary cane you done told him about."

"Sorghum."

"Yes. Israel worked hard in hopes of havin' us a farm to grow sorg'him." She stopped, and as the memories flooded back, Fannie cried out. "One day Israel got a note to meet a man needin' some blacksmithing work. He took little Parker along. That's when they grabbed 'em...my baby boy and my man."

Rebecca pulled Fannie close, her arm around the woman's shoulders. "Oh, Fannie…I'm so sorry."

Reverend Rankin continued the story. Three men had found them. Slave catchers. Somehow they tracked the family and held them at a location near Columbus for two days. When they figured it was safe, the kidnappers slapped chains on Israel and transported him and the boy south. Fannie had been ill for weeks with malaria, so they left her there. They told Fannie if she went to anyone for assistance, they would kill them both. And to taunt her, they threatened to hang Israel anyway, and sell Parker down the river.

A Negro couple had nursed Fannie, and she remained quiet for months. When she'd regained her health, Fannie came to the people she thought could help. The little bit of money they'd saved to buy a farm was used for living expenses and her travel to Ripley.

"Are you recovered now?" Rebecca asked as she tenderly squeezed Fannie's hand.

"Still weak…but better."

Rebecca turned to the pastor. "Do we know where they

are?"

"No," Reverend Rankin said. "But my guess is that the tobacco plantation owner across the Ohio—"

"Franklin Wills is behind this." John Parker jumped up from his seat. "Sure as every Confederate is a traitor to freedom."

Rebecca cringed. She still struggled with Jonathan's alliances in the war, but she stopped short of condemning him to the gallows.

"Remember how he sent his thugs after we helped Israel and Fannie to escape?" John Parker asked. "They threatened to follow the family to the ends of the earth. Said the family should never rest easy."

"They showed up on my front porch too," Rebecca said. "Go on."

"That dog, Wills…my guess is he found them."

Despair fell upon the room.

Thirty-Four

The Glue

"Are they on the Wills plantation?" Rebecca asked.

The day before, John Parker had crossed into Kentucky to peek around the tobacco farm from a distance. Israel and the boy were nowhere to be found. The blacksmith shop appeared empty. Rebecca guessed the plantation owner had cut a deal with slave traders to collect a profit, as the future of the trade was now in doubt.

"The abduction happened almost a year ago," John Parker said. "They could be anywhere in the Deep South."

Rebecca was undaunted by such odds. "We must find them."

"That's why we sent for you," John Parker said. "We're of one accord to mount a rescue."

A palpable silence gripped the room. They all looked to the abolitionist pastor, revered by many, hated by some. Everyone assembled that day adored him. The grandfather clock announced the arrival of the noon hour, breaking the stillness. There existed great danger in the South at this time, and Reverend Rankin spoke to it.

Atlanta had fallen, and Petersburg and Richmond were in Grant's sights. Phil Sheridan had laid waste to the Shenandoah Valley. The Feds put a final stranglehold on the Confederacy, and soldiers from both armies were scattered throughout the Confederate states. Despite the proclamations from Washington that all slaves in seceded states were free, most slave owners clung to their so-called property, and would do so until the bitter end. To travel south to rescue Israel and the boy would involve great danger. Still, they must try.

"I've no right to involve you in this, Rebecca," Reverend Rankin said. "But I'm old, and John Parker here is liable to have someone slap him in chains before he gets very far."

"I'm the only other person who knows Israel. I'm the logical one to go." She glanced at Fannie and squeezed her hand. "Of course, I'll go."

Reverend Rankin would not allow her to travel alone. She needed a male companion, a trusted friend willing to risk such a dangerous mission. The party might encounter Union and Rebel soldiers and need to gain acceptance from both sides.

He'd devised a scheme to secure the confidence of the Federals if they stopped the rescue party. Well-acquainted with Allen Pinkerton, owner of the famous detective agency headquartered in Cincinnati, the reverend would obtain papers identifying Rebecca as a federal spy employed by the Pinkertons. These documents would grant her passage through Union lines on a secret mission to gather military intelligence. They still needed to resolve the problem of potential encounters with Confederate forces.

Rebecca smiled at the mysterious workings of heaven.

"I may have a solution. There is a man who has been working on my place over the past few months. Goes by Jonathan Woodard."

"Who is this man? Can he be trusted?"

Trust. She thought about the word for a moment. Could she believe Jonathan after his tricks? He had pleaded with her to let him prove his loyalty. Jonathan could certainly navigate the issues that might arise with Confederate soldiers or belligerent Rebel sympathizers. This may be the best chance to get Israel and little Parker back north. Maybe even a chance for a fresh start with the man she still loved.

"Yes, I believe so, but there's a catch. Something I must insist upon."

Never one to mince words, Rebecca told them that Jonathan was a Confederate soldier, decommissioned when he lost part of his leg in the war. She recounted how Jonathan had escaped from Johnson's Island, details he wrote about in his longer second letter, and how he risked death to come north and assuage one Union family's grief. In return for Jonathan's willingness to help, she demanded assurances from those assembled around the room that he would maintain his independence.

"I am intrigued, Rebecca." Reverend Rankin studied her. "This man is special to you. I trust you, my dear, and if you say he can be trusted, that's good enough for me. We can only hope the papers I've procured from the Pinkertons will keep him safe from any Union retribution. As for us, every effort will be made to ensure his continued freedom."

First, she'd need to contact Jonathan. She would write him that day and ask him to return to Ripley.

She had pledged to help him find the unnamed girl, a mission that brought them together and launched their budding relationship. She'd agreed that finding this family would be the elixir to ease his pain and make him whole. It meant the world to him, or at least it had before they met.

Now she would ask him to search for another child, a kidnapped Negro boy named Parker Rankin, and his father. Two people who meant the world to her. This would require him to delay his quest and join her on a dangerous mission. Would he agree?

Their lives had been shattered into little pieces. Maybe this would be the glue to make them whole again.

Thirty-Five

The Plan

Rebecca's request was his best shot at reconciliation. The day Woody received her letter he'd written back that he would book rail passage to Ripley as soon as possible. First, he and his daddy would help a neighbor to rebuild his barn after it had burned to the ground. His best pal, Lucas Halverston, would accompany him north, and he told her to watch for their arrival in two weeks time.

The time had passed at a snail's pace, but he and Lucas finally stepped off the wharf boat and back onto the streets of Ripley. They stopped at the livery, rented a buggy, and made their way to Rebecca's farm.

He breathed in the surroundings. The earthy smell of the forest, the trees that clapped their hands and danced in the breezes, triggered memories of his time here. The blooms of September had faded to brown, but the purple Chicory flowers and cheerful yellow of the Evening Primrose still livened up the damp earth. Woody's hope took flight in this place.

While recuperating, Adele Myers taught him one of her favorite poems, written by Emily Dickinson, which he had committed to memory. He pictured her reciting it many times at his bedside.

Hope is the thing with feathers, that perches in the soul,
And sings the tune without the words, and never stops at all,
And sweetest in the gale is heard; and sore must be the storm
That could abash the little bird that kept so many warm
I've heard it in the chilliest land, and on the strangest sea;
Yet, never, in extremity, it asked a crumb of me.

He gazed up at the clouds, rippled high in the sky, with alternating lines of white and gray, and an occasional swirl. A harbinger of change in the weather.

"Rain's a-comin'," he said.

Lucas cast a quick glance upward and nodded. The winds blew stronger than usual from the south, tousling the treetops. The whispering trees and an occasional birdsong brought him back home to the comfort of his hammock on a Sunday afternoon. There he would swing to the gentle tunes of the wheat stalks that danced against the mild early summer breezes.

"Yep," Woody said. "A good soaking is fine by me, especially under the cover of that porch roof. Let's get a move on." Woody picked up the pace.

As they pulled in front of the farmhouse, Yankee announced their arrival. The door opened wide. Woody stood facing Rebecca as Yankee barged out of the house and jumped onto him, knocking him back a step. The dog bathed him with happy kisses. *If only.* He'd dreamed of a welcome like this from her.

"Hello, Yankee," Woody said. "You're such a good watchdog."

Lucas murmured, "Hope this Yankee is peaceful." An unwise comment. Woody shot him a glance. *Watch your words.*

Almost as an afterthought, Yankee shifted his attention to Lucas and sniffed his front and back. Lucas easily passed inspection, after which Yankee continued his reunion with Woody.

The dog dropped to the porch and rolled onto his back, and Woody stooped to give him a belly scratch. Two hind feet twitched and kicked the air.

Woody looked over at Rebecca, Yankee still in his clutches, and caught a smile. A deep hunger for her embrace surged up, but he suppressed his need.

She tentatively stepped to the porch.

Proper introductions were in order, and he had looked forward to this moment. He would correct the record and bury the fib in an unmarked grave.

"It's good to see you," Rebecca said. "Thank you for coming. Both of you."

Woody removed his fedora and ran fingers through the crop of hair that had grown over his ears and down to the nape of his neck. "Time we did this the right way. Rebecca, meet my best friend in the world, besides Yankee. This is Lucas, or Luke as I sometimes call him."

"Luke…"

He took two steps forward. "Ma'am." At Woody's glare, he removed his bowler hat. "Proud to make your acquaintance. Woody's told me all about you as well."

"And I'm Jonathan Woodard. But my friends call me Woody."

She curtsied. "Then Woody it is. And Luke." She bobbed another curtsy his way.

The warmth of her response might well have melted the Sandusky winter freeze that blackened his foot beyond repair. Was it months ago, or had an eternity passed since his daring escape from that dreadful island prison? Might this be the thaw in their relationship that he had prayed for so faithfully? Perhaps the clock had been set back in time for a different beginning.

After a short visit, he and Lucas made their way to James's spread and bedded down in the barn. The heavens opened and a cleansing rain poured down. Woody was thrilled to introduce Lucas to Rebecca's daddy. Next to his own father, these were the two most important men in his life.

The next morning, they sat at a large kitchen table in the home of Reverend and Jean Rankin, high atop the hill overlooking Ripley. A group had been assembled to plan a rescue mission: the Rankins, Rebecca, John Parker, Woody and Lucas, and Fannie. A feast was served up including eggs, ham, home-baked bread, and pancakes smothered in butter and Rebecca's syrup.

The large fireplace where Jean cooked banished the early winter chill from the kitchen. As they discussed the outlines of a plan, Woody gained a strong sense of purpose with these new friends. The warmth of the fire and the fellowship around the table renewed his belief that he and Rebecca would be drawn closer in the coming days.

"The first thing we need to figure out is where Israel and the boy are and hope they're together," John Parker said. "I'm guessing Wills's cowards paraded them back to the plantation and sold them to a slave trader, maybe in Richmond, or even Atlanta, where the slave trade continues."

"Maybe even down the Ohio into Louisiana, but the traders there are being closed down by the strong Union presence," Reverend Rankin said.

A realistic, daunting assessment. "So our first stop is the Wills spread in Kentucky," Woody said.

"Yes, but that'll be tricky." The reverend's steely edge sent a signal. "Dangerous. Here's what we know."

Franklin Wills was a hard, pragmatic businessman, but also a family man with one adolescent daughter. He left the daily operations of the plantation to a cruel overseer who'd mounted an unrelenting and eventually successful hunt for Israel and his family.

"A disgusting human being, if you can call him that," Rebecca said, her eyes flaring with indignation.

Reverend Rankin nodded and continued. Certain actions, like whippings and other harsh measures for attempted escapes, had Mr. Wills's approval. Israel had told John Parker after the escape that some of the hired hands had their way with the women, but Wills never did, as far as he could tell. He seemed devoted to his young wife. Reverend Rankin figured Israel's value as a smithy led Wills to search for the family and bring them back, and then sell them at a tidy profit. That was the plantation owner's intention all along, and the reason Israel and his young wife had decided to run.

"We must confront Wills in his home, in the dead of night, and convince him to give up the bill of sale," Reverend Rankin said. "That will inform us where Israel and the boy were initially sent. John will shuttle our party across the river in his boat, but only Woody and Lucas will advance to the plantation. Rebecca will wait for y'all in Ripley. The trick will be to skedaddle before

Wills can follow."

Harsh winter weather loomed around the corner. Travel across the mountain passes would become increasingly more difficult. To make matters worse, the military activity in the Shenandoah and around Richmond and Atlanta had intensified over the past few months. This would increase the possibility of being detained, or worse. Get back to West Virginia, and they should have clear sailing. If circumstances did call them down Richmond way instead of Louisiana, and if they needed assistance inside the Confederate capitol, Woody's contacts there would prove helpful.

The Rankins had taken a collection from friends and Underground Railroad supporters to help finance the search. Times were hard, but people gave what they could. In Richmond, Woody would have access to additional federal dollars from a favored uncle for the trip home.

Before he turned the money over to Woody, Reverend Rankin asked his final questions.

"Will you and Luke, before God and these witnesses, commit to do everything in your power to rescue this man and his son? Will you protect our dear Rebecca, even with your lives?"

"Her life before mine," Woody said. He cast a glance meant only for her eyes.

She blushed. The rest of them smiled.

Lucas said, "Yes, sir."

"Okay. We move tonight," John Parker said. "Dress warmly. Carry one bag, and bring supplies for bedding down outside. Fannie will gather the same for Israel and little Parker."

Reverend Rankin closed the meeting with a prayer for protection. Woody favored petitions to the Almighty. But he also believed a dose of good old-fashioned luck wouldn't hurt.

They would need both.

Thirty-Six

Woody's Crusade

Woody parked the rented buggy in Reverend Rankin's barn. As he and Lucas descended the one hundred steps into the shadows of Ripley, Woody considered the crusade before him. The nobility of their mission transcended ideas about institutions. A man and his boy needed saving, if they were even still alive, and he had been sent to rescue them. The chance of success dangled by the thinnest of threads, but with Rebecca and Lucas by his side, his courage swelled.

The skiff floated at the shoreline, dancing a waltz with the Ohio. John Parker huddled nearby, trying to ward off the biting cold when Woody and Lucas approached.

"I should have followed my own advice to dress warmly," John said.

They boarded the craft and set out. The stars were hidden beneath a thick blanket of clouds. A single lantern fought through a thin fog hovering over the water, guiding them forward on the short ride to the Kentucky side of the river.

When they neared, John and Lucas jumped from the skiff into the shallow water, and pulled the boat ashore. Woody stepped out, and they walked up the hill leading to a wooded area. Woody and Lucas would walk down the road until they found two horses tethered to the bushes on the left side, courtesy of a Kentucky farmer sympathetic to the abolitionists. Another couple of miles down, the scent of tobacco and a good-for-nothing named Wills would lead them the rest of the way.

John handed each man a pistol. "I hope you won't be needing these. Godspeed."

The men set out, making good time, given Woody's disability.

They'd been walking ten minutes when Woody said, "What's your plan to convince Wills to give us the information we need, and to not follow us?" He couldn't imagine Wills sitting still after two armed strangers invaded his home. "Wills won't go down without a fight."

"We'll give him good reason to back off," Lucas said.

The details of their break-in plan were set by the time they reached the horses. As Woody climbed his mount, waves of pain pulsed into his missing foot. They rode at a moderate pace, and within thirty minutes reached the plantation. Woody checked his watch…near midnight.

He surveyed the fields and the various quarters, the quiet relieving his jitters. He wondered about Israel. Slave owners like Franklin Wills were willing to fight, even kill, to retain what they considered their legitimate property, lawfully purchased.

They walked the horses from the edge of the plantation to the main house. After they secured their rides, they sneaked around to the back door and found it unlocked.

"Perfect," Lucas whispered.

They edged the door open and tiptoed upstairs to where Fannie said the master and his wife slept. Woody slipped off in one direction and Lucas the opposite, both with loaded pistols at the ready. As Woody approached Wills's bedroom, the man stirred in his bed. His open-mouthed snoring sounded like stampede of horses.

"Wha...who's there?" Wills said, muddled.

Half asleep, Mrs. Wills mumbled. "Franklin, what's the matter?"

At the familiar cocking sound of Woody's six-shot revolver, Wills sat up instinctively. "What the dickens—?"

"Hold it there, Mr. Wills," Woody said. "I have a pistol

trained on your wife, and I would hate to discharge it. Get up nice and slow like. Light the lamp next to your bed. I promise you, once we've conducted our business, we will be off and no one will get hurt."

Wills followed instructions. The lamp reflected light on a confused man, sleep still dripping from his eyes. He appeared to be in his mid-forties, average height with a receding hairline. A thick, long handlebar mustache curled up into pointed ends that nearly reached his ears.

"Who are you?" he asked. "What's this about?"

Woody scanned the room. He noted the opulence, the glass-paned windows with expensive fabrics as coverings, the wood-framed canopy bed with an end table on each side, the table and chairs for a private breakfast at the foot of the bed, and the elaborately carved armoire and fancy dresser that filled out the room.

All obtained on the backs of forced laborers. His neutral stance on slavery had already changed as a result of his time spent with Rebecca. The injustice before him, and watching Fannie recount the pain of losing her family, continued to strip away his casual opinions about the institution.

While Woody fought to protect Virginia against invasion, unprincipled men like Franklin Wills fed at their tainted troughs, enriching themselves and their hired hands. The thought turned his stomach in knots.

"Seems you've done okay for yourself, Mr. Wills," Woody said. "Can't imagine the slave quarters over yonder being quite as nice."

Wills scoffed at the intruder. "So you're one of them Negro-lovers."

Mrs. Wills started to rise from the bed, indignant at the intrusion. "Be gone from my house. How dare you—"

Woody walked over to Wills's wife and placed the barrel of his gun against her temple. That silenced her. She began to whimper.

"Mr. Wills, I'm certain your young spouse here wants to survive this encounter. Give me what I want, without dawdling, and keep your ugly remarks to yourself. Believe me, sir, I will start with her so you can watch."

"What is it you seek?" Wills asked.

"A blacksmith named Israel. You recognize the name?"

The man said nothing, but his scornful expression shot arrows of contempt at Woody.

"I believe your henchmen brought him and his son back here. Is any of this ringing a bell, Mr. Wills? Tell me where they are."

"Slaves by any reckoning, and my property," Wills said, his retort smothered in self-righteousness. "Bought and sold in a fair business deal. That's what they were, and I retain the rights to what belongs to me."

The callousness of such an arrangement, justified as normal and within the boundaries of acceptable human behavior, left Woody speechless.

"I'm the one wronged here," Wills said. "I paid top dollar for those slaves, and someone thieved my property."

"So you do recall them, you good-for-nothing rogue," Woody said. "They're people, like you and me. An innocent child, no less."

"They were contraband, so I stole them back and I make no apologies. I sold them. A fair business deal, one you can't undo."

Lucas walked into the bedroom, his pistol pointed at the back of the head of Wills's daughter, Abigail.

"Daddy..."

Woody retrained his six-shooter on Wills. "Sir, give us the bill of sale, and we'll leave."

The slaveholder looked from his wife to his daughter, then blew out a resigned sigh. "They're in my office."

He started to get out of bed.

"Hold it," Woody said. "Move slowly, you in front of me. And remember, my pistol is aimed at your head."

Lucas motioned for Abigail to sit on a chair at the foot of her parents' bed. "Stay put over there, darlin'."

Wills led Woody to the next room, where he lit another lamp and waded through a storage cabinet. He thumbed past several folders until he found the one he wanted.

"Here it is. Slave transactions." He withdrew the folder. After pulling all the papers out, he plodded through receipts. "A number of darkies have passed through over the year."

Woody became more disgusted by Wills's cavalier attitude toward the injustices he had perpetrated against Israel and his family. "You make me sick. To think we've been on the same side in this war."

"So you're a Reb soldier," Wills said. "Don't that beat all? I've been visited by a traitor—a scalawag."

Woody raised the pistol high. His need to punish Wills with a smashing blow burned within him like molten lava. *No.* He would not stoop to violence to satisfy his pride.

"I'm already sorry that I haven't killed you yet. There's still plenty of time, should you give me an excuse. Find the papers. Now!"

Wills found the record and handed it over.

Woody glanced at it and saw Israel's name and the name of another man, the purchaser. "Back to the bedroom." They gathered again in the master suite, where Woody waved the documents in the air.

"We'll be leaving now so you can get your rest," Lucas said. "As insurance we won't be bothered, your daughter will ride with us for a piece. I'm sure you understand."

Mrs. Wills begged for the men to take her instead. Wills sneered at Woody, angered by the apparent double-cross. "You said no one would get hurt if you got what you came for. So now leave us be."

"We're not hard men like you, Franklin, so I'll allow Mrs. Wills to ride along instead of your daughter. Look for her on the road about two miles south of here."

Woody expected Wills would quickly follow so he issued a false warning. "Other less considerate men will be watching the house for the next two hours. Move before that time, and we can't predict what they'll do."

He directed Mrs. Wills to dress in warm clothing behind the room divider in the corner. When she had finished, the three of them walked out the front door. Woody mounted his horse and pulled Mrs. Wills up to sit behind him. She latched onto the sides of his jacket once the horse began to trot. They rode south for a half-mile and then dropped her off.

"Now, Mrs. Wills, our men are watching, so you best stay put until your husband comes for you," Lucas said.

"Understand?"

"Yes. Just don't hurt me, please."

"We don't hurt people," Woody said. "But your husband does."

Lucas and Woody continued south, so Mrs. Wills would relay the wrong direction to her husband. Once out of sight, they circled around to the north and back to the shoreline where they met John.

"Distasteful business," Woody said. "But we got it. We'll be Richmond bound."

At four in the morning, Rebecca, Woody, and Lucas began the forty-mile ride to Parkersburg. Woody figured another five hundred-plus miles from there to Richmond, but much of the distance would be covered by rail to Harpers Ferry. He allocated three days at most for this first leg of the trip. They would take a day of rest in Shepherdstown, then travel another six days by buckboard from Winchester to Richmond. Under the best conditions, it would take ten days to get to the Confederate capital. They should be there by November twelfth.

Precious little time was left to execute their mission and get back through Rockfish Gap in the Blue Ridge Mountains before the first winter snow. Even if they freed Israel and little Parker, Woody suspected what this would come down to in the end.

A race against the weather.

* * *

They stepped off the railroad car at Harpers Ferry, bags in hand, tired from the long, twisty and soot-filled ride, and daunted by the prospect of a twenty-mile walk. Woody would be hard pressed to keep up even a moderate pace, his gait slowed by his leg device.

"Lucas, head over to the Gruber spread, about a half-mile northeast from here. See what he can do to help us get to my farm. Gerhardt and my dad are friends and sometimes business associates."

About ninety minutes later, Lucas returned with a horse-drawn buggy and an extra horse hitched to the back. "Hop on, Rebecca," he said. "You, sir, may ride the mount, compliments of Mr. Gruber. By the way, he needs all of this back in two days."

Woody enjoyed a grand reunion with his family. His parents fell in love with Rebecca, and she with them. Mama took her arm in arm on a tour of the house, sharing the few photos of the family on display. They stopped in the room where Woody and his brother slept when they were boys. He followed along to dispute the stories Mama always told about his and Lucas's mischievous antics as young men. Rebecca seemed to savor the intimacy with Mama, giving Woody a glimpse of the rich life that lay ahead if he and Rebecca claimed it.

At the table, Mama set a bountiful feast, and Papa regaled his guests with the history of his family dating to the late eighteenth century when the Woodards arrived in America. Lucas told Rebecca that everything she had heard about Woody was true, and then some, but he was blameless.

After dinner, Woody and his daddy retired to the barn to supply the wagon they would take.

"The rig is sturdy, son. With two horses and four wheels, hopefully she'll get you through the Blue Ridge without much trouble. Mud is always an issue, so hope for clear skies."

"If one of us drives and the other two ride horseback, at least through Rockfish Gap and the mountain range, we'll be okay. It'll get tricky when we add Israel and his boy to the mix."

Woody read the foreboding on his father's face, but expected he would not speak about his concerns. "Don't worry about Gruber's property," his daddy said. "On the morrow, I'll return everything."

The two of them walked back to the farmhouse in silence.

Early the next morning, they said goodbye and left.

After a day of travel, they arrived in Winchester, the junction of the Northwest Turnpike and the Shenandoah Valley Turnpike. Unlike Parkersburg, the sleepy town where Union General George McClellan located his headquarters, a place virtually untouched by the war, Winchester was the most contested locale in the Confederacy. The side that possessed this ground held the key to the valley's vast agricultural resources, unlocking the doorway to possible invasion of either Washington or Richmond. The Union had taken control after the third battle for Winchester several weeks before.

This place had worried Woody the most, but they managed to slip around the Union-occupied town undiscovered. A few miles south of Winchester, they found a spot suitable for a camp where they built a fire. Exhausted from the travel, they climbed into one tent beneath multiple blankets. Their thick clothes added a protective layer between their skin and the frigid temperatures, and they were able to sleep.

The next day, they continued on the Shenandoah Valley Turnpike, on their way to New Market. They would pass Weyer's Cave and eventually roll into Staunton.

* * *

Woody drove the party hard, four hundred miles in seven days. On the ninth of November, they were right on schedule. Along the way, a traveler shared the news about President Lincoln's re-election, the last nail in the coffin of the Confederacy. Atlanta had fallen, and Grant squeezed Lee at Petersburg, the back door to Richmond, the capitol of the Confederate States of America.

The war's conclusion seemed imminent. What was around the next corner? The prospects both thrilled and frightened him.

For now, they would continue toward Richmond to call upon a renowned slave trader named Robert Lumpkin.

Lumpkin's slave jail

"Lumpkin was accustomed to imprison the disobedient and punish the refractory."

- Charles H. Corey's A History of the Richmond Theological Seminary with Reminiscences of Thirty Years' Work Among the Colored People of the South (1895)

Thirty-Seven

The Burning

Shenandoah Valley Turnpike

Woody's attention remained fixed on the pike for any evidence of troop movements. He glanced at Rebecca seated next to him on the wagon, and decided to voice his thoughts about President Lincoln's re-election.

"The war can't last much longer. Reconciliation will follow. It must be lenient."

He looked over at Lucas who rode horseback and saw him flinch.

If Woody and Rebecca stood any chance at becoming a couple, they too would have to reconcile their views on reunification. To shy away from disagreements would only turn them into ugly spats down the road. They'd supported different sides in the national conflict, and the national peace process would require families to bind old wounds too.

Rebecca appeared lost in thought. He didn't press her. They rode in silence until Rebecca finally said, "Slavery must die an immediate and permanent death."

With its economy destroyed and its principle labor force disbanded, how could the South ever recover? Still he knew, this was non-negotiable for a reunified country, and for he and Rebecca. "On that I believe we can agree."

"I think we should welcome back the people of the South with open arms, as long as they lay down their arms and pledge allegiance to the Union," she said.

Most folks would do that.

She thought for a moment. "And as long as the colored people in their lands are given the same full and equal rights as the whites."

The country could legislate this idea, but it couldn't abolish bigotry with the stroke of a pen. He simply nodded. Lucas glared at him, a warning to tread lightly in this conversation.

Rebecca wasn't finished. "The Confederate soldiers should be allowed to…I mean, most of them should…" She stammered, and her shoulders tensed.

Woody filled in the gaps. "Be allowed to return to their homes and farms, right?" She nodded. "Most of them…?"

She straightened in her seat. "The government officials and the army officers must pay a price for their disloyalty." She breathed in and exhaled deeply.

What kind of price?

"And what would you advise? Throw General Lee in a drafty federal prison? Feed him stale bread and rancid meat?"

The thought was abhorrent.

"No, Woody. I mean…that would be for our elected leaders to decide. But you must admit, General Lee's military actions brought a lot of pain and suffering to our people. He made a choice to wage war against the government that trained him. Should he not face the consequences?"

And what about Ulysses S. Grant? The Union general had committed atrocities against the Rebel armies and the Southern people caught in the middle. Soldiers on both sides had been butchered under his command. Maybe they should share a prison cell. Woody didn't want to argue, but his first instinct was to protect General Lee.

"Robert E. Lee tried to sue for peace," Woody said. "He prayed that God would—"

"Hey, you two. Stop…and look." They both shot a glance at Lucas, but he redirected their attention by pointing to their left. "Over there."

In the distance stood a brick chimney, naked, the dwelling

that once surrounded it, burned to the ground. Only cinders remained. The surrounding acres were charred, torched to prevent earth's bounty from being delivered. They slowed their horses and gazed at the burnt fields on both sides of the turnpike.

Field crops, farm implements, barns, and mills had been burned to the ground. Farther down the pike, evidence of warehouses, sheds, and bridges—all rendered useless. Some farmhouses sustained little or no damage. Indiscriminate destruction.

The group traveled for a time in silence, shocked by the scorched land, the deliberate desolation of a fertile and productive agricultural region.

Lucas spoke with a slight tremble in his voice. "I read about this in the papers." Union General Philip H. Sheridan and his army had destroyed this breadbasket several weeks earlier. It stretched from Winchester to Staunton, a swath of land seventy miles long and thirty wide.

As he viewed the devastation, Woody recalled the sweat and blood poured out by so many soldiers on both sides to own the Shenandoah Valley. Control of this ground had seesawed between General Lee's army and Union forces. In the end, the valiant efforts of the Stonewall Brigade and others to protect this land came to naught.

Woody stopped the rig near the ruins of another farmhouse and pointed his finger to all that remained—the frame of a doorway into someone's private life.

"Take a look, Rebecca. Man's inhumanity goes both ways in this godforsaken war."

Rebecca had no response.

They rode on in silence.

Thirty-Eight

Bushwhackers

Woody found the perfect place away from the old pike to bed down for the night. He and Lucas had traveled these parts with Jackson's brigade many times before. The paths and roadways intersecting the toll road were familiar to them. After a morning meal nestled in the trees and bushes, they set off again.

The journey proved uneventful until three shadowy figures appeared on the turnpike a few miles north of New Market, halfway between Winchester and Staunton. One man moaned and writhed on the ground. The second man stooped over him, and the third waved his hands to get Woody's attention.

Woody drove the rig with Rebecca at his side, while Lucas rode horseback. He cast a cautious eye, an inaudible signal for Lucas to stay focused. Lucas nodded, his hand over his holstered pistol. Stories abounded about bushwhackers, marauders who preyed on passersby for food, money, and weapons. Woody halted the buckboard.

"Rebecca, stay by my side," Woody said, softly taking her arm. "There are desperate men roaming this valley."

"Oh, thank God," one of the strangers said.

They were all dressed in civilian clothes, and Woody noted the two huddled over the man on the ground wore pistols. One wore a Confederate kepi. Three horses stood by the side of the pike, waiting.

"We was riding back to our little camp when Karl's horse got spooked by some critter. Threw him right down on this hard road. Mind you, I'm no sawbones, but I think his leg is broke. Been praying for someone to come along."

Before Woody could answer, Rebecca climbed down.

"Rebecca, don't…" But she was on the ground before he got his warning out.

She walked toward the injured man. "May I examine him? Perhaps I can help." The man nodded.

She knelt at his side and carefully ran her hands over the man's legs. Woody stood, hand on the gun at his side. This was a classic method used by bushwhackers to finagle an upper hand on their victims, and now she was an easy target.

"Please come back here," Woody said.

The first man drew his pistol and pointed it at Rebecca's head. Karl, the man who feigned injuries, rose and restrained her. Trapped, she struggled, so the man struck her on the side of the head.

She collapsed.

Woody jumped to the ground, his anger clouding his judgment. Pain surged up his leg from the impact.

The man whose pistol was pointed at Rebecca cocked the hammer and Woody froze.

"Back down, if you care about this fine lady's physical well-being," the man said. He trained his gun on Lucas. "You on the hoss. Better toss your pepperbox down to the ground before you decide to spray lead on one of us."

Lucas pulled out his pistol and tossed it to the ground far from the men. "We're veterans who are no longer in the battle, minding our own business," he said. "Let us pass and you can go your way."

"Oh, we'll be on our way soon enough." The apparent leader, the man who did all the talking, looked to one of his cohorts. "Silas, kindly retrieve the gentleman's shooter." He turned back to Lucas. "You ought not to have tossed it like that. Tricks like that could get you killed."

Silas fetched the pistol while the leader now kept his barrel trained on Woody. With the odds still stacked against them, Woody decided that Lucas's attempt to separate the men would not give them enough time to take action. One or both of them were likely to get shot. He would have to find another way to gain the upper hand. Silas stopped and disarmed Woody, then brought both guns to his boss.

The apparent leader, a bit unsteady on his feet, checked both directions on the turnpike to make sure no travelers approached. Satisfied, he turned his attention back to the unfolding drama. "Now you on the horse, kindly step down and join your friend here." Lucas complied. "Both of you can take a slow walk over to the left side of the road."

Woody saw no option but to comply. His quick nod signaled for Lucas to do the same. The outlaw's lack of hygiene and grooming told Woody they were desperate and unlikely to strike bargains.

"Please take me instead of the lady," Woody said.

"Special to you?"

"She is." Woody breathed a sigh, hoping the man would take it as a sign of weakness that he could use to his advantage.

"Might let her go in due course," the leader said, now swaying like the treetops caught in a mild Virginia breeze. "We're not deadbeats. Just patriots who've fallen on tough times."

Drunken lout. Woody crawled out on a limb.

"I'm guessing you boys are in Jeff Davis's army." He glanced at the man wearing the kepi. "So are we…or we were," he said, with an easy smile. He showed the men his bad leg in hopes of gaining some sympathy. "Stonewall Brigade. Let's part as brothers, united in our great struggle."

A big grin crossed the ringleader's face, followed by a scowl. He came close to Woody, his gun aimed right at his groin. The odors from his body and mouth would have made a buffalo bilious. In his drunken stupor, the stranger might pull the trigger. By accident or intentionally, the result would be the same. Woody decided not to push his luck.

The outlaw was not moved by proclamations of Confederate brotherhood. "So you assume because we're in Lee's army, we're all comrades in arms."

"Something like that," Lucas said with a steely edge.

Easy, Luke.

"Well, Johnny Reb, you're right. We are butternuts, like you," the outlaw said. "Except President Jeff Davis is doing a mighty poor job of caring for us, so we're taking matters into our own hands."

Woody searched again for an opening that would allow him and Lucas to take the fight to their captors before they ran off with Rebecca to God knows where. The foul commander barked new orders for Silas, his henchman, to search them one at a time. "Karl, don't just stand there," the leader said. "Help your brother." Silas found a wad of greenbacks and turned them over to the boss. Silas and Karl didn't speak much. The leader grinned, this time wider, revealing a partial set of yellow, crooked teeth.

"Now this here's a heap'a the good currency," the leader said. "As fellow Rebs, I know you'll understand my need to relieve you of these resources. I'd leave this nice rig with you so's you can get on back home, but I can't trust y'all won't follow us, now can I?"

He ordered Silas to tie Rebecca's hands and help her back onto the buckboard. After securing her in the passenger seat, Silas sat beside her and took the reins. The other henchman, the man he called Karl, tied Lucas's horse to the back, where Woody's mount had followed since they began their journey. Karl gripped the reins to Silas's horse and mounted his own ride.

Woody watched it all happen, helpless to do anything to stop it.

"Your generosity is most kind," the leader said. "A lovely lady to keep us company, a nice buckboard, and a pack of fine horses. The thoughtful cash donation will keep us liquored and fed a while longer. Thank you, my brothers-in-arms."

The reference dripped with derision.

He ordered Woody and Lucas to lay face down on the road, hands behind their heads. As a courtesy, one Confederate to another, he did not bind them. But if they rose before the wagon traveled beyond the horizon, the leader promised to shoot the woman. Ruthless men like these did not make idle threats.

The bandit bid them farewell with an air of false courtesy.

"A fine day to you, gentlemen."

The bushwhackers made their way south.

Woody and Lucas hugged the pike as ordered. "There will be no dickerin' with the likes of them," Lucas said. "Some killing's required here. Are you prepared?"

Woody had prayed for guidance. "There's a time for war and a time for peace. This is a time to fight. Rebecca's now the object of our mission, and I mean to get her back. The fault of any killing will rest on their souls."

The thieves were out of sight, so Lucas rose and put his good arm down to help Woody up.

Woody brushed the debris from his clothes. "We've got to move fast, and you're quicker on your two feet than me."

"What're you thinking?"

"Our only chance to catch up with them is to find a couple of horses, even if we have to steal 'em."

Lucas agreed, but the challenge before them was clear. Union forces had stripped the Shenandoah of its bounty weeks before, slaughtering livestock where they stood or carting off animals as spoils of war. Mounts would be hard to find, and every minute that ticked by lessened the chances of Rebecca's survival.

"The spread about a mile or two back—the one that seemed to survive this mess," Woody said. "That's our best hope."

"Been thinking the same thing. I'll hightail it back there and see what I can find."

"Hurry, Luke. Run like the wind."

Thirty-Nine

Against All Odds

The men spoke about Rebecca as if she wasn't even there on the buckboard.

"Hey, Jesse. I knew we was gonna take the horses, but what we gonna do with her?" Silas asked.

Finally, she had a name for the ringleader. Jesse. That might prove useful in whatever events were about to transpire. "If you don't know, boy, then you got bigger problems than I thought."

"That ain't what I mean," Silas said. "They might let them horses go, but they're gonna come after a woman. You saw how that one was sweet on her. I don't mean to be shot over a lover's mission."

"What're they gonna use to shoot ya with?" Jesse asked, as he kicked his horse and rode out ahead of the wagon.

Rebecca calculated they'd traveled another five or six miles before they turned off the Valley Turnpike and headed east on a narrow path through a thickly wooded area to a clearing with a small encampment.

The kidnappers had erected four large tents for cover. Canvas tarps had been laid over wooden frames kept in place by stakes in the ground. Two supply tents were open and stocked with plenty of blankets and chopped firewood to last them through the winter. From the look of things, they'd been in this location for some time. No one would think to look for them so far from the road.

As they helped her down from the buckboard, she took a mental note of the axes, shovels, lanterns, and other tools that would be handy in a seasonal camp. A cache of firearms in one tent off to the side caught her attention. The weapons might prove useful. Thanks to George, Rebecca was an excellent shooter, and she'd do whatever she thought necessary to survive.

Jesse gripped her arm and pulled her into a closed tent. His tent, she presumed. She sat on the ground, alone and scared. Even if Woody and Lucas found a way to pursue her and found weapons to help her get out, how would they find this place?

Her captors engaged in a conversation outside the tent. "Go down to the stream and bring up some water for the horses," Jesse said. "Take that half-wit brother with you. Karl's got four more horses that need tending now."

"Don't call my brother a half-wit," Silas said.

"Or what?" The question went unanswered as the two men stormed off.

Drunk and becoming more intoxicated by the minute, the ringleader entered her tent with a half-empty bottle of whiskey. He knelt beside her, his eyes fixed on her face. She turned her head to avoid his stare, but he grabbed her chin and turned it back in his direction. He pulled at her bun until her hair fell to her shoulders. Like a dog, he sniffed her neckline, his nose brushing against her skin.

His hands were scabbed, and he stunk like a putrid swamp. Still bound at the wrists, she attempted to block his touch. "You're a pitiful drunk, and a skunk's spray smells better than you."

"Ain't you the feisty one?"

He stood and slowly circled her, taunting her with his silence and occasional belches. Seconds slipped away like a bank of fast-moving clouds—time that would either lead her into an awful encounter with this disgusting man, or result in such drunkenness that he would simply pass out. He moved in front of her, scratching his hand, trying to remove some annoyance with his fingernails. Ticks, maybe. The opened scabs released red splotches that collected around the yellowish wounds. Her abhorrence mounted.

She turned away and fought the urge to retch.

"Damned bloodsuckers," he said.

He swallowed another mouthful of cheap whiskey, the residuals dribbling down his chin.

"Join me?" He held out the bottle. "Some of this here creature comfort makes for good times. Put some whiskey down your gullet, and you might even enjoy what's coming."

She ignored him. When he stepped toward her, she spat in his direction, but the spittle fell short of its target. He sniggered in reply and walked to the opening of the tent to yell for Silas before turning back to face her.

"We're gonna get real close, you and me."

His grin turned to shock.

What in the world?

"Okay, back out and do it slowly."

Woody? That was his voice. Her heart leapt at the sound.

Woody's tone sounded harder than she'd ever heard. "I'd love to gut you like a Tennessee trout. Don't give me any more of a reason."

Her joy was interrupted by the sound of a gunshot from outside the tent.

The ringleader pulled his firearm and turned, aiming point-blank at Woody. Rebecca rose and stepped toward them.

Woody sank an oversized knife deep into the man's stomach. Stunned, the ringleader's eyes fixed on Woody with a confused stare. He fired a round into the ground, and then the gun fell uselessly from his hand. The two men stood locked in a death embrace.

Woody pulled the blade free.

The man released a deep groan and sank to his knees. Then he fell face forward to the ground, dead on arrival. Outside, a gun battle had ensued after the first shot.

Woody rushed to Rebecca, who wrapped her bound wrists over his head and clung to him. Tears welled up in her eyes. "I'm so sorry," she said. "This is my fault."

"Ssh. You didn't cause this. These men did, and now we're going to finish it." He freed himself from her embrace and wiped the bloody knife against the outlaw's blanket. Then he severed the ropes binding her and placed one hand on her shoulder. "Promise you will stay here and keep low until this is over. Until I come to get you."

She nodded. Woody joined the gun battle.

The idea of remaining in this tent alone while Woody and Lucas might meet their end in a blaze of glory terrified her. The fight raged on from opposite ends of the camp. Unable to track all the action, Rebecca could no longer sit idly by. She crept out of the tent and over to the storehouse of arms. Without being noticed, she slipped in and examined the range of weapons.

She grabbed a Colt six-shooter, made sure its chambers were full, and crept out of the tent and behind some trees. She circled and pressed ahead until she was ten yards behind the two brothers. She'd nearly gotten to where she could shoot one when she tripped on a branch and fell forward.

Silas stood and turned around as Rebecca rose to her knees. He got off one shot. At almost the same instant, Rebecca fired a round that struck Silas between the eyes.

Karl stood to finish Rebecca, but a volley of bullets cut him down.

It was over. Thank God. She started to stand, but a sharp pain in her shoulder shocked her, and she dropped to her knees.

Woody ran to her. "Oh, God, you're hit." He pulled her into his arms as he shouted, "Luke, she's shot. Bring me something to stop the bleeding." Lucas ducked into a tent and brought one of the outlaw's shirts. He tore it in half and handed it to Woody, who examined the wound. "Looks like a graze below your left shoulder."

Woody tied the material around the wound, then scooped her into his arms and showered kisses on her mouth and face.

"You crazy...I thought I'd lost you again."

"Gonna take a lot more fight to take this scrapper down," Lucas said. "Mighty good shooting, ma'am."

"Guess I learned to hold my own along the way." The crimson stain on the bandage sent an urgent message to her brain. She clenched her jaw.

"This hurts."

* * *

They examined the provisions in the camp. Rebecca found the money stolen from them and discovered a larger bundle the highway robbers had taken from other victims.

"There's a farmer and his family near here who can use some cash," Lucas said.

"What farmer?" She had so many questions. "How did you get to me so quickly? When we left, both of you were stranded face down on the pike."

Woody explained how Lucas ran almost two miles back to a farmhouse they'd passed before their encounter with the bushwhackers. He pleaded with the kind family for help, for horses and firearms to hunt down the attackers.

"I told them we're Virginia farm boys, and these vermin fed off innocents in the valley," Lucas said. "Turns out, they been working these parts for a while. The farmers considered it a gift if we'd rid them of this pestilence. They made me promise, my hand on the Bible, that I would restore their property. In return, they loaned me two faithful nags and these guns."

As an afterthought, they'd thrown in one family heirloom, a bowie knife handed down by the farmer's daddy.

Woody and Lucas loaded the corpses over three of the horses. They walked the dead men deep into the woods until they stumbled upon an ideal spot. The graves would be hidden. They dug three holes using the bushwhackers' own shovels, laid their bodies in the ground, and refilled the pits.

They decided not to report the incident. They didn't have time for delays, and rescuing Israel and his son was more important than these three devils.

"I suppose it would be fitting to say something, even though vermin is too kind of a word to describe these characters," Lucas said. "They had mamas somewhere."

Woody lowered his head and prayed. "Lord, judgment is left to you. In regards to these men, your will be done in the end. For our sins this day, we pray for your forgiveness and continued mercies. Amen."

On the walk back to camp, Rebecca asked, "How'd you find us here, in the middle of nowhere?"

Woody called it a miracle. He explained how after several miles, he and Lucas had come across a lone traveler headed in the opposite direction. When Woody asked the driver if he'd seen a vehicle fitting their description, the man said yes and went on about how his neighborliness was met with grunts and an unkind comment. Silent cries for help leapt from the woman's eyes, the man had said, and he feared she was being held against her will.

"Do you recall passing him, Rebecca?" Woody asked.

"He was my one shred of hope."

"The man happened to look behind him just as the bandits turned off the pike and headed into the woods. Without that information, we never would have found you."

* * *

As they re-entered the camp, Woody took stock of the delay in their journey.

"We'll bed down in these tents for tonight, but with our own blankets," he said. "Tomorrow morn, we'll make good on our promise to the farmer. The extra cash and horses, and all these camp provisions, should go a long way toward repaying the man's kindness."

He paused for a moment, deep in his own calculations. They had been put through the mill and lost one precious day. "Come tomorrow, we'll make up time by driving ahead faster."

A wet and cold mountain pass stood between them and Richmond, threatening to derail the rescue. He was determined to slip over and back before bad weather could lock them into a standstill.

Forty

Richmond

They rode hard the next day and decided they would enjoy the comfort of a warm bath and a bed in Staunton, the last town on the Valley Turnpike before they turned east on the old Three Notch'd Road.

Woody led them to the American Hotel, where he'd stayed on previous visits to the city. Union forces several months before had ransacked the town. One of the finest spots between Cincinnati and Richmond, the American Hotel survived because it had served as an officers quarters. The blackened ruins of the train station across from the hotel left a stark reminder that for a time, the Feds had controlled the city. They had withdrawn and taken the torch to many structures, after which the Confederates reasserted control.

As Woody soaked in a soothing bath, he calculated the remainder of their journey. Tomorrow, the twelfth, they'd make their way to Charlottesville, assuming they didn't run into any problems. From there, it was another two days to Richmond, if the trip remained trouble-free along the way. They were forty-eight hours behind schedule, and the Blue Ridge Mountain pass, Rockfish Gap, still loomed ahead. Progress depended on clear skies, and little or no mud.

As he scrubbed his body clean, he imagined how much Rebecca was enjoying her bath. His visions drifted further. He pictured her in the water, and then stopped himself cold. Someday, he and Rebecca would be intimate, as husband and wife. For now, despite his need, he would control his wandering thoughts of her.

* * *

Woody watched Rebecca dip her head and huddle beside him. The frigid air flowing through the Blue Ridge pass slammed them.

He and the biting cold shared their own history. The hard slogs over the mountains with Stonewall's boys, pitted against the ice and mud that swallowed their feet. Trudging through the bitter winds and snows that whipped through Northern Ohio with a vengeance last winter, praying for the comfort of a deep sleep that would have killed him. He shivered the memory from his mind.

He leaned closer and wrapped his arm around her. "I'm sorry it's so cold. You all right?"

She smiled up at him. "A little chill won't kill me."

The woman was a marvel.

The first night into the mountains, the temperature dipped to the point of freezing their drinking water. They set up a tent and gathered as much firewood as they could without wandering far from the small camp. The heat warmed them in the early evening hours and cooked the squirrels Woody and Lucas had shot for dinner. After their meal, they huddled together under multiple blankets inside the tent.

Two days later they rolled through the Virginia Piedmont, an open region of farms, villages, and towns that lay between the Shenandoah Valley and the Washington-Fredericksburg-Richmond axis. The weather had warmed considerably.

They approached the outskirts of Richmond, where a Confederate Cavalry patrol, forty or so soldiers still in their saddles, approached them. "Manure spreaders," Lucas said. "Four buggers on the ground, two officers."

The soldiers on the ground walked toward the buckboard,

one of them lifting his hand. Woody halted the rig. "Greetings Lieutenant. Your men are a sight for sore eyes. What's the condition of our capitol city?"

"To whom am I speaking, sir?" the officer said. "State your business in Richmond."

"I am Jonathan Woodard, a proud soldier of the Stonewall Brigade. My service was cut short when I escaped from Johnson's Island prison. Lost a foot in the process. My friend here is Lucas Halverston. He left active service after a cannonball shattered his arm at Gettysburg."

The officer removed his hat. "I am First Lieutenant William O'Reilly, serving under General Custis Lee in the First Battalion Virginia Cavalry, Local Defense. Pleasure to make your acquaintances. You boys of the Stonewall Brigade served the Confederacy with gallantry and grit. You have my admiration and great respect."

"Thank you, sir." The officer glanced at Rebecca and bowed. "My apologies, Lieutenant. Allow me to introduce my wife, Mrs. Rebecca Woodard."

Rebecca raised an eyebrow and gave the soldier a genteel smile.

"Madam." O'Reilly turned his attention back to Woody. "These are dangerous times. What brings you to Richmond?"

Woody told him that they represented Kentucky plantation owner Franklin Wills on a potential slave-trading matter. He reached into his jacket pocket, but the move alarmed the three men who accompanied the lieutenant. One of them drew his pistol. Woody pulled his hand back, and this time asked permission. "May I?" Seeing a nod from the lieutenant, Woody withdrew the record they'd taken from Wills and handed it to the officer.

He unfolded the paper and quickly reviewed the details. "A bill of sale for two slaves to a Mr. Robert Lumpkin. This transaction happened six months ago. Your business now?"

The revelation shocked Woody. He had failed to examine the date on the paperwork. Wills kept Israel and little Parker on his plantation for six months after he'd abducted them.

"A follow-up visit," Woody said to the officer. "We'd like to interest Mr. Lumpkin in another sale. Mr. Wills continues to transition his main crop away from tobacco. He has no need for the same number of slaves."

"I understand." He handed the paper back to Woody.

Lieutenant O'Reilly outlined the military situation around Richmond. General Lee and his Army of Northern Virginia had formed a wedge-shaped position north and east of the capital, and extending south across the James and Appomattox rivers. They'd held Grant at bay, with additional fortified emplacements running east and southwest of Petersburg.

"The Yanks are entrenched behind, hugging close to Lee's formation," the officer said. "Lee is locked in place, but his position is far too strong for Grant to move. They are pressed cheek to jowl south of the James River."

"A stalemate," Woody said.

"Right."

"Is Richmond safe to visit?"

"I can assure you Richmond is protected from Union attack." He explained that inside the city, the population had swollen to over a hundred thousand. The locals were threatened with petty larceny and assault, mostly from juvenile gangs. "Keep your eyes open, and don't loiter late at night."

"Good to know, Lieutenant. How are things during the day?"

Woody played the role of a sympathizer down to a tittle, while Lucas sat tall in his saddle with folded arms. These lies could be excused. The existence of a man and his boy depended on a daring rescue.

"You will find the streets filled with normal city life during the day," the lieutenant said. "People like you still going about their business. Did you secure a place to stay? Most hotels are full."

"Yes, we did, and thank you for the fine job you and your men are doing to keep Richmond open to loyal Southerners."

Woody bade the officer goodbye. They entered the city on Brook Avenue and turned left onto Broad Street. They arrived late in the day on the fourteenth of November, but the street traffic bustled with horse-drawn buggies, buckboards, and street rail cars. The Richmond, Fredericksburg and Potomac Railroad tracks ran down the middle of Broad Street, a wider thoroughfare built to accommodate a variety of dry goods stores and retail shops. Pedestrians filled the streets, seemingly unconcerned about the close proximity of the enemy, or perhaps overconfident in the ability of the Confederate soldiers to keep the opposing army deadlocked.

They reached the intersection at Seventh and Broad, where the railroad tracks ended. The New Richmond Theater, which replaced the one that had burned down two years before, sat on the corner.

Woody stopped the rig and stared at the building, an amazing structure compared to the old theatre. In better times, he had enjoyed a performance by Peter Ritchings as George Washington. In the middle of the performance, the stage manager stepped onto the stage to announce the result of the 1860 presidential election. Abraham Lincoln would preside over a national government that stood on thin ice. That was the last time Woody had visited Richmond.

He turned right on Seventh Street. A look of curiosity bounded from Rebecca's face. "Woody, back there, when the officer mentioned Custis Lee. That's—"

"The eldest son of Robert E. Lee. Also related to George Washington."

Lucas inquired about having booked accommodations in the city, a question Woody didn't answer. They would understand soon enough. After turning on Capitol Street, Woody stopped in front of the square, the lifeblood of the Confederacy, where President Jeff Davis had plotted the South's strategy for war.

People strode in and out of the capitol building. They dressed in fine suits, and many wore stovepipe hats. Most of them sported beards or mustaches. Generals and lower-level officers, resplendent in their best military dress, also made their way around Capitol Square.

They traveled east on Main, turned left onto Twenty-Fifth. Much of Richmond appeared shabby, uncharacteristic of the way this grand city had been. Roofs and fences needed repair, and many middle- and upper-class homes desperately cried out for a new coat of paint.

Woody led them onto Leigh and rode down the block past the Leigh Street Baptist Church where he occasionally attended services in years past.

He pulled up to an elegant two-story Greek revival mansion on a huge lot with outhouses and stables. Rebecca asked, "Who lives here?"

"Just wait. You're about to find out."

He led them up to the front door and knocked. The door opened and revealed a stately gentleman in his middle years wearing a ruffled dress shirt and trousers with stripes running down the outside seam. His sideburns ran thick and long, and he sported a bushy goatee that covered his chin. Smoke from his pipe wiggled upward, casting a mild and pleasant aroma.

"Hello, Uncle Reginald," Woody said. "Surprise. Please meet my friends."

Reginald Woodard led the group into his exquisite home, Woodard Manor. Astounded, Lucas entered the foyer and murmured, "Knew you had kin down this way. Didn't realize he's sound on the goose."

Woody whispered back. "He's wealthy in more ways than one."

* * *

Rebecca had never been inside a home so grand. She entertained a horrible thought. Had Woody's uncle built his wealth on the backs of slaves like Franklin Wills?

Woody's uncle instructed his servants to care for the wagon and horses and after introductions, showed the trio to their rooms. They would gather in the dining room in two hours after everyone had rested and freshened up.

The bedroom that Reginald had offered her showed a woman's touch, impeccably decorated with fine fabrics on the window and bed, ornate wallpaper with a floral pattern that looked like it belonged in a governor's mansion. She looked forward to meeting Reginald's wife.

Rebecca was the first to come downstairs for dinner, self-conscious that she'd be underdressed for dinner. She wandered into the parlor, where she stared for some time at the picture in a simple gold frame, displayed on the grand piano. A much younger Reginald sat beside a beautiful woman with high cheekbones, haunting eyes, and a thick head of hair.

Reginald walked up behind her. "My wife, Miranda, and me. Taken soon after we married."

"I'm anxious to meet her. Will she be down soon?" Rebecca remembered her manners. "How inappropriate of me."

"Not at all." Reginald smiled kindly. "This is my favorite likeness of her. Miranda died three years ago of pneumonia. We spent twenty-seven glorious years together. Raised three girls, all happily married. They live in West Virginia and Washington, and their husbands are all serving in the Union army. I'm very proud of them."

"Has that been difficult for you? I mean…you live within the heart of the Confederacy."

"At times, yes." He'd been called everything from a Lincoln loyalist to a Tory by the local citizenry. He'd opposed secession, and rather than move when his sons joined the Union Army, he chose to stay in Richmond and remain neutral. "I'm still in good standing with most of Virginia's elected leaders. I've helped to build Richmond over the years."

He asked if she had wed.

"I am widowed. My husband died fighting for the Union. As a widow and a widower, we share a common experience, Mr. Woodard."

"I insist you call me Reginald." He offered her an arm and led her to the dining room, where Woody and Lucas joined them. After dinner, while they enjoyed coffee and dessert, they reflected on the state of affairs in Richmond.

"Uncle Reginald is one of the original investors in the Tredegar ironworks back in the '40s," Woody said. "He gained a tidy profit after selling his interest a few years later. Other business endeavors since those days have also contributed to his success, right Uncle?"

Reginald nodded. He appeared preoccupied.

"Suffice to say," Woody continued, "the mills have shifted production during the war. My uncle can speak to this."

Reginald shared his disappointment about Tredegar. He'd worked to build an engine of construction, a force that would build up, not destroy.

"I abhor that it currently produces military ordnance,"

Reginald said. "Our glorious Richmond suffers under the distinction of being the seat of the Confederacy. This saddens me."

A servant refilled the coffee cups. Reginald sipped his beverage and removed a chocolate from the dessert plate as the French grandfather clock announced the eight o'clock hour. "Common household items from three years ago, like these chocolate treats or the coffee you are enjoying, are now unavailable. Or they are so highly priced due to inflation, most do without these days."

He had met that day with a consortium of officials and businessmen to seek solutions to these shortages, which went beyond food. The Union blockades also prevented much-needed medical supplies from reaching the Confederacy.

Earlier, Woody had mentioned their purpose in Richmond, a mission Reginald thought to be noble. He'd been disappointed that his brother, Woody's father, had sided with the South when the rebellion broke out, and that Woody had chosen to fight in Lee's army. But for the Woodards, family superseded political differences, and both sides decided they'd learn to live with the other's decisions.

Rebecca redirected the subject of their conversation, hoping to loosen whatever had been preoccupying Reginald.

"One area of interest to me is the slave trade," Rebecca said. "We understand Mr. Lumpkin and a few others are the last traders left."

"Perhaps you've been reading my troubled mind," Reginald said, casting her a knowing wink.

He shared about Lumpkin's operations in the slave trade. Lumpkin ran his business on a deplorable plot of land called Shockoe Bottom, a swampy cluster of tobacco warehouses three blocks from Capitol Square. The place had been aptly dubbed Devil's Half-Acre. Lumpkin worked hard to whitewash his heartless reputation, but Reginald and others had witnessed the direct testimony of Anthony Burns about the nefarious activities within the compound. The most famous inmate in Devil's Half-Acre, Burns had been released when abolitionists bought his freedom, and he provided lurid details about an operation most folks preferred to ignore.

Lumpkin lived in the upper story of the main house with his wife, Mary, a former slave who'd bore him five children. Mary was said to be a kind woman by most accounts. Sympathetic to the poor souls in the buildings below, where Lumpkin kept his stock of Negroes ready for sale.

"My final word to you is this—beware of Robert Lumpkin," Reginald said. "Expect an untrustworthy, hard-bargaining man."

"Duly noted, Uncle," Woody said. "I reckon we'll be getting a first-hand look at his operation in the morning."

Reginald seemed unsettled. Rebecca probed.

"Is there anything else you wanted to share, Reginald?"

He looked at her, then at the table, and heaved a long sigh. "The activities reportedly taking place in the building at the corner of the plot concern me most. A vile place of unspeakable cruelty, where man's inhumanity to man is practiced with great precision. A slave jail."

Rebecca trembled.

After dinner, Woody insisted that she remain at Woodard Manor while he and Lucas would pay a visit to Lumpkin's despicable place of business.

Despite her fear, she refused.

Forty-One

Devil's Half-Acre

Tuesday, Nov. 15

Woody drove Uncle Reginald's horse and two-seater carriage while Rebecca sat by his side and Lucas rode horseback.

A few autumn clouds partially bathed the coppery sun, and intermittent gusts rustled through the neighborhood. An increased chill rode on the back of the wind, slapping against his face. Winter approached, and Woody was mindful that it could take several days to find Israel and little Parker, assuming Robert Lumpkin agreed to point them in the right direction. Even if he did, stealing them from a plantation seemed an insurmountable task with the tight timeline.

Rain would come and obstruct Rockfish Gap and other passes. The longer they remained in the Deep South, the greater the chance of being swept up in the final dance between two armies.

Woody approached Lumpkin's compound from Franklin Street. He pulled onto the narrow, crooked lane that descended down to an old two-story brick house, surrounded by a high-standing fence. Trash, leaves, and dirt lay strewn about the road. A small whirlwind lifted some debris into a funnel that twirled like a ballerina and then scattered into the air.

Woody jumped down from the buggy. "Rebecca, I'd prefer that you wait here with Lucas. Let me handle Lumpkin."

"No chance, Mr. Woodard. Let's go." He wasn't surprised. Her bullheaded insistence frustrated him.

Resigned, he walked to her side and helped her down. He muttered, "Dad-blamed stubborn woman with an independent..."

She responded with a blank stare.

"Rebecca Johnston, you can be so dad-blasted…" Woody gave up and signaled for Lucas to join them.

Contact with Lumpkin, the bully trader, would distress her, and exposure to his inner sanctum would fire her indignation. This building served as the holding pen for his inventory, where Lumpkin would surely traipse Negroes before them, stripped down as merchandise for review. Success depended on keeping cool heads.

Rebecca knocked. A light-skinned Negro woman dressed in a black-and-white pinstriped skirt and blouse with a black velvet belt around her waist answered with a smile.

"Ma'am," Lucas said, with a slight bow.

"Good morning. Is Mr. Lumpkin available?" Woody asked.

"Whom shall I say is calling?"

"Tell your master that Jonathan Woodard is here, with his wife and business associate. We're calling on behalf of Kentucky plantation owner Franklin Wills."

"Wait here for a moment."

They stood on the porch, quiet, each adrift in their thoughts. Woody feared that Israel and little Parker were lost to them. If Lumpkin proved unwilling to offer useful information about where they might be, should he and Lucas gain it by force, like they did with Franklin Wills? In a large metropolitan city, the authorities would certainly respond to Lumpkin's demands for justice. Woody became impatient.

"What's taking that servant?" Woody said.

He looked over at Lucas who shrugged his shoulders.

Upon returning, the woman welcomed them in. "Mr. Lumpkin's calendar is busy with previously scheduled appointments, but he bids you to join him for an introductory meeting. Follow me."

She led them to a large open court, where a casually dressed, overweight man sat with his chair tilted back and a cool drink in his hand. Late fifties, Woody guessed. Lumpkin stood to welcome his guests.

"This is Mary, my wife," Lumpkin said. "Please," he motioned to the chairs around the table, "have a seat."

The woman who let them in was not a servant. The assumption embarrassed Woody.

"Which of you is Mr. Woodard?"

Woody stepped forward, his hand outstretched. "Jonathan Woodard. With me are Rebecca Woodard, my wife, and my associate, Lucas Halverston."

Lucas shook hands with the renowned trader. Rebecca curtsied.

"A pleasure," Lucas said. "We're hoping we can do business on behalf of Mr. Franklin Wills of Northern Kentucky."

The slave trader thought for moment. "Can't say as I recognize the name."

"Very understandable, given the size of what must be an impressive client list," Lucas said.

They all took a chair. The rotund man was sweating profusely. Wet rings circled his underarms, and droplets fell from the fatty flesh below his chin to his shirt collar. Jovial in manner, Lumpkin appeared perfectly comfortable with his untidy appearance.

"Please tell him I appreciate his business and am pleased he chooses to do business with my establishment once again," the slave trader said.

He beckoned Mary to bring his guests some iced tea. Woody examined the grounds from his vantage point, noting the other buildings that were separated by a brick retaining wall. One structure on the easternmost corner, next to a creek adjacent to the compound, caught his eye.

"This is quite an operation you've developed here, Mr. Lumpkin."

"Thank you, Jonathan. May I address you by your first name? Please, my friends call me Robert. Actually, all of these parcels existed here when I bought the land in the forties."

He explained how he turned the unused buildings into a profitable enterprise and that his trading services benefited the strong agricultural sector in the South. As he elaborated, bemoaning the gradual decline in their way of life and the once vibrant trade, Mary returned and served each of them a glass of tea.

"Thank you, my dear. Now you can leave us to our business."

"Mrs. Lumpkin, you are most kind," Woody said.

After she left, Lumpkin said, "Now, my friends, how can we do business today?"

Woody shared the business proposition. He handed the bill of sale to the slave trader and explained that Mr. Wills had a third slave related to the two Lumpkin had already purchased. If he was agreeable, Mr. Lumpkin might purchase the third slave at the much-reduced price they were offering, and also reunite the family.

"These days, with the noose tightening around Richmond, and the trade a trickle of what it once was, I'm afraid I've become somewhat lax in these matters." Lumpkin examined the bill of sale involving Franklin Wills, scratched his head, and confessed the transaction had faded from his memory. "Yes…I see here that one of the slaves is a child. Curious…I don't recall showing a child to any recent buyers. You say the third slave in question is a relative."

Woody nodded. "The mother of the little boy."

Lumpkin promised to consult his accountant, who kept strict records of all transactions to determine the name of the buyer on his end, if there was one. In the meantime, he insisted on showing them some of his prime stock. "We may be able to do some separate business before you leave," Lumpkin said.

This was the invitation Woody had expected and had hoped to spare Rebecca from.

"Actually, we—"

"Come, I insist."

Woody had to think fast. At that moment Mary came back to the courtyard to offer her guests more tea.

"Rebecca, now would be a perfect time for you to ask all your questions about Richmond society," Woody said. "Perhaps

Mary might entertain you while we conduct some additional business."

Rebecca tried to conceal her displeasure, but Woody saw through the mask.

"Please, Mrs. Woodard, come this way and I'll take you on a tour of our living quarters," Mary said.

Lumpkin led Woody and Lucas deeper into the property, pointing to the kitchen building and the boarding house that accommodated his clients, the white slave traders and the Negroes who served them. He offered rooms for the night, but Woody declined. He played the role, but his disgust for Lumpkin's operation increased with each step. Lumpkin led them to another brick building that housed his showpieces—the Negro men, women, and children who had been primped and readied for sale. The overseer unshackled three of his fittest young men and one female whom Woody estimated to be around sixteen years old.

On some plantation, this young girl had slipped from her mother's grasp. Carted off in some trade, the child would likely never be reunited with her mama again. He steeled himself from an overwhelming wave of sadness for the girl. The overseer suffered no such emotion, as he lined the Negroes up and ordered them to strip naked and stand tall.

The males removed the older suits they wore to impress potential buyers. None of them spoke. The female hesitated, so the cruel foreman struck her calf with the handle of his whip. She buckled.

The girl slipped off her dress. Lumpkin stood before them, highlighting their positive features—full sets of teeth, muscular physiques, and clean hair. They had washed and greased the faces of the males so they would shine. The heartless overseer poked at the female's breasts and private parts. With a wicked grin, he pointed out the side benefits of ownership. "Wide hips, very suitable for childbearing."

Woody forced himself to speak up. "Yes. Excellent stock."

The words left him empty, but he had to say something to stop the overseer's violations. The monster relished his work. Lumpkin promised the human stock was healthy and would make good workers in the fields. The woman could be used for multiple purposes. He smiled to punctuate his meaning.

Woody pointed outward to beyond the field. "The brick building off in the back, near the creek. How is that structure used?"

"Some of our more difficult individuals are housed there. That part of the operation I leave to my overseer." Lumpkin started to walk back to the courtyard. "Come by tomorrow at around eleven. I should have the paperwork I need to discuss Mr. Wills's request. Perhaps we can do some additional business as well."

"A delight." Lucas shook hands with Lumpkin and shot a look at Woody, who followed suit with a handshake.

"The pleasure has been all mine," Lumpkin said. "So, until tomorrow, a pleasant day to you all."

Mary and Rebecca joined them at the front door. Mary slipped a small folded piece of paper into Woody's palm as she shook hands and bid them goodbye. Before he boarded the buggy, Woody opened the slip of paper.

"Oh, my God. This is from Mary." He showed them the note. "You both need to hear this."

He read, "Mrs. Woodard's appeal for the child has moved me to act. I don't believe you are slave traders. Come back at midnight, but enter from the rear side of the property, where I will meet you by the gate."

He caught Rebecca's sly grin as the buggy lurched forward.

* * *

Rebecca was certain. Israel and little Parker were in Richmond, right under their noses. She'd appealed to Mary Lumpkin's sense of Christian charity for the sake of the child. The risks were enormous, but she took the gamble of opening up to Mary, and now it appeared they might find Israel and Parker.

Woody, Lucas, and Rebecca stocked the wagon with food and other items and hitched two fresh horses. If her hunch bore fruit, they would be making a hasty escape under the cloak of darkness. Late that night, they said goodbye to Uncle Reginald and set out for Devil's Half-Acre again. The wagon and Lucas's mount moved slowly in hopes of not alerting anyone on the street of their presence.

Woody reminded Rebecca that he'd stowed a loaded gun under the seat in case they ran into any resistance. Suddenly, danger greeted them in the pitch-black night.

A group of hoodlums blocked the road. The horses stopped. Woody made no attempts to evade the trouble waiting to be unleashed. He and Lucas sized up the circumstances without speaking, as she had seen them do on the Shenandoah Valley Pike.

The pack surrounded the wagon. As a dozen of them moved toward the rig, Lucas stood. "Back off if you'd like to make it home in one piece tonight."

A boy of no more than fifteen spooked Lucas's ride. The move caught Lucas off-guard, and the horse bucked and threw him to the street. Woody glanced at Rebecca, who told him, "Go help Luke." The delinquent grabbed the reins of Lucas's horse, while Woody jumped from the wagon to aid his friend. Bruised and bloodied, Lucas clutched Woody's hand and stood.

"You okay?" Woody asked.

"Yeah. Just a wounded ego to go along with these scratches."

"See here, boys," the young man said to his companions. "Appears I got me a new horse. A mighty fine one at that."

Rebecca reached under her seat for the loaded pistol. The gang of twelve surrounded Woody and Lucas, taunting them as broken down invalids and circling as they prepared to assault.

Rebecca burned inside. She'd seen enough injustice on this trip. It was time to even the odds. She raised the gun and cocked the hammer. The noise stopped the mob in its tracks.

She aimed at the leader. "I will shoot you where you stand, so help me God."

The gang backed off a few steps. He looked around at his cohort to make sure they still backed him. "There's six lead pills in that there pistol. Twelve of us. Besides, I don't think you have the guts to fire."

"Maybe," Rebecca said. "But if you're wrong, the first bullet goes into your brain, and my friends here will tell you. I'm a damn good shot."

The leader pulled a knife and lunged at Woody.

Woody knocked the attacker's knife-wielding arm high and hammered a blow to the face. Rebecca grimaced at the crackling of bones. The punch had broken the young man's nose, disabling him. He dropped to the ground, moaning, his hand on his face and his head tilted back, trying in vain to stop the stream of blood.

The gang's mood for mischief waned. A gang member checked on the disabled leader who waved him off. Another raised his hands. One ran from the scene and another two followed him. The rest backed up and moved to the side of the road without another word. Lucas remounted his horse and plowed into the middle of the group to further disperse them, as Woody climbed back onto the wagon. He winked at her, and she winked back.

"Better move fast," she said. "We're going to be late."

Mary would not wait all night.

Forty-Two

Lumpkin's Slave Jail

Woody parked the buckboard at the Broad Street entrance to Lumpkin's Alley. One of them had to stay with the rig, and he couldn't leave Rebecca on the streets of Richmond at midnight, by herself.

They needed to move or risk missing Mary at the rear entrance to the property. "Luke, if we don't come back in forty-five minutes…"

"I'll come a-lookin'."

They walked up Lumpkin's Alley, the way before them lighted by a small lantern that Rebecca carried. Unlike the gradual downward slope from the Franklin Street entrance, this direction led them up a steep mound. Woody's prosthetic slowed him down, and the climb challenged his stamina. His leg ached from the vigorous exercise, but he clenched his teeth and trudged through the pain. When they reached the property, they circled around to the back, as Mary had instructed.

Woody shivered in the night air, but the chill that racked his muscles must have paled compared with the frigid conditions Lumpkin's slaves experienced.

He and Rebecca found Mary in front of the gate that led into the compound, a lantern in one hand and a set of keys in the other. She unlocked the gate.

"Sorry we're late," Rebecca said. "Some ruffians on the street—"

"This is common in Richmond these days," Mary said. "I am glad Robert sent our girls to boarding schools, away from all this."

The night clouds cast a black veil over Devil's Half-Acre. A howling dog interrupted the quiet. Woody heard the muffled sounds of rodents or large insects that crept and crawled, probably infected by the cocktail of disease that flowed in the creek waters nearby. He'd backed up a few steps to allow Rebecca through the entry when a screech sent his stomach to his throat.

A cat scuttled past him.

"Lots of strays these days," Mary said. "Come quickly."

She led them onto the property. The mysterious structure that had caught Woody's attention earlier stood before them.

Mary used a different key to unlock the door to the old brick building. A wave of noxious odors swept over them. Woody and Rebecca covered their noses and retreated back into the fresh air. He wavered between hope that Israel and Parker were incarcerated here and a prayer that they'd never experienced the conditions in this slave jail.

"I pitied them when they came," Mary said. "The boy—so small, so innocent. The father so desperate that his son remain by his side."

With a face of anguish, Mary recounted what happened that day. The father was uncooperative from the start, so the overseer placed him in the slave jail. The boy was taken to the holding cells under the main house where the slaves were readied for sale. Mary had tried but could not comfort the child, so she conceived of a plan to keep the father and son together. She paused her story.

After deep breathes of fresh air, they stepped inside. It took a moment for their eyes to adjust to the darkness. Woody knew when Rebecca's had because she gasped, "Sweet Jesus, how can anyone be so cruel?"

Rebecca's eyes filled with tears, as she grabbed Woody's arm.

He slipped it around her back, and they followed as Mary passed a dark and terrifying space.

"The whipping room," Mary said.

One Negro, fettered by iron, lay stretched out on the cold floor. He'd been flogged, and all the flesh on his back was raw like a cut of meat. The shackled man attempted to speak, but in his weakened state could only make a muted appeal.

As Woody expected, Rebecca moved toward the man to offer assistance or a kind word, but he held her back. Mary promised to fetch some fresh water for the poor soul once they left the compound.

Rebecca appealed to Mary. "Can you not release him?"

"The overseer will notice when he comes in a few hours. Best to leave things as they are. This will give you a better chance of escaping Richmond. Trust me."

Her voiced cracked.

Rebecca held her lantern up. The silent tears in Mary's eyes revealed a desperate need to be forgiven for the cruel actions undertaken in this den of sickness. "This way."

Mary continued with her story. Weeks before Israel and the boy arrived, she'd discovered that the overseer had been stealing from her husband. When she confronted him, he begged her not to tell Lumpkin and said he would owe her the favor. So at her behest, he brought the boy to his father in the slave jail and promised not to speak about the arrangement to his boss.

Israel was flogged many times over the course of several months, but he still refused to cooperate. He would not become a beast of burden again, not for Robert Lumpkin or anyone else. Mary could do little to help him, but she did watch over the boy.

They stepped through the prison. Other rooms, each with sturdy iron bars covering a small window, housed many prisoners. They lay crammed inside, almost on top of each other, bound in chains. Mary stopped in front of one of the cells.

"How can you stand by and watch this?" Rebecca asked.

"I am a Christian woman. I do not sanction my husband's actions." She unlocked the door, and they held lanterns out to light a narrow and unventilated space. A single bucket of water, cloudy and foul, sat in the middle of the damp floor. They stepped over the people sprawled on the ground, trembling from the cold, as Mary led them to a corner.

Woody flashed back to his time in the prison camps. Dysentery, whooping cough, and pneumonia. Sickness that ran rampant. Bugs flourished alongside these disease-ridden Negroes, just as they had at Camp Chase. Foul food and water no doubt contributed to their illnesses.

Huddled in the corner in ripped and soiled clothes with a single old and tattered blanket around him lay a bearded, emaciated man. A little boy was nestled deep within the man's protective arms. The boy clung to his protector, shivering even as he slept.

The man tried to shelter his eyes, as flickers from the lantern reflected off his dark irises. He pulled the child closer, waking him.

Rebecca fought through her tears. "Israel, it's Rebecca Johnston. Do you remember me? We're here to deliver you and your boy to Fannie."

He shook his head and clutched his son.

"Remember, in Ohio? I showed you my sorghum mill. You wanted to start one yourself one day. Do you remember?"

Israel coughed several times but showed no signs of recognition.

Mary stepped forward. "They're here to take you and the boy. Get up."

He seemed to recognize her and struggled to sit upright, uncertainty etched on his tired and weathered face.

She unlocked the manacles around his ankles. The absence of the chains revealed swollen feet and raw, torn flesh.

Israel peered long and hard at Rebecca until he trusted the vision. He spoke with a low, gravelly voice. "Miss Rebecca? Is this really you?"

Rebecca knelt by his side and gently put her arms around him. "It's me. God has led us here."

He heaved a sigh. Tears blossomed into belief, as he lifted his stick-thin arms to heaven and cried out praise, barely audible, to the great Deliverer. After holding his boy close in a prolonged silence, he looked up at Rebecca.

"This here's Parker."

Rebecca drew the boy to her, and without hesitation, he wrapped his arms around her in a full embrace.

"I told him about you," Israel said, "and how we became free people."

Woody noted that somehow Parker seemed nourished, unlike Israel and the others in the cell. Woody helped Israel to stand, but his legs wobbled and he collapsed. Woody caught him before he hit the ground. The second time Woody placed Israel's arm around his shoulder for support, unfazed by the extreme odors emanating from his body. Israel moved a few steps toward Mary, bringing Woody with him. He looked deep into her eyes. He sought to hug her, so she met him halfway, and he fell into her embrace.

"I am so sorry," Mary said. "May God forgive us for what happened here."

"No, Mary," Israel said. "God will bless you, and I will never forget what you did here. Thank you."

Rebecca continued to hold Parker, and Woody steadied Israel as he walked under his own strength. The other prisoners in the room looked on in silence. One older man simply smiled and raised his head toward heaven. Mary led them out of the rancid building to the back gate. As they passed through, Woody turned for one last look. After his encounter at Lumpkin's slave jail, he couldn't believe he'd ever justified such behavior. History would uncover the truth about this horrible place. He pledged to do his part to ensure it.

Woody realized that Mary would be left to face Lumpkin's fury. "Will you be all right? You humbugged your husband. Will he hurt you?"

Remorse rolled down her cheeks. "I did nothing, and for this, my Lord is who I fear, not Robert. Anyway, he doesn't believe me capable of much beyond pouring tea and bearing children. I doubt he'll suspect me."

Woody sent Rebecca ahead with Parker while he assisted Israel.

Mary closed and locked the gate behind them.

He admired the woman's courage but doubted she would emerge from this unscathed. There was nothing he could do for her now. They must hasten their retreat from Richmond before the overseer discovered two slaves had gone missing.

Forty-Three

Freedom

As they made their way back to the wagon, Woody caught a glance at Israel's back through his bloodied, shredded shirt. His flesh had been ripped open. Some of his stripes were scabbed over and some remained raw, infected. Red, swollen welts surrounded them, evidence of previous whippings. Israel's face was drowning in sweat from a high fever. He needed a doctor, but they couldn't risk that, not until they reached Charlottesville. Israel had survived this long. Woody prayed the hope of freedom would give him strength.

The boy was well dressed and fed, all things considered. He must have received special treatment. Woody gave thanks for that.

Israel's breathing became more shallow and raspy, so he slowed his gait. Woody did not want to push the sick man, but danger lurked close behind them.

He realized they had not been introduced. "By the way, I'm Woody, a friend of Rebecca's. In a minute, you will meet my good chum, Lucas."

"If you are Rebecca's friend, you are mine as well," Israel said. "For what you did...I..." He coughed, reminding Woody of his own bloody, odorous, racking cough that almost killed him in the snows of Northern Ohio. "I...will be...forever in your...debt."

They reached the hill he and Rebecca had climbed earlier. Woody could see her and the boy talking with Lucas below.

Woody asked about Mary, and Israel's heartfelt thanks to her as they left, but as they descended the steep hill, Israel stumbled to the ground. Woody lunged for him, hoping to grab an arm or a handful of clothing, but then he too lost his footing and tumbled down, rolling halfway to the bottom. Woody caught up to Israel, frantic.

"Are you okay?"

The man grimaced. "I am fine. Didn't...you..."

This time a violent spate of coughs shook Israel. Lucas brought him water from the rig, offering small sips. Finally, Israel finished his sentence. "Didn't you ever roll down hills when you was a boy?"

Woody and Lucas helped him to his feet and continued to support his steps to the wagon. Fresh blood soaked through what few fibers existed in his shirt. They got him onto the seat and laid Parker in a cozy spot on the hay made into a bed with several blankets. The boy fell fast asleep.

"Now listen, Israel," Woody said. "This is hard, and I'm sorry…but I must shackle you with these manacles and chains one more time, and it's going to be uncomfortable. We may get stopped along the way. We need folks to believe we purchased you and the boy and we're transporting you to a new master."

Rebecca had suggested the irons, and an ever-resourceful Uncle Reginald had secured the props. Israel clenched his teeth as Woody bound him. The horse carrying Rebecca walked to his side.

"This will be the last time, my friend," she said.

Stocked with provisions and powered by fresh horses, the steady rig carried them into the stillness of the night. The early morning hours of the sixteenth had arrived, and still no rain fell, but good fortune had overplayed its hand.

Woody figured they'd find a stream away from Richmond where Israel and Parker would bathe. They would dress father and son in the clothes Fannie had purchased in Ripley the day Woody and Lucas had visited the Wills plantation. Then he'd push hard to Charlottesville, where they would seek the medical treatment that Israel required. As the wagon slowly moved beyond the city, Israel's cough began to subside.

"An angel of mercy," he said.

The statement came out of the blue.

"Who is an angel of mercy?" Woody asked.

"Back in Richmond, you asked about Mary."

"Yeah...?"

Israel told him about how the incarcerated men in Lumpkin's slave jail were fed rancid bacon and other putrefied food. They ate to avoid starvation, but the spoilage made them sick. At the risk of harsh punishment, Mary had often brought little Parker fresh scraps from Lumpkin's table. She also sidled into the jail twice a week in the early morning hours to clean the boy. Sometimes she even brought him fresh clothes. Lumpkin never knew, for he'd refused to enter the jail.

"An angel of mercy saved my boy's life."

As Woody drove on, he wondered how long it would be before Lumpkin discovered that one of his slaves had escaped right under his nose.

Would he send men to find them?

Could they stay ahead?

Forty-Four

Charlottesville

Friday, Nov. 18

Woody steered them into Charlottesville. As they traveled, both Lucas and Rebecca had kept a close lookout behind for riders in pursuit, but as far as they could tell, they hadn't been followed. Israel's need for proper medical care became urgent, as his fever had spiked and the sputum he coughed up turned bloody. Rockfish Gap still loomed before them and a light rain had begun to fall.

Due to its strategic location in this theater of war, Charlottesville overflowed with wounded Confederate soldiers. They had converted the University of Virginia into a medical facility and the Charlottesville General Hospital into a makeshift military medical center. Woody chose not to take Israel to either place. Even though the Negroes made up a majority of the population in this town and county, and a significant number of them were free, he left nothing to chance.

The chains remained on Israel for now.

He thought of one other place that might be helpful, the bi-racial First Baptist Church. He'd worshipped in that house of God in 1860 while traveling with his family to visit Uncle

Reginald. He headed for Park Street. With any luck, someone might direct them to a doctor for treatment and shelter. He parked the rig in front and told the others to wait.

Finding the front door unlocked, he walked into the dark sanctuary. Candles and one lantern cast a sparse light on the altar. No one appeared to be there, so Woody turned and started to walk away. Across the shadows came a voice.

"Can't a man get a night's sleep 'round here? You looking for someone?"

Woody turned back toward the altar and encountered a shabbily dressed old man, balding, with a prominent forehead. He had popped up from one of the first pews. His slurred speech made it difficult for Woody to understand him…probably sleeping off a day of drinking. The man's lack of teeth didn't help his enunciation.

"Perhaps," Woody said. "I'm transporting a slave back to Kentucky, but he is in urgent need of medical attention. Do you know who might be able to help?"

"Hardly no darkies at this-here church anymore," the drunkard said. "They done started their own. You can try there."

He lay down again in the pew.

"Pardon me, sir, but where would there be?" Woody asked.

The man lifted his head one more time. "Land sakes, man … the old Mudwall building, the brownish one. Used to be the Delevan Hotel."

Woody thought he knew the location. He headed back to the Three-Notch'd Road, which turned into Main Street through the town. Sure enough, they approached a yellowish-brown building resembling a hotel. Caution told him to park behind the building rather than on this major thoroughfare.

He left the others and walked in the open front doors, where he passed rows of cots filled with soldiers who could not walk, and others who milled about, their bandaged injuries not as grievous. From somewhere else came the sound of singing. He followed it to the top of a staircase.

He stepped down quietly and came into a large area illuminated by candles and several lanterns. Multiple rows of chairs had been set up, in front of which a chorale of twenty-five colored men and women sang a gospel song. Woody listened for a few minutes, mesmerized. He had never before witnessed such passionate worship, joy oozing from every member. They smiled, lifted hands high, and swayed in almost perfect time. He closed his eyes to experience the music with no distractions.

A voice jarred him from his exaltation. "May I help you with something, sir?"

He opened his eyes and removed his hat. "Powerful worship. I found myself lost in the sounds of God's praises."

"I'm sorry to disturb you."

"I'm sorry to intrude on your practice. My name is Jonathan Woodard."

They shook hands. "I'm Pastor William Gibbons. You're not from Charlottesville."

"No, I am not, Pastor Gibbons. I have a man with me who desperately needs medical help."

The pastor's eyebrows lifted. "I see."

Woody told the whole story about Israel, how he and his infant son were abducted from their home in Ohio and ended up in Lumpkin's slave jail in Richmond. "We got them out of that hellhole, but he desperately needs doctoring."

The pastor's expression turned grim.

"Well, God brought you to the right place. Four men are searching the town as we speak. They stopped here a couple of hours ago—wet, hungry, and saddle-weary. Desperate-looking fellas, asking about a party like yours."

Lumpkin's posse had somehow gotten ahead of them, maybe when they pulled off the road to bathe Israel and the boy. The city was small. A few thousand at most, and it wouldn't take long for the searchers to discover them. Woody needed to act fast.

"Pastor Gibbons, can you help us?"

The pastor wasted no time. "I know the right person, a medical woman on the east side of town. But we have to get your party out of Charlottesville now. The trick will be convincing her to come with us."

"To where?"

"A little village north of here called Rio Mills."

The pastor retrieved his coat, and they circled the Mudwall building to the back where both their vehicles were parked. The pastor stared at Israel's chains, and then at Woody. He cast another glance at Parker, fast asleep in the back of the wagon.

"I need to tell you that we're moving about under the ruse that he is a recently purchased slave," Woody said. "I hope that doesn't dissuade, and that you'll be willing to agree to that untruth if we are stopped."

The man smiled. "Sometimes deception can be an act of kindness."

Forty-Five

The Way Home

Rebecca joined the pastor in his buggy. Woody drove the wagon with Lucas at his side. Israel lay behind on the hay with his body over Parker's to protect him from the cold.

Tired after the long day of travel, Rebecca longed for a bed and was anxious to get Israel and Parker out of the misty night. On Main Street, white citizens braved the damp, flitting about on some errand or necessary outing, but there were almost no Negroes. She found this unusual.

"Where is the Negro population?"

Pastor Gibbons explained that most free Negroes resided on the east side, around Vinegar Hill, and the slaves stayed off the streets to obey the nine o'clock curfew. Some prominent leaders had enacted an ordinance because they feared many traditions in their post-antebellum culture would slip away. Important men like Uriah Levy, who kept twenty-one slaves on Monticello, former-President Jefferson's home, clung to the old order. So the local authorities rounded up slaves who didn't possess written permission to be away from their master's land. Many free coloreds, blue-collar workers who owned their own homes, followed the curfew to avoid confusion.

Another regulation prohibited Negroes from smoking in

public. If caught in the act, slaves would receive ten lashes, and free coloreds would pay a ten dollar fine.

Rebecca railed against such discrimination. "This is so foreign to our founding principles, our Christian roots."

When would such backward ways become unacceptable to good people?

He looked to her and smiled. "You are a follower of Jesus?"

"Yes, I'm a believer. And I believe slavery must be abolished, and women must be given equal rights."

"So you are an ardent devotee of many good things."

Traveling along the primary mercantile street, they passed a brickyard and a number of eating-houses, barbershops, and other commercial establishments. Modest homes on small lots formed a community of working-class people. Pastor Gibbons said they would seek help from a close friend, Mrs. Annie Foster, a widow who worked in one of the local food markets.

"You will like her. But we cannot stay at her home. She'll have to bring her medicines to a place north of here."

"But if she works in a food market, how can she—"

"Help your friend?"

She nodded.

A protégé of another anti-slavery, women's rights activist, Annie had studied with Dr. Orianna Moon, the former Superintendent of Nurses in the Charlottesville General Hospital. Dr. Moon married and moved away after the war broke out.

"Seems Charlottesville's not ready for Negro medical professionals," the pastor said, "so she works at the market."

Pastor Gibbons pulled the buggy to a halt in front of a small house, and Woody parked the wagon behind them. The pastor knocked on the door. A middle-aged Negro woman opened it, hugged him, and looked beyond to the people waiting outside. They spoke for a few moments, after which the woman closed the door behind her and the pastor returned to his buggy.

"So she's unwilling to help?"

"On the contrary, she'll be right out." A few minutes later, Annie Foster emerged again, this time carrying a large bag. Lucas jumped from the wagon and helped the nurse up to the seat. He untied a horse from the back of the wagon and mounted, following close behind as the party made its way north.

They came to a river that separated them from a small village on the opposite bank. "The Rivanna River and Rio Mills on the other side," the pastor said. "Bridge was burned by the Yankees a while back, but local folks been using flatbed boats to cross over."

Woody looked over to Lucas. "Check downstream." Lucas rode off while Annie took the opportunity to evaluate her patient under the partial cover of a tree.

"Israel, you best take off your shirt," Annie said. She examined the wounds on his back, her eyes first widening then tearing up.

Rebecca could hardly bear it. "Please, can you help him?"

"His fever is high, and that cough don't sound good."

* * *

Rebecca heard the footsteps behind them, but the four men emerged from the trees before Woody could draw his pistol. Lumpkin's hunters must have followed them to this remote area to avoid making a scene in Charlottesville.

"Drop it," one of them said. "Don't try to be a hero, or this night might be your last." Woody let his weapon drop to the ground. "Don't mean you any harm. Just here to collect the property you stole from Mr. Robert Lumpkin of Richmond. He's none too happy with y'all taking his Negro."

As the men entered the clearing at the river's edge, the sound of a rifle being cocked caused all four of them to turn around. "Now you can drop it. All of you." Lucas sat tall in the saddle, his rifle balanced on his short arm. They appeared to comply until one reached for his gun. A shot rang out. The man grabbed his hand as the gun fell to the ground. A line of smoke rose from Lucas's barrel.

The other men discarded their pistols. Woody looked over to Pastor Gibbons. "Please, sir, if you would collect those firearms." Then he addressed Rebecca. "Kindly retrieve the ropes in back of the wagon and bring them over."

Woody tied their hands and feet together, and then bound them in a circle around a tree trunk. Lucas confirmed that a wooden bridge connecting both banks had been burned down, along with some mills on the other side. But many of the village homes appeared unharmed.

"That's where we need to go," Pastor Gibbons said. "My sister and her family live on that side."

"Saw one'a them boats a ways down on this side," Lucas said. "We can leave the wagon and horses here and proceed on foot."

Rebecca watched as Woody conferred with Lucas. He nodded his head several times and said, "Uh-huh. Don't worry about me. Just get Israel patched up." It was clear Lucas would remain and make certain the posse stayed put.

Uncertainty weighed heavily on Rebecca's spirit, but she cast off her doubt and embraced God's promise. *I will never leave you or forsake you.*

They helped everyone else to the boat and pushed off the shore and the river bottom with the long poles stored on the vessel. On the opposite side, the pastor led them to a home set in the trees away from the village. There the gifted nurse-turned-store-clerk swung into action. Annie assembled her simple tools—a basin of warm water, clean cloths, bandages, and several ointments and tonics to treat Israel's ailments. Rebecca helped, and they worked for an hour cleaning Israel's wounds.

He moaned and gasped with every intrusion. Annie kept up a constant melody of whispers. "Almost done," and "Ooo-ee, that's a bad one" and "You been strong this long. Just hang on a little longer."

When all the wounds were clean, Annie applied a poultice made from dogwood, an herbal healing agent. "We don't get any traditional medical supplies, what with the needs of the army. The Yankee blockade limits our access, but these homespun remedies work quite well."

Once they had bandaged his back, they decided to let Israel sleep in a warm bed for one hour. Annie pulled Rebecca aside. "Get him to eat this dried persimmon fruit. It will ease the diarrhea. Be sure he drinks plenty of this tea made from persimmon bark. The tea will help break his fever. Israel has a powerful will to live. I believe he will, if we can get him through the night."

After Israel had rested, they thanked Pastor Gibbons's family and made their way back across the river. They collected Lucas, cold, wet and tired. "In the morning, someone will find these men and untie them," the pastor said. "Best if you travel around Charlottesville and make your way through the mountains."

Woody and Lucas bid him farewell. They helped Annie onto the pastor's buggy.

Rebecca looked up at her and said, "You are my hero, and I'll never forget you. Someday, you will become a great hospital nurse."

"Lord willing. Bless you on the rest of your journey."

Then Rebecca pulled the pastor into a tender hug. "Thank you," she whispered. "How can I ever show my gratitude?"

He looked at Rebecca with kindness as he climbed up to join the nurse. "Return home safely," Pastor Gibbons said, and drove into the wet night.

Mercifully, the rain soon let up.

They covered Israel with all of the blankets they had in an attempt to keep him and the boy dry. Burning with fever, Israel tossed and turned on the wagon bed for most of the night, moaning with pain as his wounds objected to the jarring movements. She forced him to eat the persimmon fruit and drink the tea that Annie had packed.

* * *

They drove hard and made it to Staunton, the first city on the Shenandoah pike leading north to Harpers Ferry. The drenching rain turned the city into an oasis in Rebecca's eyes.

Dear God, what a welcome sight.

After securing rooms, they rested the entire next day, Sunday.

Thanksgiving fast approached and she counted her reasons to be thankful. Though still very sick, Israel had rallied, his high fever breaking as the result of the constant rest over the course of the day. The friendship she and Woody shared had blossomed into a love she once thought impossible to experience after George's death. Her purposes in life became clearer—to be a wife and mother, and to work for causes that would right the wrongs in the American fabric of life. And she gave thanks that they'd reached the Shenandoah Valley before the heavens unleashed this downpour.

The continued doses of the remedies Annie provided performed their magic on Israel. On their second day in Staunton, Rebecca found another reason to be thankful. As she undressed Parker to wash his clothes, he smiled for the first time since they'd left Richmond. He hugged Rebecca and shouted, "Papa!" Then he scampered across the room, climbed onto Israel's bed and jumped on the mattress. When he recovered from the jostling, Israel smiled at her and said, "I'm blessed because of you."

Israel remained weak and needed consistent bed rest without being moved, but they had to complete the final leg of their journey. Weary and out of food and necessary supplies, they pulled into the Woodard family farm on the twenty-fourth of November, Thanksgiving Day.

The exhausted but thankful entourage walked through the front door and was met with a boisterous welcome. Apparently, they'd arrived just as the Woodard's were about to sit for their dinner. After the reunion, which included Woody's brother, Robert, who was home nursing a gunshot wound that had almost healed, Rebecca tucked Israel into bed and brought him a plate of home-cooked food. She was heartened to see his appetite had returned.

When she sat at the table, Woody's father raised his glass to both his sons. "To Robert...to Woody. To the best Thanksgiving ever for the Woodard clan." Everyone lifted their glasses and drank.

Woody leaned toward Rebecca. "It's been several weeks, and I haven't opened the golden case. Even longer since a nightmare interrupted my sleep."

More reasons to be thankful.

* * *

January 1865

A large group of passengers stepped onto the wharf boat at the Ripley dock. Rebecca gently bit her lower lip with anticipation. It'd been more than a year since Israel and Fannie held each other, talked about their futures, played with their son together.

The reunion about to take place almost cost Rebecca her life, but it also created a new heart in her. One that could love another man unreservedly. Woody had asked her to marry him, and the answer was a resounding yes.

She glanced to her right at Israel, still too thin and suffering a lingering cough, but the last few weeks in Shepherdstown had set him on the mend. He carried little Parker onto dry land, surrounded by Rebecca, Woody, and Lucas.

Suddenly, Israel stopped, his eyes fixed straight ahead. There in the distance stood Fannie with Reverend Rankin, Jean, and John Parker.

"Go to her, Israel." He looked at Rebecca, his eyes wet and his lips quivering. Israel walked toward her. When they met, little Parker held his hands out to his mother. As she took him, Fannie dropped to her knees, overwhelmed with raw emotion.

"My baby, my baby," she cried, over and over.

After several moments, Rebecca walked to her side and held the boy. Fannie rose and came face to face with Israel.

The embrace that followed must have made angels cry with joy.

Forty-Six

New Beginnings

Georgetown
Brown County, Ohio
May 1865

New beginnings. That's what Rebecca called their journey into Pleasant Township.

Winter retreated and new life sprang forth, for the nation and for the Israel Rankin family, who'd returned to Columbus focused on Israel's full recovery.

The elusive end to the long, bloody war finally came. The country licked its grievous wounds and hobbled toward an uncertain future without its courageous leader. Despite his assassination, President Lincoln's vision would continue. One united nation, liberty for all. But the execution of this ideal faced a mountain of challenges, starting with the reunification of North and South.

In Red Oak, Ohio, Rebecca viewed this as a metaphor for Woody's life. His complete healing from the ravages of war would also be long and difficult, beginning with the delivery of an ambrotype to a Northern family that had suffered a great loss. She'd decided a final chapter needed closing before they launched their new life together. The time had come to find the unnamed girl.

She'd contacted her network throughout the county, and a reliable tip came back. A family with the last name of Brown resided in Georgetown, and a ten-year-old girl lived with them. She and Woody packed their bags, filled the buckboard with essential supplies, and launched yet another new adventure together.

The landscape before her spoke about the constants that would continue despite man's folly. The tumult that tore the nation's fabric had left this land in Brown County untouched. Hills rose several hundred feet, some limestone-laden and covered with tobacco crops. They leveled out to rolling land, and finally farmlands. Precipitous gorges dropped further into ravines, narrow and deep with rocky sides. Out of the moss-covered bedrock grew the purple blooms of waterleaf wildflowers. The tree canopy had closed, signaling the looming finish of the wildflower season, but other late bloomers—like geraniums and orchids—still colored the landscape, adding to the visual feast.

* * *

As they approached Georgetown on the northern end of the township, Woody thought about how far he'd come. Lee had surrendered to Grant the month before, and the end of the hostilities were near. Rebecca had set the wedding for July. His nightmares had abated. The few that dared to poke through his subconscious mind were shadows with no definition. She and Lucas, and the likeness of the girl to a lesser degree, helped him to bury scarring memories in an unmarked grave.

And now…transitions. The processing. The adjustment to a new life. Lucas had decided to spend some time in Cincinnati to take a taste of big city life. Woody expected him to return to Ripley soon. They were small town boys at heart.

Each sunset brought forth a new and better day.

So he and Rebecca went.

When they turned onto Main Street, Woody stopped the buckboard and called out to a local citizen passing by.

"Pardon me, sir. We're from out of town, searching for a family that may live in this region. With whom might we make inquiries?"

The man scratched his head. "Might start at Mayor Patterson's office, up the street. If'n he can't help you, try old lady McCain. Been around these parts since the dawn of time. Lives outside of town. Passed her place coming in, I s'pect."

"Thank you kindly, sir."

He looked at Rebecca, and her smile was as wide as his anticipation. When his runaway heart settled, he questioned the mission. The unnamed girl had already served her purpose in his life. She'd helped him survive. Wouldn't it be best to leave well enough alone?

Nerves…? Then he reminded himself again why they had come. The girl's father had never come home from the war. Woody must tie this final knot.

Rebecca encouraged him on. "Okay, Mr. Woodard. Off we go to visit Mayor Patterson."

He stopped the rig under a wooden shingle that read, Mr. D.V. Patterson, Mayor. The sign, held aloft by small chains on both sides and attached to a metal anchor, wobbled in the breeze. The squeaking noise held him in a trance. A buckboard or two, and a few horsemen, passed them. The only sound that registered came from the signboard. A moment of truth arrived, but he remained glued to the seat, his eyes fixed on the swaying sign.

"Woody…?" Her voice echoed through his foggy thoughts. "Come, dear."

"Okay, Rebecca. You got us this far, and now it's time for me to finish."

He jumped from the buckboard and circled around to the other side. She placed her hand in his and carefully lowered herself to the street's surface. Arms linked, they stepped up to the wooden walkway. He knocked on the door and waited. Nothing. He rapped again, this time a little louder.

A voice boomed from inside. "Come in already!"

Rebecca smiled and said, "Unusual welcome."

Inside, a formally dressed older man sat behind a desk, hunkered over a stack of files. He removed his spectacles, rubbed the bridge of his nose, and peeked up for the first time. "Oh goodness, please forgive me for my boorish behavior. I wouldn't be rudely shouting out if I'd known visitors were in town."

"Looks like you are buried in business." Rebecca pointed to the mound of paperwork before him.

"Very boring. Please take a seat. To whom do I have the pleasure?"

"My name is Jonathan Woodard, and this is my fiancée, Rebecca Johnston."

The mayor rose to shake hands. He was possibly the tallest man Woody had ever seen. "Welcome to Georgetown, a wonderful place to consider relocating, now that this business between the states is over."

"Indeed," Rebecca said.

Mayor Patterson began to heavily promote the town, launching into a soliloquy about their most famous former citizens, the Jesse Grant family. Jesse Grant owned a local tannery, and lived in a house on the corner of Main Cross and Water streets. At another time, Woody might have taken interest in the town's claim to fame, but his attention remained fixed on how close they were to solving one of the great mysteries of his life.

"Their boy, Ulysses, was only a year old when the family came to town," Mayor Patterson said. "U.S. Grant lived here until his appointment to West Point in 1839. Young Ulysses, quite fond of horses, found employment in teaming. He'd ride his horse at full speed and stand up, sometimes on one foot, to the astonishment of his friends."

Rebecca jumped in. "Mr. Mayor—"

"Please, Miss Johnston. Less formal. Call me DV...everyone else around here does."

"DV, do you possess any information about a family named Brown living hereabouts?"

"Brown. Hmm…let me see. The husband's name?"

"Clancy Brown," Woody said, reaching for her hand. The gentle touch calmed him.

"Why yes, of course. That would be Mrs. Amanda Brown and her daughter. They moved to Georgetown in '63. Tried to recover after her first husband, Clancy, died in one of the Shenandoah Valley battles—Port Republic, I believe."

Woody could hardly contain himself. Might this really be the end of his search?

"Do you remember the little girl's name?" he asked.

"Her name? Why, yes…Charlotte. A wonderful young lady."

"Charlotte," he said in a whisper. He couldn't believe it. Finally. "Charlotte."

The unnamed girl now had a name. Lightheaded, Woody responded again when Rebecca squeezed his hand. "A perfect name. Please, sir, can you direct us to their location?"

Mayor Patterson inquired as to their relationship with the family. Woody gave him a quick version of his story and showed him the ambrotype.

"That's her all right. A beautiful likeness of young Charlotte."

Rebecca squeezed Woody's hand again, and he turned to her. Tears hovered in her eyes, blurred by the tears in his. After all this time, he'd finally found her.

"You folks all right?" the mayor asked.

"Yes," Woody said. "Perfect."

The mayor explained that Amanda's extended clan lived up north in Sandusky. "That's on the shores of Lake Erie, near that Confederate prison. Ever been there? The place is damnably cold in the winter."

"Are you telling me Mrs. Amanda Brown and Charlotte now live in Sandusky?"

Of all the places he would not want to visit. He held his breath waiting for the response.

What a cruel twist of fate this would be.

Forty-Seven

Charlotte

"No, no," Mayor Pearson said. "Amanda's remarried. She's now a Clayburn. The family lives on a horse and cattle ranch five miles out of town."

Woody glanced at Rebecca, and both of them broke into a deep laugh over the connections to Sandusky.

Sandusky, the city across the bay from Johnson's Island, where many Confederate officers, and even a few privates, languished within a certain compound. Some died on the island. A handful launched a daring escape one blustery New Year's Eve. All were soon recaptured, except for one. The mayor asked about the joke, but they declined to answer.

They thanked the mayor, promised to consider Georgetown if ever they chose to move, and headed out.

The Clayburn spread was a vibrant ranch.

Men herded horses from nearby grazing lands into corrals. Hooves kicked up gritty clouds that lingered in the air, settling only after the last horse had crossed the wooden gate.

A group of hired hands watched in another corral as a man rode a bucking bronco but lasted just ten seconds before the horse cast him to the ground. His fellow hands jeered as he rose and slapped the dirt from his shirt and pants. Other workers busied themselves with menial chores around the ranch.

Woody parked the buckboard in front of the expansive ranch-style house.

"Can I help you folks?"

A middle-aged man of stocky build walked toward them from one of the barns. His dark, heavily lined face spoke of a life wrangling in the sun. His graying hair, extending to his shoulders, waved in the gentle breeze.

"Name's Jonathan Woodard, here to see Mr. Quincy Clayburn. This here's my fiancée, Miss Rebecca Johnston."

"I'm Quincy Clayburn, owner of this ranch." He stopped beside their buckboard. "What can I do for you?"

Woody tipped his hat. "Very pleased to meet you, Mr. Clayburn. Quite an operation you've got here." He told the rancher about their visit to Mayor Patterson's office, and how their inquiries about Amanda Brown led them to the ranch. "We have crisscrossed much of Brown County to find you, sir."

"What led you to take such a journey?"

Woody stepped off the buckboard and helped Rebecca down. They joined Clayburn inside at his invitation and entered into a large room with a high-beamed ceiling. The furnishings were simple but tasteful, nothing like the ostentatious décor inside the Wills plantation. The main room led both to adjoining rooms and the kitchen.

After a few minutes of small talk, Woody explained the purpose of their visit. Rather than tell his complete story, he pulled the gold case from his haversack and handed it to Clayburn. Taken aback, the man looked at it, then back at Woody.

"Charlotte," he said, raised eyebrows betraying his shock. "What—"

The double doors to an adjoining suite opened, and everyone turned as a woman emerged. She struck a commanding pose. She had jet-black hair parted down the middle and braids that extended past her shoulders. Her lips were painted ruby red. To Woody's surprise, the woman was pregnant.

"Ah…my wife, Amanda."

* * *

They sat for more than an hour, as Woody said all the things he had rehearsed countless times in anticipation of this moment.

The resemblance between mother and daughter struck him as Amanda shared the long seesaw of emotions she and Charlotte had experienced after Clancy went missing in action. As Woody expected all along, the not knowing had become a daily sadness. After the passing of months and years, she gave up hope of ever knowing.

Then, at her lowest ebb, she met Quincy Clayburn. He had promised a new life for her and Charlotte, starting with adopting the girl after she and Quincy married.

"I came all this way, through battles and marches, and times when I thought I would not survive another day, to give this to you, Amanda." Woody rose and handed her the likeness. "I called her the unnamed girl. To know her now as Charlotte takes me beyond my expectations. I feel as if I've known her all of her life."

The woman looked at the ambrotype for a moment, and then held it close to her heart. "This is where I know Clancy held her." She smiled and gave the image back to him. She walked into the next room and returned with another case. She handed it to Woody, who looked down at a slightly different version of the same picture he had carried for so long.

"Mr. Woodard, may I gift the likeness of my daughter to you? That is, the same ambrotype you carried all this time."

A tear slipped from his eye, which he caught and wiped away. "Amanda, I can't tell you how happy that would make me."

"Wonderful. Now to the most important reason that I believe you came. Would you like to meet Charlotte?"

He feared his voice would crack, so he cleared his throat to answer. Rebecca jumped up. "He would like that very much."

Woody and Rebecca followed Quincy and Amanda outside, where Amanda pointed to the top beam of a corral. There sat a young girl in a calico dress. She watched, clapping her approval, as a ranch hand climbed on the back of a wild stallion.

They walked toward the girl, and as they did, Woody recognized her face. A more mature version of the young girl who'd posed for the photograph.

When they reached the girl, she smiled at the group. "Hello, Mother. Daddy." Her hair hung in ringlets down to her shoulders, just like in the photo.

"Charlotte, please come down so I can introduce some very special friends."

The girl jumped to the ground and stood beside her mother.

"This is Mr. Woodard and his fiancée, Miss Johnston."

Woody looked down at her, recalling the comfort that God had given him in the midst of turmoil…a hope he could not fully fathom at the time. Indeed, all had been righted in due time.

"Mr. Woodard, such a pleasure to know you," Charlotte said.

"So good to know you too. But please, call me Woody."

Woody and Rebecca visited with the family for hours and became fast friends. To Woody, it seemed like only minutes. They enjoyed a barbecue in Woody's honor that night and then stayed the evening. When they parted company the next day, he had inherited a new little sister.

* * *

Ripley, Ohio
July 1865

Woody and Rebecca held the wedding at Red Oak Presbyterian Church. Pastor John Rankin conducted the ceremony.

There was standing room only in the church. Little Parker and Israel sat in the front row. The couple's extended clans, along with the Halverston family, John Parker, and many others from the community, filled the pews. Even the Myers and Bond families made the long trek from Toledo, joking that a swirling blizzard could not keep them away.

Lucas stood as best man, and Fannie and Charlotte as Rebecca's matron and maid of honor. The reception turned into a joyous celebration of two people so much in love, both of whom fought mightily against the forces aligned to keep them apart.

They honeymooned on a fancy steamer that made its way down the Ohio River to Cincinnati, where they stayed at the Burnet Hotel for several days. The couple retraced the steps that led him to Over-the-Rhine and the widow Braun. They even paid a visit to Tildee McPhearson, who expressed great pride in having led Woody to his new bride, and to the girl named Charlotte. They didn't reveal his identity as a former Confederate soldier. Maybe in time.

The first night after they returned to the farm, they sat before a crackling fire and basked in the warmth from the flames. After being together in a comfortable silence, Woody brought the search for the unnamed girl to an official close.

He dug into his army haversack and carried the ambrotype over to the hutch in the parlor. He placed it in a prominent spot, where Charlotte's likeness might compel him to regale their guests with the story of a young girl who'd helped him survive the war.

He gazed at his wife with adoration.

"Behold what arises from the ashes of the great national struggle," Woody said.

Rebecca answered, "Thanks be to God for the unnamed girl."

The End

If you enjoyed The Unnamed Girl, I'm guessing you'll probably like my other stories too. Sign up for my (not so frequent!) free newsletter to get special deals and hear about all my newest works before anyone else. You can get on the list here: mikehmizrahi.com. For joining my preferred readers list, I'll send you my newest short story for FREE!

Author's Notes…

On June 11, 2012, the Museum of the Confederacy in Richmond, Virginia, released eight Civil War photos to the public in hopes someone could identify the long-deceased subjects captured in time. I love a mystery, and I love the Civil War period of our nation's history. So on that spring day in 2014, when I typed the words "Civil War mysteries" into the Google search box and hit enter, I soon found the inspiration for my next novel.

I read in wonderment the Associated Press story on the New York Daily News site, and others published in different outlets, about a little girl in a hoop dress seated on an ornate chair, ringlets spilling to the sides of her face. The photo was spellbinding, at least to this Civil War enthusiast, and there was an interesting backstory to its discovery.

It seems a Private Thomas W. Timberlake of the 2nd Virginia Infantry, Company G, a soldier in the famed Stonewall Brigade commanded by General Thomas "Stonewall" Jackson, was walking the June 9, 1862 battlefield of Port Republic (the AP story mistakenly identified it as the Battle of Port Royal) after the fighting was over. He came upon the ambrotype in question, on the ground between two dead soldiers, one a bluecoat and the other a Confederate. Timberlake picked up the photo and kept it until his death in 1914, and sometime afterward his family donated it to the museum. And the real "unnamed girl" has gone unnamed to this day. Or so it seems.

Private Timberlake became the inspiration for my main

character, Woody Woodard. There aren't any other parallels between Woody and the real life Timberlake, other than the discovery of the ambrotype and their involvement in the first Shenandoah Valley Campaign of 1862, and other Stonewall Brigade engagements. Although, as you will read in Timberlake's following obituary, he had a lifelong friend who fought by his side throughout the war. (Enter Lucas Halverston!)

Timberlake was born on March 7, 1840, on his family farm, Sherwood, on the Shenandoah River in Warren, Virginia. He was married to Fannie Greggs on Sept. 20 (or the 25), 1865, and he died on April 1, 1914. He left this life at the same place he entered it, his beloved Sherwood.

For so many soldiers in that horrific war, their Bibles, photographs, and letters from family and loved ones were often the only comfort and peace that sustained them from one battle to the next. This was the case for my fictional character, Jonathan Woodard, whose obsession with the ambrotype in the story, and his need to deliver it to the family after the war, leads him on an unexpected journey. A search that allows him to reclaim his spiritual and emotional health. In the process, he also finds the love of his life, Rebecca.

As far I know, there are no records that disclose Private Timberlake suffered from what we now call Post Traumatic Stress Disorder. Many Civil War veterans did. I'm also unaware if the ambrotype was anything more than a war memento to him.

This was the point of departure between what I learned and what I dared to imagine. This fictional story is what flowed through my fingers and onto my computer keyboard.

Obituary

Thomas W. Timberlake
Confederate Veteran Magazine
Published July 1914

Thomas W. Timberlake died on April 1, 1914, at his ancestral home, Sherwood, on the Shenandoah River. His father was Capt. Richard Timberlake, and his mother was Amelia H. Andrews, of Spotsylvania County, Va. He was a medical student at the University of Virginia in 1861, and would have graduated in a short time, but when the tocsin of war sounded he left the school and at once volunteered for the war in Capt. William Nelson's company, G, 2nd Virginia Infantry, Stonewall Brigade. He was a tall, delicately constituted man, yet by force of will was in Jackson's famous Valley Campaign and on to Seven Pines, below Richmond, thence to Cedar Mountain, where his brigadier general, Walker, was killed; on to Second Manassas, where he was severely wounded in the neck (which bullet was never extracted) while fighting in the railroad cut on August 28, 1862. He was again wounded at Mine Run on November 27, 1863, in the left leg, and this incapacitated him for further infantry duty. He then joined Company B, 12th Virginia Cavalry, Gen. Turner Ashby's old brigade, commanded by Rosser, then known as the Laurel Brigade. While defending the middle ford in the Cedar Creek fight on October 19, 1864, he was shot through the right lung. He soon recovered from this and rejoined the company. In the last of February, 1865, he captured Lieut. S. H. Draper, of

Sheridan's staff, a noted Jesse scout of the Union army, clad in gray, defeating his twenty-five men with eleven.

[J. R. Rust, of Haymarket, Va., sent this tribute to his comrade, to which he adds: "I am proud of his heroic, patriotic life. We were reared on adjoining farms, were friends in boyhood, comrades in many hard-fought battles and starving, strenuous marches in snow, heat, and dust from 1861 to 1865. Never a cloud or blot on his manly character reached my ear. He is survived by a lovely Christian wife, who was Miss Fannie Greggs. He was an elder in the Presbyterian Church for years. As a Christian neighbor and devoted husband he had few peers. Peace to his noble dust!"]

T. W. TIMBERLAKE.

Private Thomas W. Timberlake

The real Unnamed Girl

ABOUT THE AUTHOR

Mike H. Mizrahi and his wife, Karen, reside in Poulsbo, Washington. They have two grown children, Lindsay and Matthew, and have been active in church and community service. Mike's first historical novel, The Great Chattanooga Bicycle Race, can be purchased at his website, mikehmizrahi.com, as well as Amazon.com. His upcoming projects include a compilation of short stories and a novella about the harshness of life in war-torn Congo. Mike is an avid blogger. Visit him at mikehmizrahi.com and facebook.com/AuthorMikeMizrahi/.

Made in the USA
Middletown, DE
16 February 2019